Wicked Ugly Bad

A Kinda Fairytale

Cassandra Gannon

Text copyright © 2013 Cassandra Gannon
Cover Image copyright © 2013 Cassandra Gannon
All Rights Reserved

Published by Star Turtle Publishing

Visit Cassandra Gannon and Star Turtle Publishing at
www.starturtlepublishing.com!

Or like us on Facebook for news on upcoming books and promotions!

Or email Cassandra Gannon directly: **starturtlepublishing@gmail.com**

We'd love to hear from you!

Also by Cassandra Gannon

The Elemental Phases Series
Warrior from the Shadowland
Guardian of the Earth House
Exile in the Water Kingdom
Treasure of the Fire Kingdom
Queen of the Magnetland
Magic of the Wood House
Coming Soon: Destiny of the Time House

A Kinda Fairytale Series
Wicked Ugly Bad
Beast in Shining Armor
Coming Soon: Happily Ever Witch

Other Books
Not Another Vampire Book
Love in the Time of Zombies
Vampire Charming
Cowboy from the Future
Once Upon a Caveman
Ghost Walk

If you enjoy Cassandra's books, you may also enjoy books by her sister, Elizabeth Gannon:

The Consortium of Chaos series
Yesterday's Heroes
The Son of Sun and Sand
The Guy Your Friends Warned You About
Electrical Hazard
The Only Fish in the Sea

Other Books
The Snow Queen
Travels with a Fairytale Monster
Nobody Likes Fairytale Pirates
Captive of a Fairytale Barbarian

For Maizie
My Tyrannical Princess

Chapter One

The Tuesday share circle is, by far, the least responsive group to therapy. Even for villains, they're antisocial, uncooperative, and selfish. Until they begin working together, none of them will get anywhere.

Psychiatric case notes of Dr. Ramona Fae

If she hadn't been insane before Cinderella tossed her into the nuthouse, she'd definitely gone full blown crazy since she'd been there.

For six weeks, Scarlett Riding had been locked inside the Wicked, Ugly and Bad Mental Health Treatment Center and Maximum Security Prison. She knew what crazy looked like. Letty had spent the past month and a half staring at ink blots, making macaroni necklaces, and doing calming jigsaw puzzles of baby ducks, so she recognized all the signs and she accepted the truth.

She was legitimately, one hundred percent certified out-of-her-mind, now.

It was almost a relief.

Scarlett knew she was nuts, because she no longer cared that she *might be* nuts. Whatever dark thoughts swirled inside of her head, she preferred them to the doctors trying to "fix" her into some brainwashed zombie. From the minute they'd dragged her into the WUB Club, Letty's only focus had been getting out and getting even. No one was going to make her sane without one hell of a fight. She was willfully choosing Bad over Good.

Actually, no. It wasn't really a choice, at all.

Scarlett was fighting for her life. They wanted to erase everything that made her Scarlett and remake her into one of *them*. Only worse, because she'd *never* be one of the Good folk and no one knew it better than her oppressors. They wanted to make her into an obedient worshipper of the status quo. Someone who bowed as the pretty people went by and then dutifully built them their damn castles.

She'd sooner die.

Letty stared down at the little paper cup full of pills that the nurse handed her and tipped them into her mouth. Smiling vacantly, she took a second cup full of water and pretended to swallow. "Thank you, Glinda."

The fairy nodded, already passing out meds to the next patient in line.

Ahhh... The ever-changing, undertrained staff of the WUB Club. Once a mere annoyance and now a vital part of Scarlett's plans. Thanks to the prison's substandard conditions, it was almost too easy to trick the lazy Good folk staffing this place.

She slowly made her way over to the TV and sat down on one of the plastic, orange chairs. The recreation room was always busy this time of day. Insane villains liked talk shows. Not surprisingly, Scarlett herself found the programs more hypnotic with each passing day. She listened as some nice, ordinary bears accused a snotty little blonde girl of breaking into their house and sleeping in their beds. Of course, the simpering host was on Goldilocks' side.

Good folk stuck together.

The stupid pills were already dissolving under Scarlett's tongue and they tasted terrible. Still, she kept her expression neutral, until she finally felt safe enough to pretend to drink the last of the water. Actually, she used the opaque sides of the cup as cover and just spit the pills into the waxy little container.

She'd been pulling that trick for a week now and it worked like a charm. Under other circumstances she'd be appalled by how easy it was, as a matter of fact. The gloomy apathy of the hospital worked in her favor, but you'd think they'd be a little more vigilant in this dump. Who wanted crazy lunatics off their meds?

Well, besides the crazy lunatics.

Still, with every hour without the drugs in her system, Letty could feel herself returning to normal. Soon, she'd be getting out of there and making her stepsister pay.

She *had* to. Time was running out.

Once Cinderella got the ring on Charming's finger there would be nothing to stop her from killing Scarlett and Dru. If they didn't escape soon, that blonde bitch would come for them and this time she wouldn't be content with just straightjackets and armed guards. This time there would be blood.

It was escape or die.

Letty crumpled up the cup and got to her feet. "Time for group." She announced to no one in particular, although an elf named Merle gave her a vague nod.

She casually tossed the paper cup full of pills into the trash as she strolled out the door and waved at an orderly. It was better to be friendly and agreeable. She'd figured that out in the second week. You couldn't successfully plot anything if they *suspected* you were plotting. So she *tried* to act browbeaten and complacent.

Most of the time.

The WUB Club was housed in an industrial box of a building, completely different from the beautiful palaces and charming villages in the rest of the Four Kingdoms. Lots of long, dingy corridors flanked by doors with frosted windows and plastic name plates. Everything was painted the same ugly green as her elementary school auditorium and smelled like mold mixed with heavy-duty cleanser. Since very little cleaning went on, Letty assumed the scent had just worked its way into the walls and linoleum.

Nothing but the best from dear Cindy.

Scarlett's stepsister had sent her to a place of hopelessness and despair. Given the low standard of care and lack of food, it wasn't surprising that so few Baddies ever left the WUB Club alive. Suicides were the biggest killer, claiming a least one person a week. No doubt Cinderella was hoping that Letty would eventually be among the ones who just gave up.

Unfortunately for her, Letty didn't give up easy.

She stopped at the last door in the hallway and took a deep breath. Group therapy was one of the worst parts of being adjudicated criminally insane.

Firming her jaw, she marched inside the windowless room and took her seat in the share circle. God, she hated Tuesdays. The only positive part of the whole humiliating spectacle was that she got to spend time with her sister.

Drusilla had been tossed in the WUB Club with her and imprisonment was even harder on Dru that it was on Scarlett. She sat listlessly in her chair, staring at the wall. Her red hair was unwashed and lank, her unpretty face blank. Neither sister had ever been beautiful, but now Dru looked like a hollow, gaunt shell of the person she'd been.

Shit.

Scarlett needed to find a way to get Dru off the meds. Unfortunately, Drusilla and Letty were kept apart as much as possible, so it was impossible for them to really talk. It was yet another way for Cindy to try and break them.

It wouldn't work, though.

Letty had always taken care of Dru and she always would. But, the best way to ensure that her sister lived a long and happy life was to stop Cindy from getting what she wanted.

Scarlett tried to catch Dru's eye but her sister was lost inside her own mind. Maybe it was for the best, right now. Scarlett still didn't have an actual plan to get them out of there, so she didn't want to get Dru's hopes up.

She sighed and looked around the rest of the Tuesday share circle. A bridge ogre, a troll, a wicked witch, a deposed prince, and that insufferable wolf. So, everyone else had shown up, which meant that nobody had disappeared into the bowels of the institution since last week.

For some reason, Scarlett was glad about that. So often, prisoners would just vanish, never to be heard from again. It bothered Scarlett how no one else seemed to care about that or asked where they went. The people locked up in the WUB Club were all Bad, but they were still *people*.

It made Scarlett wonder if anyone would notice when her turn came to disappear. As soon as the royal wedding was over, Cindy would have Scarlet dragged off in the night, never to be heard from again. There wasn't a doubt in her mind.

Dr. Ramona Fae, their "facilitator," stood by the whiteboard, drawing a complicated mass of circled words and connected lines. Something about apples and wands being triggers for magic addictions... God! Why did psychiatrists all love diagrams? That incomprehensible web of steps was supposed to curb violent impulses, but it just made Scarlett want to punch someone.

Plus, she'd forgotten her feelings journal back in

her room, so Dr. Ramona was going to be pissed when they got started. Actually, Scarlett hadn't "forgotten" it so much as she'd deliberately tossed it out the barred window. She might be crazy, but she sure wasn't crazy enough to give a shit about a "feelings journal." Although a big part of her did want to write "kill, kill, kill" on every page, just to see if Ramona's condescending expression finally faded as Scarlett shared *that* with the group.

God, she *really* needed to get out of this place.

Still, the guy beside her was eating the pages of his journal, so Scarlett wasn't too worried about falling behind the rest of the group. She watched as Benji the bridge ogre ripped a spiral-bound sheet free, crumpled it up, and popped it into his mouth. No one stopped him. The monster was eight feet tall, covered in blue fur, and built like a –well-- a bridge ogre. Sweet as he was, it was best to just let him snack.

"Lookin' a little stressed there, Red." A deep voice drawled. "Anything you wanna share with the rest of the class?"

Against her will, Scarlett's eyes traveled over to the bane of her already miserable existence. If there was one person in this place who *should* be locked up and away from society, it was Marrok Wolf.

He smirked at her, slouching in his seat with typical lupine grace, looking completely gorgeous and completely immoral. Even in his human-form, Marrok retained a wildness that commanded attention. His unevenly cut hair fell forward over the exotic angles of his face, his golden eyes constantly watching her through the tawny strands.

Marrok was the best looking man in the Four Kingdoms, Good or Bad. If he hadn't been born evil, he would have been a perfect knight. Even his body was custom-made for charging around on horseback, slaying monsters. Tall and broad-chested, with muscles that didn't come from a gym. His looks were so... gallant. So heroic. Such a shame that a dashing, valiant exterior was wasted on a complete asshole.

Everyone in their group was assigned the same solid red uniforms, but Marrok was one of the few who looked stunning in the familiar sweatpants and t-shirt that read, 'EVIL.' It annoyed Scarlett that she was on the same security level as that maniac. Firstly, because the crimson color of her "EVIL" outfit clashed with her red hair and secondly because she *wasn't* evil.

Ugly, yes. Wicked, sure.

But, she wasn't like the *wolves*, for God's sake.

No Baddies were popular in the Four Kingdoms, but Marrok and his brethren were some of the least respected. They were only tolerated for their entertainment value and then quietly disposed of when they stopped being useful. They were usually "drafted" into televised athletic competitions, because of their size, aggressiveness and camera-ready faces. They were bet on and bought and treated like prize-winning racehorses. Except, unlike horses, women often paid to sleep with the wolves.

Marrok was the best player in the Wolfball leagues, but he caused endless problems both on and off the field. Even Scarlett knew that and she refused to follow the brutal mix of wrestling and football that always seemed to leave someone broken on the ground. He was brilliant at his assigned role as the... whatever the player who tackled people and tried to kill them was called. If the different positions even *had* names. The sport gave every indication of being a rule-less melee, so maybe the players were all interchangeable.

It seemed to Letty that the Good folk of the Four Kingdoms just liked to pit their teams of semi-enslaved Baddies against each other out of sheer random bloodlust. Most wolves accepted that as their lot and made the best of it for as long as they could, soaking up the limelight and relishing their pseudo-celebrity.

Marrok had taken a different path.

He'd been uncooperative to the point of madness, dismissive of everything the Good folk held dear, and unrepentantly Bad. In return, the audience loved him... even if his inability to follow orders got him thrown in jail a lot.

It helped that he was gorgeous, of course. And charismatic. And a fantastic liar. He was constantly in and out of the WUB Club for violating rules. But, he always returned to the field with a shining smile and a promise to do better... which he absolutely didn't mean.

It was *completely* ridiculous that Scarlett was lumped in with the biggest, Baddest wolf in the Four Kingdoms. Letty had never done anything wrong and they treated her even worse than someone with fifty counts of Badness on his record. She'd formally protested the unfairness of it when she first arrived, which in retrospect had been a mistake.

It just meant she'd caught Marrok's attention.

He gazed at her with cruel delight from across the share circle. "I was thinking about you last night." He drawled, ignoring the fact she was ignoring him. "As you know, thinking of others takes us outside of our own problems. I think about you *a lot*." His unsettling yellowish eyes glowed. "Now... did ya ever consider that maybe you *wanted* Cinderella to climb into that pumpkin and steal the guy from you? Maybe it was your way out."

Scarlett kept her gaze on his and didn't respond

to his idiotic theory. Reactions encouraged him. Marrok preyed on the weak, so you just had to stare him down like any other animal.

"I mean, maybe you knew Cinderella was the mysterious girl at the ball the whole time. Maybe you *wanted* her to have that dipshit Charming. Maybe you were *glad* when she jammed her foot into that shoe, because it got you off the hook."

Scarlett wasn't going to say one word about the glass slipper to anyone. Her stepsister had spies everywhere. Still, Marrok's smug words pissed her off.

"Off the hook?" She scoffed. "The hook where I'd get to marry the handsome prince and rule a kingdom with my piles of money, you mean? We should check with your doctors, because they need to adjust your meds, Wolf."

His mouth curved at that, understanding the threat.

Ever since she'd stopped taking her pills, Scarlett had developed a sixth sense around other patients who'd started their own secret rehab programs. Just looking at him, she knew Marrok was keeping himself clean and sober, which frankly scared the hell out of her. She came from a long line of famous criminals and even she was impressed with his potential for villainy. She had no idea what he was capable of.

Especially, since he knew *she* was abstaining from her tranquilizers, too. She could see the awareness of it in his gaze as he leaned forward.

"I think we're both doing okay with this dosage." He murmured. "And I didn't mean to upset you, by bringing up your past. I'm sure you told yourself you wanted to be the trophy princess for that dickhead. But, in the end, your..." He hesitated thoughtfully. "Hmmm.

Hey, Doc, what's the politically correct phrase for not gettin' any, again?"

God, Scarlett hated him.

Marrok didn't bother to glance in Ramona's direction as he pretended to remember. "Oh, yeah!" He snapped his fingers. "Your *repressed sexual desires* got the better of you, Red."

She wasn't sure whether the nickname derived from her hair, the group's color designation or "Scarlett." Whichever reason, it bugged her. "If I offered you some kind of dog treat, would you finally shut up?"

He ignored that. "Your instincts subconsciously drove you away from that limp-dicked man-boy, for your own good. You secretly wanted some evildoer to fuck you into the ground, even while you were pouting that you didn't get a fairy godmother to whammy you a pretty dress for the party." He snorted. "And, by the way, why the hell would you want a guy *that* hung up on women's clothes? I think it hints at unresolved issues in your childhood, don't you, Doc?"

"Wonderful." Avenant waved a languid hand towards the wall clock. "The wolf just beat his own record for beginning the weekly barrage of sexual harassment." He looked over at Ramona and arched an imperious blond brow. "I'd like to once again petition for a class system to be implemented in this institution. I should be in with a more elite group of villains, rather than with this rabble."

"I'll pass your complaints on to Dr. White." Ramona agreed quickly.

She always quickly agreed with everything Avenant said. The former Prince of the Northlands had a commanding presence and a habit of talking at everyone like they were his servants. Even the hospital staff jumped to attention around him.

Tall and lean, with shoulder length white hair and the face of a Nordic god, Avenant looked *exactly* like a prince of the Northlands *should* look: Even with his fall from grace and condescending attitude, women in the WUB Club, Good and Bad, drooled over him.

Well, the ones who didn't spend an hour a week in a share circle with the bastard, anyway.

"Did you just call us 'rabble,' again?" Esmeralda the witch snapped. "Because we discussed hurtful words last week and I remember adding that one to the whiteboard."

Avenant lifted a shoulder in an indifferent shrug. "I'm sure sheep would rather be called elephants... But they're still sheep."

Esmeralda's crimson eyes narrowed. Like most witches, her skin was a lovely shade of green and she liked to show as much of it as possible, which took some real doing in shapeless sweatpants. She was young and at the height of her powers, so it must bug the hell out of her that she couldn't just blast Avenant through the wall for his insolence. Like everyone else in the WUB Club with magical powers, though, she wore a spell inhibiting manacle on her left ankle.

Ramona clapped her hands, trying to regain the group's attention. "Alright, let's get started, people." She was a tall, thin fairy, who wore a lab coat every day because she thought it made her look smarter. "We'll start with Marrok's thoughts about Scarlet." She gave him an encouraging nod, her gray eyes eating up his handsome face. It was unprofessional the way she ogled him. Marrok really should file a complaint about it. "It's good that you're having so much insight into others." Ramona gushed at him, her gaze straying down his body.

"It shows that you're really listening in group."

Marrok modestly shrugged. Either he didn't notice Ramona's inappropriate attempts at eye-sex or he was just immune to them by now. God knew they happened every week. "Talking about things with friends helps us process the past and make better choices in the future."

Scarlett made a disgusted sound. Marrok had made a career out of bouncing from crime scenes to mental institutions, so it wasn't surprising that he'd memorized all the buzz words.

Every time he was released, all the officials agreed that *finally* he'd learned his lesson and was sure to play nice. Every time they were wrong.

The guy navigated the WUB Club like a shark in a goldfish aquarium. His performance reviews were spotless. He told all the doctors just what they wanted to hear. He probably filled his feelings journal with poems about repentance and kittens.

How could the others not notice he was a fiend?

He smirked at Scarlett. "Well, I was saying that my inner-self feels like Letty should prune some of the negative weeds in her mental garden and self-actualize the healing process. She needs to know that we're here to support her personal growth and to watch the flowers of her positivity *bloom*."

Only he could make that stupid psychobabble sound like an invitation to an orgy.

"That's beautiful, Marrok." Ramona sat down in the circle and looked over at Scarlett. "Anything to add?" She sounded far less interested in whatever Letty's contributions might be, but she picked up her clipboard and jotted down something *glowing* about Marrok. "Your sister would be so pleased if you're ready to show some signs of progress, Scarlett."

"*Step*sister."

"What?"

"Cinderella is my *step*sister." The words were too harsh, but Scarlett couldn't stop them. Nothing pissed her off faster than a mention of the sainted Cindy. She could see the disapproval on Ramona's face and it set her temper off like a rocket.

"You think it would be *wonderful* to be her sister, I know. Everyone does. That's because you have no idea what she's really like."

"But, everyone in the Four Kingdoms knows! She had a terrible life of subjugation, but kept her good heart and charitable..."

"*She's* the crazy one." Scarlett interrupted, leaning forward in her plastic chair. "You know, Cindy sang *constantly* just to annoy me. The noise would get into my head until I thought I'd snap if she didn't shut-up. Only she *never* did. She couldn't have been *that* mistreated, if she had time to memorize so many brain-crushingly annoying little ditties about love and rainbows. She *like*s subjugation, so I actually tried *not* to give it to her. It makes her sickly happy."

Marrok's eyes gleamed with deviance and lies. The perverted jackass loved it when she shouted. It turned him on.

Beside her, Drusilla stirred at the mention of Cinderella. Poor Dru was so drugged she was actually buying into the bullshit brainwashing of this place, which just pissed Scarlett off *more*. "Letty, if you don't work the process, you'll never..."

Scarlett cut her sister off. "And that's not even mentioning all her woodland pals lurking around, doing her unnatural bidding. Gross, creepy, human-sized rats making breakfast in the morning. *Rodents made the coffee, people!* Do you get how unsanitary that is?"

"That does sound appalling." Avenant concurred. He managed to look like he was holding court, even in his "EVIL" t-shirt. "In my castle, I didn't even allow *trolls* near the kitchens for fear of disease."

"Hey!" Rumpelstiltskin objected hotly.

Avenant rolled his eyes. "Oh, your people are grimy basement dwellers and you know it."

"I'm telling you Cindy got off on the housework." Scarlett continued. "No one *made* her do it. She has some kind of twisted cleaning fetish. She uses those rats as BDSM toys. It freaked me out every time I saw how scrubbed the floor was. I thought she was going to mop straight through the marble with her bizarre perversions."

Ramona cleared her throat disapprovingly. "I don't think it's appropriate to spread lies about the future princess."

"Oh, I do." Marrok assured her lasciviously. "Don't spare any dirty details, Red."

"It's all true. I'm telling you." Scarlett shook her head in disgust. "Every day was a nightmare with that caterwauling bitch. *Dru and I* were the victims, not Cinderella. For one night –*just one*-- we were supposed to be free of Cindy's disturbing predilections and sewer dwelling cronies... and *what* happens, instead?"

"I think it's someone else's turn to share." Ramona prompted a little desperately.

Scarlett was too wound-up to care about all the "still crazy" demerits she was earning. "Blondie crashed the party and stole poor Charming! *That's* what! But, God! How *terrible* I've been to poor Cinderella." Scarlett threw up her hands in mock despair. "She's living in a fucking castle and I'm stuck in prison, but poor *her*." She snorted. "That spiteful tramp and her tiara can *both* kiss my ass."

Esmeralda started nodding, her wild mass of black curls tumbling around her face. "I know how you feel. Bratty kids were trying to tear my house apart and eat it. I *had* to stop them or I would have been homeless. But, still they locked me up."

"Yes!" Scarlett nodded triumphantly. "That's my whole point! *We're* not the bad guys... *they* are." She pointed out one of the barred windows to the flawless world beyond. "All of the perfect, milquetoast, shiny Good folk out there, who think rules don't apply to them. That they can just *eat* Esmeralda's house. That they can break deals with innocent trolls, because *now* they're royalty and need to keep their precious heir." Her hand swept towards Rumpelstiltskin, who grunted in agreement. "Not to mention poor Benji. Hell, he's only here because some developer wanted to force him to sell his bridge."

"Now it's a condo." Benji whispered sadly.

"*I* am the rightful Prince of the Northlands, but they refused me my throne because I was born Bad." Avenant put in. "They said it was against the law for me to rule. I had no choice but to take what was mine by force and then they called *me* the villain."

"Exactly! What about you, Marrok?" Scarlett pointed at him. "Did you even get a choice about playing that ridiculous Wolfball thing? Or did they force you into it and then send you here when they didn't follow their sadistic rules?"

He said nothing, which was all the answer she needed.

"See? *We're* the ones punished, while they get to live out their happily ever afters." Scarlett looked around the share circle. "What about *our* happily ever afters?"

"You don't deserve a happily ever after when you're evil." Dru said quietly.

Scarlett's mouth thinned. It was just a matter of time before Dru got sucked under by this place. Scarlett blamed Cindy for the change in her sister's spirit. "*Everyone* deserves a happily ever after." She said firmly.

Marrok regarded her with a strange expression.

Scarlett pretended not to notice. "Besides, we're not evil, Dru."

"We *are*, though. I see that, now."

"Very good reasoning, Drusilla." Ramona said in her smarmiest tone. "You're exactly right. *All* of you were born wicked, ugly, and/or Bad. It's in your psychological makeup to do terrible things. You're here to try and suppress it as best you can, but you'll never be Good like the rest of us. You need to accept that."

Avenant gave a contemptuous snort.

"Oh, I've accepted my nature." Marrok arched a brow at Scarlett. "You should too, Red. Believe me, life gets so much better when you just give into the inevitable."

She glowered over at him. "First off, die in a fire. And secondly, there shouldn't be a '*them*.' Why are they allowed to declare us wrong and lock us away? Half the people here haven't committed any crimes!"

Ramona sighed and lit a cigarette with her star-shaped lighter. The woman smoked three packs a day. "There are laws against being evil…"

"I'm not evil! I haven't even done anything illegal. I just don't like Cinderella. That doesn't make me crazy or demented. It just means I know her better than you." Scarlett was warming to her topic. "Bad isn't evil, it's just *Bad*. My grandmother always says that."

"She does." Dru murmured. "Where is Grandma, Letty?"

Scarlett didn't think it was a good idea to answer that. "My point is, there should be justice for people who aren't born charming or beautiful."

"Justice?" Esmeralda repeated blankly. "For Bad folk?"

"Yes! There should be a real place for us! We shouldn't just... *judge* people on what they look like and say that's all they are. Whether or not they have horns, shouldn't make a difference in what kind of job they can get." She shook her head. "That's just *stupid*. Don't you think we can do *better*? That we should all be equal?"

Everyone stared at her like she really was insane.

"Fucking hell..." Marrok sounded awed. "I *knew* there had to be *something* going on, but I didn't put it together until now." He started laughing. "You're *Good*."

Scarlett blinked. Maybe he was on drugs, after all.

"Noooo." Ramona put in swiftly. "She's an ugly stepsister, remember? They can't be Good."

"It's true." Drusilla nodded. "Even as children we tormented dear Cindy."

"No, we didn't!" Scarlett snapped. "She's got some kind of kinky sex thing where she likes housework, so she's pretending to be a martyr while sleeping with her pets. The simpering sweetness is all an *act*."

Esmeralda made a note of that in her journal. "This is an *awesome* share time."

"Ugly stepsister, my ass." Marrok's gaze roamed over Scarlett's body like she was some exotic species of bug plopped under his microscope. "You're one of *them*. In fact, you're *better* than them, because no one ever told you you were better. Shit, this is just my fucking luck."

"If Scarlett is Good, then she can't be here." Rumpelstiltskin complained. He removed his pointy hat, so he could scratch his pointy head. His beard was white and curled down to his stomach. He scratched that, too. The little guy was always so twitchy. "This is supposed to be a safe place for Bad folk to talk without judgment."

"We can't kick Scarlett out of group." Benji the bridge ogre objected, swallowing the last mouthful of his feelings journal. His XXXXXXL "EVIL" shirt was stretched taunt against his massive midsection. "That would make us no better than them. They discriminate because we're Bad and we'd be excluding Letty because she's Good. It's a vicious cycle of hate and the share circle is about inclusion."

Dru glanced over at him earnestly. "That is *so* deep, Benji."

He blushed and ripped off the arm of his chair to munch on. In addition to being Bad, the guy had developed an eating disorder. It was the stress of this place.

"Scarlett's not Good." Ramona loudly assured everyone.

"I'm not Good." Scarlett agreed. "I can't stand any of you. Especially *him*." She pointed at Marrok, his crazy announcement bringing up all her insecurities. "A Good folk wouldn't be thinking of horrible tortures to visit upon his body, right now."

"Red, you can start visiting places on my body anytime you like." Marrok drawled. "Christ! I couldn't understand what the hell was going on with you, but now I get it. The meds were masking some of it, but today..." he closed his eyes and breathed in deep, "I can *smell* the Good on you."

"That's not true." But she still gave herself a

surreptitious sniff.

"Oh, it's true alright. And it explains so much. Wolves always know when nice little girls enter our woods, but your kind never suspects all the hungry things circling in the shadows."

"For the last time..."

He cut her off. "Did you really not *know* you were different from the rest of us? Do you think that witches and trolls worry about gaining equality? Do you think *he* does?" He pointed at Avenant.

"Gaining equality with any of you would be a staggering demotion." Avenant scoffed.

Marrok ignored him, his attention on Scarlett. "Do you think your sister there doesn't believe that Cinderella is *better* than her, just because she's prettier?"

"It's true. She is." Dru nodded.

"No, she's not!" Scarlett was getting really angry, now. "Everyone just listen, alright? What I'm saying is completely logical. It's about all of us having a say in the Four Kingdoms. Bad folk outnumber the Good. Why are they controlling us? Why can they just toss us in here, without even a real trial? Who represents *us*?"

Rumpelstiltskin frowned thoughtfully.

Esmeralda looked over at Ramona like she might have the answer.

The doctor stubbed out her cigarette and lit another. Her chain smoking always seemed to get worse when Scarlett shared her thoughts. "That's just the way things have always been done in the Four Kingdoms." She sputtered. "Do you not understand that?" Obviously at a loss for what else to say, Ramona launched into a quick civics recap. "Each kingdom of our land --North, South, East and West-- has a prince. The kingdoms meet in the middle, here in Centerlands. It's a free area, where we have the market and... the hospital."

"*Prison*." Scarlett corrected.

"And then there's the Enchanted Forest, which I'm sure you all know is overrun with lawless criminals. No one claims ownership of such a place, except the villains who've escaped their rightful justice."

"Are you really attempting to give *me* a geography lesson?" Avenant glared at Ramona, sounding offended. "I'm the rightful ruler of the Northlands, peasant."

"'Peasant' was on the whiteboard, too." Esmeralda muttered.

Ramona held up her hands for silence. "The point is our majestic princes make rules that are best for everyone."

"But, it's always the *same* princes." Benji said around his plastic seat cushion. "Until it's their sons. And they're always Good. Except when Avenant took over and everyone was too afraid to stop him."

Avenant smiled at that memory.

"Well, of course the princes are Good! No one wants some ugly, wicked villain in charge of a kingdom? That would be crazy!"

Scarlett arched a brow at the choice of words. "Haven't you heard? I *am* crazy. According to you and Cindy, anyway."

"You aren't crazy. I don't know *what* the hell you are, except in big fucking trouble." Marrok leaned forward, looking annoyed at her, now. "How long do you think it'll be before more Baddies sniff you out?"

Scarlett glanced at him in surprise. "What's that supposed to mean?"

"It means not everyone in here has my kink for Good girls. Word gets around this place that you're a white hat and you're sure not gonna win inmate of the month."

Her eyes narrowed at the warning.

"Oh, Grandma won't like that." Dru predicted.

"Anything we say in group is confidential." Benji complained. "That's part of the trust contract."

Avenant snorted. "And yet the good doctor writes down everything we say." He pointed at Ramona's clipboard.

Ramona frowned at him. "I told you, these notes are just for your private records. You'll be very grateful to have them when you come up before the Medical Review and Parole Board, and they see how much you've progressed in your therapy."

"Very comforting. Except, I'm here for life plus a century."

"Oh." Ramona frowned down at her clipboard and made a note of that.

"Also, he hasn't *made* any progress." Esmeralda muttered.

"Nobody's gonna have to *tell* the rest of the wolves that Letty's Good." Marrok retorted. "They'll be able to scent it on her, just like I did." He arched a brow at her. "You are ass-deep in enemy territory, right now. Whole lotta Bad folk who are locked up in here don't like your kind. No friends, no powers, no handsome prince... seems like your own people tossed you to the wolves." He drew out the last part as if he thought it was just *brilliant* wordplay.

"For the last time: *I'm not Good.*" All her life she'd been hearing things like that from her grandmother and they stung. Scarlett knew she could be Bad, if she just had a chance.

"Well, baby, you're the closest thing I've ever

come to finding it." His face got softer somehow. "The *real* kind of Good is pretty damn rare and you wear it like a perfume. No wonder I scare you." Golden eyes stayed locked on blue for a long moment and then Marrok smiled at her. It wasn't a smirk, he actually *smiled*. "Letty, do you really not know who I am?" He asked softly.

Scarlett looked away, unnerved and confused by the gentle tone.

"This topic is straying from our objective this week." Ramona flashed Scarlett an annoyed glare, blaming her for capturing Marrok's attention. "We're supposed to be discussing ways you can all make amends for you wicked ways and live decent lives. Or, at least, as decent as you're able, given what you are."

"Once again... life plus a century." Avenant's tone suggested Ramona had the IQ of a toadstool. "What possible difference could it make *what* kind of life I lead, if I'm destined to live it here amongst these hillbillies?"

"Hillbillies?!" Esmeralda threw her hands up in exasperation. "He just *said* that! Come *on*, people! Words hurt."

"No one ever gets out of here." Drusilla put in gloomily. Her eyes stayed fixed on the peeling paint. "No one ever has and no one ever will. Prince Avenant is right. It's all hopeless."

Benji's hand inched up.

Everyone ignored him.

"Avenant's an *ex*-prince." Rumpelstiltskin corrected snottily. "Being a prince and getting *fired* is worse than never being a prince, at all." He clearly wasn't over the whole "grimy basement dwellers" comment.

"I was born a prince and I will die a prince." Avenant retorted with icy distain. "That usurper may have my crown, but I am the one and only legitimate ruler of the Northlands. You would do well to remember that, troll."

Benji waved his hand like a kid wanting to be called on in class. "Doctor?"

"*No*, we're not doing this, again." Marrok dragged his gaze from Scarlett long enough to glower at Avenant. "We're not gonna spend this whole time talking about *you* and that fucking crown. All we *ever* talk about is you and that fucking crown. I want to talk about sexual fantasies, for once. Last night, I had one starring a bossy redhead and this huge caldron of vanilla pudding…"

Avenant cut him off. "Really? The pudding thing, again?" He rolled his eyes. "Ramona, there *must* be a better share circle I could join. Where did you assign that guy who touches things and they turn to gold? I should be in *his* group."

"*Doctor!*" Both of Benji's hands waved impatiently.

"Al*right*, Benji." Ramona clearly would've preferred to discuss Marrok's sexual perversions, but the ogre just wouldn't let it go. "What would you like to share?"

"Trevelyan got out of here, so it's not hopeless." Benji gave Dru a wise nod and settled back in his chair as if he was satisfied.

Half the group cringed like they expected lightening to strike at the sound of the name.

"The *dragon* got paroled from here and they locked up me and Dru?!" Scarlett shouted. That son-of-a-bitch sold magic and death to the highest bidder.

"We don't talk about Trevelyan." Ramona nervously glanced towards the door. "Just know that he was a problem right from the beginning. I had to start holding special therapy sessions *after* our group sessions, just to deal with the trauma he inflicted during the *first* session."

"They didn't *let* Trevelyan out." Rumpelstiltskin corrected. "He escaped about five years ago. They try to keep it quiet, but..."

Scarlett cut him off. "How?"

"How what?"

"*How* did he escape?"

"I don't know. I didn't really get a chance to ask him *before he escaped*."

"As if he would lower himself to talk to you, anyway." Esmeralda scoffed. "Marrok knew him though, didn't you, Wolf?"

"We met." Marrok said shortly.

"You were in the same cell!" Ez snapped. "That's more than just 'meeting' someone."

"Sad really." Avenant mused. "Trevelyan was part of a majestic race. Doomed and enslaved by lesser beings, but majestic, none the less." His gaze swept over the rest of the group with a sigh. "I know the feeling well."

Scarlett's mind raced.

Someone had escaped from here. Someone evil and way more powerful than her, but it *could* be done. You just had to have the guts to try something bold.

Letty's gaze slowly lifted to Drusilla. The royal wedding was in just a few days. This would be the last time Scarlett and Dru were in the same room together before then, so this was Scarlett's only chance. No way would Charming or her grandmother be able to help her in time. It was all up to Letty.

She *had* to do something.

Now.

Ramona made another effort to seize control of the conversation. "We really need to concentrate on our group work. Benji, why don't you tell us about some of the personal goals you've striven towards this week?"

"Well, I've been trying not to eat so many light bulbs..."

He trailed off as Letty rose to her feet.

"Scarlett, you mustn't stand during share time." Ramona scolded around her cigarette. "It doesn't show good listening-ship."

"Ya know what, Ramona?" Scarlett turned and gripped the back of her chair. "I think I'm through sharing with you."

Hefting the chair up, she swung it right into the doctor's head. She'd never hit anyone before, but it was so amazingly simple that Scarlett was shocked she hadn't tried it sooner. Ramona toppled to the floor in an unconscious heap while the rest of the group gaped at Scarlett in shock.

She stood over Ramona's fallen body, the chair held at an awkward angle, and arched a brow at Marrok. "Tell me again I'm not Bad."

Chapter Two

A high IQ and delusions of grandeur are dangerous in any Baddie. In this patient, they seem particularly troublesome, though. To my highly-trained mind, Scarlett's firebrand tendencies and inability to know her place make her the most dangerous villain here.

Psychiatric case notes of Dr. Ramona Fae

"Wonderful." Avenant rolled his eyes. "Letty's killed the doctor. Now I'll have to start all over with training another one to stand when I enter a room. It'll take weeks."

"Luckily, you have life plus a century to get it right." Esmeralda retorted. She bent down to pick up Ramona's clipboard and flipped through the pages. "Geez, look at the shit she wrote about me. 'Anger issues?' 'Lacking empathy?' 'Can't take criticism?' Hell, I'm glad the bitch is dead."

"She's not dead!" Scarlett peered down at her victim and had no idea what to do next. "I just knocked her out a little bit." She hesitated and glanced at Marrok. "Right?"

"How am I supposed to know?" He casually leaned back and arched a brow. "*I'm* not the one who beat her skull with a folding chair."

"But you're the most experienced criminal here, so I'm bowing to your expertise!" Scarlett inched closer to Ramona's still form and tried not to hyperventilate. Her grandmother would expect her to stay calm. "I think she's breathing. Oh, thank God. Don't you think she's breathing?"

Marrok barely glanced down at the woman.

"She's breathing."

"She's also unconscious." Benji said worriedly. "Should we call someone in here to help her?"

"No!" Rumpelstiltskin cast a frantic look towards the door. "That's the last thing we need! They'll blame the whole group for this. Throw us *all* in the dungeon. We have to get out of here!"

"Oh, this isn't going to look good on the weekly report." Dru lamented. "Letty, you'll be getting some demerits for sure."

"I'm not going to be *around* to get them." Scarlett dragged her attention away from Ramona. "None of us are. Rumpelstiltskin's right. We need to get out of here. All of us." She nodded, convincing herself of her new plan even as she created it. "We're escaping the WUB Club. It's the only way."

Marrok's mouth curved.

"But, I'm finally making some real progress on my confidence issues in here..." Benji began.

Avenant cut him off. "It's impossible to escape. I say we turn Scarlett in and hope that Dr. White only punishes her. It's our best option."

Marrok lazily shrugged. "Or we could blame *you* and finally get rid of your ass."

"I like that idea." Esmeralda voted.

"Two minutes ago you guys told me Trevelyan escaped." Scarlett reminded them, drawing their attention back to her scheme. "It *can* be done."

"Are you *also* capable of turning into a fire-breathing monster?" Avenant asked snidely. "Because if you *are*, now's the time to mention that. Otherwise, I don't see how you plan on getting passed the guards..."

"I don't know exactly, but..."

"...and all the alarms..."

"We'll have to work out the details..."

"...and the Lake of Forgetting..."

"Obviously, that will be a problem..."

"...and the flying monkeys..."

"*Alright!* I'm not saying it'll be easy, but neither is spending the rest of your life locked up in here." She glared at him. "Do you *want* to sit there in cheap sweatpants while someone else wears your crown around like a party hat up in the Northlands?"

Avenant's mouth thinned.

"I didn't think so." Scarlett said regaining her confidence. She could do this. She just had to convince them that this was the only way. "Life plus a century, Avenant. This moment --*right now*-- is the only chance you will *ever* have of seeing your big icy castle, again. You know that."

He watched her broodingly, but he stopped talking about turning her in to the guards.

Encouraged, Scarlett moved on to the others. "Do *any* of you want to be here? Even you, Benji. Wouldn't you be happier living under a nice bridge frightening trespassers?"

He gave a dreamy sigh. "I love a good trespasser."

"Esmeralda?" Scarlett turned to the witch next. "Don't you want to do magic, again?"

"Of course I do! It's the only thing I *dream* of. Casting spells... Turning people into frogs... Genetically engineering my gingerbread army..."

"Well, you'll never even get to say another hex unless you come with me. Wouldn't you risk *anything* to regain your powers?"

Esmeralda's expression grew fervent. "*Anything.*"

"Alright then." Scarlett looked over at

Rumpelstiltskin. "And you… while you're stuck in here, who's looking after all those cute little first borns you bargained for?"

"Nannies. It's costing me a fortune."

"Right. Don't you want to get home to the kids?"

"Mostly, I just don't want to be here when the guards find out what you did to Dr. Ramona. Right now, I'm all about the running away."

"Whatever." She didn't care *why* he agreed, just so he agreed. "Marrok…?" Scarlett finally turned to the wolf, at a loss as to what argument she could use with him.

He'd be released from the WUB Club soon, if for no other reason than he was the most popular Baddie in the tabloids. He made Good folk money and that was more important than his list of crimes. Why would he want to risk a life sentence on escape when he could just wait it out and be free to go back to his life of fame?

Marrok arched a brow at her, waiting for her sales pitch. Every time he looked at her, Scarlett felt him seeing straight through to all her secret doubts and insecurities.

"Just…" She exhaled heavily and didn't even try for cleverness or subtlety. It wouldn't work to persuade him. Even discounting everything else, she expected him to refuse to go along with this just because he liked screwing with her. "Look, do you want to escape with me or not?" It was the only thing she could think to say.

He lounged there, considering her with unreadable topaz eyes for a long moment. "What the hell." He eventually drawled. "I got nothin' else to do today, so… sure."

Scarlett blinked, amazed that it had been so easy to convince him. "Really? Because, if we're caught, it's an automatic life sentence." She wasn't sure why she was suddenly reminding him of that, but she couldn't help it. Unlike the rest of them, Marrok shouldn't go along with this plan. Logically, it was a poor decision, even for someone with such staggering impulse control problems. "In less than six months, your sentence is up anyway."

"I'm an impatient guy." He lifted a shoulder in a lazy shrug. "Let's start digging a tunnel."

If he was sure, she wasn't about to push her luck. "No tunnel. We don't have the time." She looked over at Esmeralda. "If we got that spell inhibitor off your leg, could you blast a hole in the side of this building?"

"No. The second I do anything that big, the magic sensors will go off and the whole place will get shut down with purple gas." She gestured towards the vents in the ceiling. "They'll pump it in here and everyone goes to sleep."

Rumpelstiltskin paled. "Oh God." The purple fumes of the sleeping spell could only be broken by a True Love's kiss and those were hard to come by when you were sealed in a padded cell. He glowered at Scarlett. "You've completely fucked us over! They'll *never* believe that you did this on your own! If we get caught, all seven of us will be gassed and locked up."

Scarlett ignored him, her attention on Esmeralda. "Could you conjure something smaller that wouldn't set off the alarms? Could you maybe whip up a *tiny* spell to make yourself look like Ramona?"

Esmeralda smirked. "I'm a level six witch. I could do a simple, undetected glamour that would fool Ramona's own mother. But only if I get this bling off of me." She pointed to the manacle on her ankle.

"You think no one's thought of cutting off their restraint?" Avenant snorted. "The second you remove the monitor, the guards will know it. It's all hooked up to the computers. My first day here, I had that figured out and you people still haven't..."

Scarlett interrupted him, her mind whirling. "We *want* the guards to know."

"We do? Are we stupid?"

"Some of us aren't." Scarlett kept her eyes on Esmeralda. "If you make yourself look like Ramona, can you make Ramona look like you?"

"Of course."

"Good. Benji?" She turned to the bridge ogre. "Are you strong enough to break that ankle cuff off of Ez?"

"Oh, he's strong enough." Dru volunteered hazily. "Remember how he shared that he once lifted the entire Eastlands Bridge to get those bratty goats?"

Benji winced. "I'm not supposed to use my strength to do evil, though. It's part of working my steps..."

"This isn't evil!" Scarlett insisted. "We're saving the Four Kingdoms by escaping."

Benji blinked. "Saving them from what?"

"From my wicked stepsister Cinderella, of course! Trust me, okay? This is the only way."

"It is?" Benji hesitated and glanced over at Marrok. "Are you *sure* Scarlett's really Good?"

"Oh, she's Good enough to eat." Golden eyes glowed hot as Marrok watched Scarlett pace. All this rule breaking was like a lupine aphrodisiac. "My journal entry about today's meeting is gonna be *epic*, by the way. I'm feeling a lot of personal growth in some real interesting areas, Red."

"Just sit there and be quiet." Scarlett jabbed a finger at him, all her focus centered on her rapidly developing plan. "I'm about to make you a hero."

***

"So that's when the witch somehow pulled off her own restraint and flung herself at me like a beautiful and deadly panther. I think she'd seen my stupid clipboard and realized that I'd been writing down sordid lies about her mental state. I'm very jealous of her, you see, and use my middle management position..."

"*Dr. Ramona.*" Scarlett bit off. "The guards just want to hear how we stopped Esmeralda from escaping. Not about your hard work here in group." She shined a smile at the two security dwarves who were taking a report on the incident. "They're very busy men."

"Oh, right." Esmeralda, in her magically created "Ramona" disguise, flipped back her hair and frowned when the move didn't come off with her usual flair. Ramona's short blonde pixie cut didn't swing like the witch's long curls. "So anyway, while the magnificent Esmeralda attacked me --looking *super* glamorous, by the way-- I cowered to the floor, praying for my own quick death."

"We were all praying for that." Avenant concurred.

"We're all going to be gassed." Rumpelstiltskin muttered, rocking back and forth in his seat. His gaze stayed fixed on the real Ramona's unconscious form.

Magic now had the doctor looking just like Esmeralda *usually* looked, right down to the red sweat suit. The broken manacle was strategically arranged next to her body. Unless you were a wolf, and could smell the difference in the woman's scent, no one would be able to tell who she actually was.

"That's when Marrok heroically stopped her rampage." Scarlett put in. "He knocked Esmeralda unconscious with his Wolfball skills and saved the day. Didn't you, Marrok?"

"Nope."

Damn it! She'd known his brief moment of cooperation wouldn't last. Scarlett's teeth ground together. "Yes, you *did*, remember?"

"I wouldn't hit a woman. No wolf would do that."

"You would if it meant saving the lives of others." She snapped.

"Well, that would depend on *which* others."

"It all happened so fast." Esmeralda/Ramona interjected, before Scarlett could continue the argument. "I'm just thankful the witch was caught unaware and stopped in time. It was pure luck that she didn't destroy us all."

"How did the witch get her magic inhibitor off?" One of the dwarf guards asked, taking careful notes of "Ramona's" eyewitness report. Since she was supposedly the only Good folk present, her testimony would be all that mattered to Dr. White.

Marrok kept his attention on Scarlett. "That's an interesting question." He smirked. "How *did* she get it off, do you think?"

"I don't know." Her blue eyes flashed daggers at him. "I guess it just broke."

"The witch is a cunning and brilliant foe." Esmeralda/Ramona agreed. "Who knows what kind of genius plan she had hatched. We were all too dazzled by her athleticism and by the way she outsmarted me at every turn to notice all the details."

"Well, we can check that out later on the video." One of the guards assured her.

"The *video?*" Half the room chorused in horror.

Benji scrunched his massive body down in his chair. "Uh-oh."

Drusilla winced. "Letty, maybe we should just..."

"It'll be *fine*, Dru." Scarlett interrupted with determined cheer. "Right, Doctor Ramona? The camera is *great* news, isn't it?"

"Yeah." Esmeralda/Ramona quickly scanned the ceiling, her eyes falling on a small security camera. "Sure... great." She swallowed. "Yeah, a video will clear up all the questions you have, guard. Uh... when will you be reviewing that, again?"

"As soon as we're done carting the witch down into the dungeon." The head dwarf closed his notebook with an authoritative snap. "By then, it'll have downloaded onto the main computer and we can watch it frame-by-frame in the office. See if any of this bunch tried to help her with her stupid plan."

Marrok arched a brow at Scarlett. "It *was* a stupid plan, wasn't it?"

The dwarf guard nodded at Esmeralda/Ramona like she was the one who'd agreed with him. Good folk tended to tune out the Bad like the hum of a florescent light. "Don't worry, Doc. We'll sort all this out in no time."

"Super-duper." Esmeralda/Ramona gave a weak thumbs-up as the men hefted the unconscious "witch" between them and carted her out the door. "Thanks fellas. Couldn't have done it without you. I'll just finish up here and make sure these nut-bags get back to their cells." She slammed the door shut behind them and swore in the ancient language of witches. "*Now* what do we do?!"

"I feel violated." Benji lamented. "Group is being

videotaped? What about our trust bubble?"

"I *told* you that Ramona wasn't respecting our confidentiality." Avenant reminded them smugly. "Servants always spy."

"Nobody panic." Scarlett held up her hands and felt panicked. "Let's just think this through."

"What's there to think about?!" Rumpelstiltskin shrieked. "They have a tape! The gas will come and put us all to sleep and..."

"Shut-*up!*" Scarlett snapped. "It's not actually a tape. You heard him. It's a video file. We'll just have to erase it from the computer and everything will be fine."

"Oh, that makes all the difference in the world." Avenant scoffed. "Except the computer is locked in the security office... with all the *guards and security*."

"You are the most whiny prince ever." Scarlett declared. "Charming would never complain so much."

Marrok slanted her an unreadable look. "Charming also left you here to rot, so he's possibly not the best role model."

She ignored him. "Let's just concentrate on solving the problem."

"We should just give up." Drusilla murmured, slipping even deeper into her drugged gloom. "Charming left us. Cinderella was right. Good will always beat us in the end."

Marrok put his hands behind his head like he was lounging back at the beach. "I have this fantasy where *I'm* beaten by Good with this saucy leather whip. She's wearing this little school girl uniform and we're in this thing of vanilla pudding..."

"Wolf, I swear to God, I will have Ez turn you into a toad." Scarlett turned back to Esmeralda like a general in command of her troops... her doomed, criminally insane troops. "Ez, can you do any kind of magic to get rid of the recording?"

"Not without triggering the magic alarms. I'll have to go in and do it the boring way." She smoothed her stolen lab coat over her hips and frowned. "Hey, do I look fat in this body? Be honest."

Benji started munching on a throw pillow. "This whole situation is making me stress eat."

"You're not going *anywhere*, witch." Avenant glowered at Esmeralda. "How can we be sure you'll come back?" He made a "hel*lo*" gesture with one hand. "She could just leave us here and make a run for it, all dressed up in Ramona's face. Am I the only one who realizes that?"

Esmeralda flipped him off. "I barely even considered that, jackass."

"Avenant is right." Rumpelstiltskin bobbed his head. "Esmeralda will escape and let the rest of us take the blame for this whole mess! I know it!"

"How many times must I tell you peasants to address me as *Prince* Avenant? And if the witch goes to deal with the computer, then so do I. At least *I* have some knowledge of how they work."

"Of course you do." Esmeralda sneered. "How much did you embezzle from your loyal citizens, again?"

"Those slush funds were all setup by that fucking usurper to frame me!"

"We don't have time for this bickering." Scarlett's gaze swept the room. "Our whole group is escaping. *All* of us. No one will be left behind, so long as we trust each other."

Six people stared back at her like she was deranged.

Evildoers weren't big on team building.

"Alright, maybe not *trust* trust, but trust that all of us want to get out of here." Scarlett tried a different tactic. "Look, it's simple logic. If one of us goes down, we all do. Whoever gets caught or abandoned will just rat the others, right? So, we're all in this together."

Marrok made an "aww" sound. "That's beautiful, Red. *Except*... if we're a team and all, why does it seem like you've appointed *yourself* captain?"

"Well, who do *you* think should be captain? You?"

"Why not? I work on a team professionally. Plus, you said yourself I have the most experience at being a criminal."

"You also have the most experience at being a sociopath!"

Marrok crossed his arms over his chest. "But, that was before I met *you* and learned violence isn't the way. You taught me to be peaceable and honest and... Oh *wait*... Thaaat's right. *You* just clocked an innocent fairy in the head, didn't you?"

Scarlett stalked over to plant her palms on the arms of his chair, looming over him. "If you can't play nice tell me now. Because, I need you to be serious and *help* me. Please."

His smirked faded. "I'll help you." For one brief moment, he actually sounded sincere. "You *know* I will. Baby, if you want to escape, we'll escape. But, we gotta do it smart."

"That's what I'm trying to do!"

"No offense, but you're doing a piss poor job. Now, it's not all your fault." He held up a hand forestalling her protest. "After all, what does a Good girl know about staging a jailbreak?"

"I'm... not... *Good*."

He leaned forward to inhale the scent of her hair. "You sure smell Good."

So did he.

Scarlett blinked rapidly at the thought.

Marrok moved his head to keep eye contact when she would've looked away in awkward confusion. "It's alright." He whispered. "I should have handled it better. Even through those damn drugs they were giving you, I knew who you were. I just didn't understand why *you* didn't know and it pissed me off. I didn't understand that you couldn't *possibly* figure it out."

Scarlett swallowed. "Figure what out?"

"Poor Letty." His tone was all warm honey and promises. "You've spent your whole life locked in a castle being Good, haven't you? You've never been near any *real* Baddies, at all. You have no idea how we operate."

"I come from a notoriously wicked family!" She insisted. "I'm telling you, I'm very, very *Bad*. Look at what I'm doing, right now."

"Baby, I see you. I see you talking about trust, and saving the Four Kingdoms, and all-for-one-ing it with the rest of these idiots, when you *should* be figuring out a way to save your own cute little ass. It's so erotically Good, I feel like you're just torturing me with how adorable you are."

He had to be messing with her. No one ever called ugly stepsisters "adorable." "When I torture you it will be painful, not erotic."

"Oh, I'm hoping it'll be both."

Scarlett pulled back, refusing to be taken in by the seductive smile he leveled at her. She crossed her arms over her chest and cleared her throat. "Alright, this isn't getting us anywhere. If you have something to add to this escape plan, feel free to speak up."

"Please, do." Avenant muttered. "The woman clearly needs all the help she can get."

"Well, first off, we're not fucking around with a computer system." Marrok arched a brow at Scarlett, resuming his normal sarcastic tone. "Seriously, you watch too many movies. None of us have any idea how to hack into security mainframes and erase encrypted video files. Especially not him." He pointed at Avenant. "I guarantee Prince Asshole didn't commit his own cybercrimes. Any money he electronically stole from his poor oppressed people, he had some *other* poor oppressed person electronically steal *for* him."

"My people loved me!" Avenant lifted a shoulder in an arrogant shrug. "And when they *didn't*, they paid for their disloyalty. That's how you build *real* citizenship."

"And how you wound up here." Esmeralda said sweetly.

Scarlett disregarded their bickering, a skill she'd fine-tuned through many looooong group sessions with them sniping at each other. "Fine, Wolf, how do you suggest we fix this mess, then?"

Marrok leaned over to grab Ramona's star-shaped lighter, which had fallen on the floor. "We use nature's eraser." He held out his hands "ta-da!" style. "Arson."

Chapter Three

Everyone's afraid of The Big Bad Wolf. And for good reason.

Psychiatric case notes of Dr. Ramona Fae

Why would fate give him the goodiest Good girl in the Four Kingdoms as his True Love?

It just didn't make any sense.

When he'd thought Scarlett was evil, Marrok had been bewildered by how... pure she seemed, but at least he could comfort himself with the knowledge that she was probably faking her naiveté. Now that he knew she was *Good*, though, he felt like he'd been handed a spider web made of crystal and told not to break it. It would've been funny if it wasn't so damn frustrating.

Letty believed in happily ever afters for Baddies, for God's sake. What was he supposed to do with someone like that?

Marrok glanced down at her and stifled a sigh.

Still... wolves could always scent their True Loves and this girl was definitely his. Everyone in the Four Kingdoms was born with a True Love and most Bad folk had some kind of innate knowledge when they met their other halves. No one knew exactly why, but Marrok suspected that it was a protective measure to keep them from accidentally harming their True Loves before they realized who they really were. Bad folk weren't so great at *not* killing people who annoyed them and True Loves could be pretty damn annoying.

From the second Scarlett had shown up in the Tuesday share circle, Marrok had known who she was and it had severely pissed him off that she'd so clearly rejected him. That she'd watched him warily, and tried to ignore him, and pretended not to notice their connection.

Except she hadn't been pretending.

The woman had no way of recognizing him, because she was Good straight down to her spotless (yet kinda of scheme-y) soul. Good Folk couldn't sense much of anything beyond their own moral superiority. It was a biological fact. Plus, his aggravating little True Love was doubly blind because she didn't even *know* she was Good. ...Of course, she *also* didn't know how to be Bad.

No one had prepared her properly for either world.

What kind of damn idiots had raised this girl that they didn't notice she wasn't wicked, ugly or Bad? That they'd allow her to be dumped in prison with men like him? Seriously, what the fuck was he supposed to do with a woman like this?

And things would be even worse now that the drugs were out of her system. He hadn't been lying to Scarlett earlier. Now, the other wolves would be able to scent the Good on her and her kind weren't real popular in the WUB Club. It was a wonder she hadn't been eaten already.

This stupid escape plan really was their only option if Marrok was going to keep her alive. And -- against his better judgment-- he was *determined* to keep her alive. He'd fucked up enough in his life. He wasn't blowing this, too.

Trevelyan would be laughing his ass off if he saw this.

Marrok's jaw firmed. He had to get Letty out of there, no matter what it took. Good or Bad, you only got one True Love, so this redheaded pain in the ass was vital to him. Granted, he'd always imagined that his True Love would be some delightfully evil she-wolf, who laughed as she broke hearts and severed limbs, but Little Miss Save-the-World would have to do.

At least she smelled nice.

"This is never going to work." Scarlett whispered. "We should come up with a different idea." She leaned closer to him to peer around the corner of the hall. The security office was only ten feet away, but it was bolted from the inside with a camera setup to record anyone who came close to the door.

Since she was too distracted to notice that she was almost touching him, Marrok took the opportunity to lean down and breathe in the scent of her hair. The spiced apple fragrance shot right to his groin.

"Of course it will work." He murmured. "I'm a master criminal. My plans always work."

"Really? Then, why are you in jail?"

Despite himself, Marrok's lips twitched upward at her bitchy tone. At least it was *something*. "My evil stepsister set me up. I swear."

Scarlett leveled a look of death in his direction. Good or not, the girl did have a delectable mean streak. "Just remember who's in charge of this escape, alright? I'm going along with this part of the plan with some *extreme* reservations."

"Uh-huh." Marrok barely heard her words, his attention on watching her lips move.

His sexual fantasies had been getting increasingly graphic lately and some of the best ones starred her mouth. The girl probably had no clue what to do in the bedroom --which was a shame because the she-wolf vixen of his imagination had always been incredibly limber-- but his body didn't care about Scarlett's lack of skill. He just *wanted* her. All his instincts told him to claim her right now, rebelling at the unnaturally long wait he'd already endured.

What other wolf could spend six weeks locked in a confined space with his True Love and not even *touch* her? He deserved a damn medal for his restraint. Not that she appreciated it. God, he couldn't have found a more difficult girl if he'd tried.

"Are you listening to me?" She demanded.

"Nope."

She made an exasperated sound. "I *said* I'm in charge. Just do what I tell you, alright?"

"This just turned promisingly kinky. Do I have to call you 'Mistress?'"

Scarlett gestured towards the security office. "Just get on with it. And remember not to murder anyone."

"No promises on that front." He grazed her temple with a kiss, his smile growing wider as she jolted. Then, she quickly remembered she hated him and shoved him away. "Stay right here where I can see you. Understand?" He said.

She blinked up at him in confusion, still not getting it.

He'd been discreetly keeping an eye on Scarlett from the first day she'd shown up in the WUB Club, making sure that no one so much as cut in front of her in the cafeteria line. If people in the WUB Club knew how important she was to Marrok, she'd already be dead. He had so many enemies that Scarlett would be a target just because she belonged to him. Especially among the other wolves. He'd either played Wolfball against or with most of them, and his brethren weren't great at leaving rivalries on the field.

God, he hated his fucking job. Coming to the WUB Club was like an annual vacation he took when he just couldn't stand it any longer. Only this visit, he'd found the one person who could finally change *everything* for him.

If he could keep her alive, Letty would save him from his life.

He knew it with everything in him.

Marrok didn't want the girl more than two feet from his side until they were safely outside the prison walls and away from all the insane killers who hated her kind. Then, he'd be willing to renegotiate the distance to a generous four feet.

Well, maybe three.

Marrok pointed a finger at her, his voice growing serious. "Don't do anything stupid, helpful, or violent until I get back."

She glowered up at him, looking irritated and flustered and very, very innocent. Jesus, how could he have ever thought a woman with eyes like that was evil? Even narrowed in anger, the blue of them was as clear as a wishing well.

"I'm not stupid, helpful, or violent, you jack..." She stopped mid-swear. "Wait. What's wrong with being helpful? How is that an insult?"

"See, you wouldn't ask that if you were really Bad. Now stand back and let the professionals deal with the crime spree." Marrok playfully waggled the bottle of cleaning fluid he'd pilfered from the supply closet using Ramona's key. "You're in good hands, Red. At least three of my felony sentences were for arson."

"What about the other forty-six?"

"Forty-*seven*. Fifty counts of Badness on my record. Easy number to remember." Marrok untwisted the top of the bottle and inserted a tightly wound rope of paper towels.

"Don't worry. After I take the crown from Cindy's head, I'll make sure you get a pardon." She promised.

"Last time I checked, a crown was also attached to a certain dickhead in tights. You planning to take him for yourself, too?" Hopefully not, since Marrok would be dead in the ground before he let that royal ass-wipe touch his True Love.

"I can handle Charming." She assured him.

"The guy has the IQ of a banana, so I'm sure you *can* handle him, but..."

"He does not!" She interrupted hotly. "Charming is a sensitive and intelligent man. He's very interested in villains' rights and other social justice issues."

Marrok edged into the hallway. "He told you that?"

"Yes, as a matter of fact he *did*. Many times."

"Then, he was trying to get laid."

"Oh, he was *not*. He's very sincere about..."

Marrok cut her off. "...about getting laid. While you were explaining your crackpot theories, I'll bet sincerity was coming out of his ass. Trust me, he was mindlessly nodding and picturing you naked." At the other end of the corridor, he could see Avenant waiting with Benji. Marrok gave a signal and he swore he could hear the Prince of the Northlands sighing from twenty feet away.

Showtime.

"Oh no." Avenant called in the worst acting performance since what's-his-face the giant had starred in the WUB Club's production of *Cats* last fall. "Someone come quickly. This poor blue ogre is dying."

Benji obediently toppled to the floor, clutching his

stomach and groaning. "Ow. The pain. I'm dying."

"Oh for God's sake." Scarlett muttered. "We should have practiced this part more."

Marrok had to agree. He rolled his eyes as Esmeralda entered stage left, still disguised as Ramona.

"Stay calm!" She bellowed to no one in particular and posed for maximum dramatic effect. "I'm a doctor!"

"You're a psychiatrist." Avenant corrected sourly.

"That's a doctor!"

"Not a *real* doctor."

"Then why am I called *Doctor* Ramona, wiseass?"

"Still dying." Benji prompted.

"Shit. Sorry. Right." Esmeralda got back on script and crouched down beside him. "Oh no! He's dying!" She laid one palm on Benji's torso and the other against her forehead in tragic repose. "I cannot bear to see my patient suffer like this. We must rush him to the infirmary. Guards!" She looked up at the camera over the security office door. "Come quickly and help me carry him. We haven't a moment to lose!"

"He's dying." Avenant reiterated in case they'd missed the point.

"*Dyyyyying.*" Benji wailed, getting into the spirit of the show. "Help me! *Help!*"

Thankfully, the WUB Club didn't employ rocket scientists. The door to the security office opened and one of Dr. White's dwarf henchmen came out. "Are you sure he's not faking it, Dr. Ramona? A lot of times these fellas play sick in order to get a few days rest in bed."

"I think I know when someone's faking an illness." Esmeralda scoffed. "I'm a *doctor*."

"Psychiatrist." Avenant corrected, even as he covertly used his foot to block the office door from closing. "Are there any other guards in the office that can help carry the ogre?"

Letty had insisted that they ask that. The woman was adorable.

"No. Just me." The dwarf looked a tiny bit intimidated by that fact.

Avenant gave Marrok a thumbs-up sign.

"*Finally.*" Marrok flicked Ramona's stolen lighter, creating a small flame. "Next time we escape a loony bin, Red, we do it without the amateurs." He lit the paper towel wick and moved purposefully down the hallway.

The guard was now gamely trying to heft up a portion of Benji's massive body weight, while Avenant criticized his lifting methods and Esmeralda listed reasons why psychiatrists actually saved more lives than useless medical doctors. Benji himself had gone limp, his giant body all akimbo as he continued to wail.

The dwarf never saw Marrok grab the handle of the open office door and lob the makeshift Molotov cocktail inside. It took less than a second. Marrok kept walking as the door swung shut, his pace never faltering as he executed a neat U-turn and rejoined Scarlett.

Avenant moved closer to Esmeralda and away from the door.

Benji squeezed his eyes shut.

Wham!

The explosion blew the door right off its hinges. Trapped inside the security office, the blast was contained, but it effectively destroyed all the computer backups and surveillance equipment in the WUB Club.

Scarlett used Marrok's arm for support and gave a bounce of delight as all the evidence of Ramona's attack burned. "We did it!" She whispered loudly.

Marrok glanced down at her and realized having a Good girl for his True Love wasn't *completely* bad news.

No Baddie could ever smile with that much joy. "Go team." He drawled.

The guard was hopping around ineffectually trying to put out the fire with his stupid hat.

"I'm feeling better." Benji declared and sat up. "It must have been something I ate."

"Thank God I was here to save you." Esmeralda helped him to his feet. "Now, tell me about your mother."

The guard took off, yelling for someone to bring a fire extinguisher.

"There's no way we're going to get away with this." Avenant reported, looking Marrok's way as he and Scarlett moved out into the open. "When questioned, I'll be explaining that you forced me into this idiocy at gunpoint."

"If I had a gun, you wouldn't be alive to explain anything." Marrok assured him. "Now stop being a pussy and accept the fact that my plan worked." He gestured towards the smoldering office. "Maybe they *are* gonna figure out who torched the joint, but by that time we'll be long gone."

Or at least Marrok and Scarlett would be. He didn't care what happened to the rest of the Tuesday share circle, regardless of what his den mother of a True Love had in mind.

"Besides, it wasn't like we had a lot of time to come up with a better idea, Avenant." Scarlett pointed out, in what Marrok thought was a promising show of solidarity. "That tape would incriminate us all. We had to get rid of it fast."

"Exactly." Marrok nodded. "Now, the video surveillance is taken care of and we're in the clear. That's the only…"

A voice came over the intercom, cutting him off: *"Marrok Wolf report to Dr. White's office immediately. Marrok Wolf report immediately to Dr. White."*

Marrok sighed. "Aw... fuck."

Scarlett looked up at him in horror.

Avenant instantly headed for the arts and crafts room. "I was never here."

"Marrok, what are we going to do?" Scarlett demanded, wide eyed.

"I'm gonna report to Dr. White and you're not going to do anything until I get back." The last thing he needed was Scarlett coming up with the next step of her escape without the proper evil guidance.

"What if she somehow knows you just set that fire?" She pointed to the burning office in horror. "What else *could* she want from you?"

He didn't even want to think about it...

Chapter Four

Marrok, like most wolves, scores extremely high on the "loyalty potential" portions of his mental testing. With training, he could be taught to heed commands and follow orders. Unfortunately, he resists all efforts to properly channel his impulses. At this point, he gives his allegiance to no one.

Psychiatric case notes of Dr. Ramona Fae

"How would you like to get out of here?" Dr. Snow White leaned across her desk and smiled like she was prepared to sell him some magic beans.

Marrok settled into an uncomfortable office chair and tried not to scoff at the out-of-the-blue offer. "Wow, you really think I'm rehabilitated? I *have* been feeling a lot more in touch with my inner child, but I thought release was still a ways off."

"Don't try to bullshit me, Wolf."

Snow White looked like a china doll, but she hadn't enslaved the dwarves through her charms. She was tough as nails and always seeking ways to acquire more power. The walls of her dimly lit office were lined with the heads of various creatures she'd hunted and ripped the hearts out of. Also, there were mirrors. Many, many mirrors.

To Marrok's way of thinking, the chick was just as crazy as everyone else in the WUB Club, she just hid it behind diplomas and too much lipstick.

"We test the blood of everyone who comes through the door." She continued, her ruby red lips pursed smugly. "Budgets cuts mean it sometimes takes weeks for us to get the results, but today Scarlett Riding's came through. Guess the *first* thing our medical staff saw when they plugged her data into the computer?"

"Knowing that girl, whatever it is I'm betting it wasn't sexually transmitted."

"She's your *True Love*." Dr. White smiled as she delivered that news, but there was no humor in it. Just greed. "It popped up on the mystio-physiological screening. We always run those, to make sure True Loves aren't lodged together. But, I have to say I was surprised to see *your* name attached to the most notorious ugly stepsister in the Four Kingdoms."

"She's not ugly." Marrok delivered that massive understatement with an admirable amount of equanimity considering his mind was racing. What was this really about?

"But she *is* notorious." Dr. White arched a black brow. "If some of the rumors about her family are true, it's no surprise she's unrepentantly evil. Blood will tell, after all."

He had no clue what she was talking about, but it didn't matter. "Wolves can't choose their True Loves. Notorious or not, Scarlett is mine."

A wiser person would've heard the warning in that statement, but Good folk always thought they were the smartest people in the room. Dr. White kept talking.

"I know you're probably feeling... *something* for the girl." She waved a hand, dismissing the cornerstone of any wolf's life like it was a high school crush. "But, Scarlett's got enemies that go straight to the top. Nothing can save her and you don't want to get mixed up in her mess. You're a smart guy, for your kind."

"Not smart enough, apparently."

She disregarded that. "And, really... there are True Loves and then there are *True Loves*." She flashed him a knowing look. "You're the most famous wolf alive. You've reportedly had princesses in your bed. Women who would ordinarily *never* let a Baddie touch them, offer huge sums to have you. Surely you had someone… *more* in mind for your wife."

Actually, he'd had someone *less* in mind.

Less wholesome. Less aggravating. Less… Good.

But, there weren't True Loves and *True Loves.* To wolves, there was just MINE.

Good folk would never understand that or comprehend the lengths any self-respecting Baddie would go to keep what was theirs. Until Marrok knew where this meeting was headed, though, he was willing to play along with this insanity. His annoying little True Love was being insulted and threatened, two things wolves didn't take kindly to. Still, he needed to know why Scarlett was so important that the Powers That Be were apparently even willing to let *him* go free if it meant getting what they wanted from her.

What the hell was Letty mixed up in?

"If I were you," Dr. White continued, "I'd make the best of this situation and use that girl to get out of here."

"How could I do that?" Marrok spread his hands as if he was stymied.

"Well, I can help you. I happen to know that her stepsister is very eager to find something Scarlett has. If you were to help us get it back from her…" Dr. White let her voice trail off enticingly.

"Right." Marrok pretended to ponder the weird offer. "I could do that, I guess. Would it be hidden in her bedroom or…?"

"No, I've searched everyplace in the hospital. She has to have it stashed outside somewhere. You need to get her to tell you where it is."

"Alright. First I need to know *what* it is, though."

"A glass slipper."

Marrok squinted. "Like *the* glass slipper?"

"*Exactly.*"

"How did Scarlett get Cinderella's shoe?"

Better question: Why would she steal used footwear? Why not a golden scepter or something that was worth real cash on the secondary market? Letty wasn't an idiot, so she had to have a reason, but damn if he knew what it was.

"Who knows how she got her hands on it." Dr. White shrugged. "Cinderella had the shoe locked up, in preparation for the royal wedding, and somehow Scarlett got through the security. I don't know how *any* of you Baddies commit your crimes. Like the rest of your kind, she's just evil and fiendishly cunning, I suppose."

Scarlett was the least evil person in the Four Kingdoms. Now that Marrok saw the truth, it shocked him how easily everyone else wrote her off as wicked, ugly and Bad, without noticing she was really idealistic, beautiful and irritatingly virtuous. Even for Good folk that was pretty fucking blind.

And no *way* had she stolen that shoe. It was way above her criminal skillset. Granted, Letty was clever and scheming, but a successful B&E of the palace...? He could more easily imagine her leading the town's people on a strike for unionization than ninja-stealthing into a castle to crack a safe.

Something was very wrong here.

The door to Dr. White's office burst open and Ramona stumbled in. It only took Marrok half a second to know that Esmeralda was no longer driving the good doctor's face and body.

Now, Scarlett was.

He would know that spiced apple scent anywhere.

Marrok's eyebrows climbed, trying to figure out how they'd pulled off this new trick. Like some kind of bizarre three card monte game, he supposed it meant that Esmeralda was now disguised as Scarlett and the real Ramona was still in the dungeon disguised as Esmeralda. Letty couldn't do magic, so there was no spell inhibitor on her ankle to prevent the witch from using a glamor on her, but why had they bothered?

Or rather why had *Scarlett* bothered, since there was no doubt in his mind whose plan this was. His True Love was the only one in the share circle with the balls to try a stunt like this. Was she worried that he was going to rat out the escape plot? If so, why in the hell would she dig herself in even deeper with this Ramona disguise? What was she up to?

The woman was a fount of new and interesting ideas.

"Dr. White. Hi." Scarlett/Ramona straightened her lab coat. "Right. Ummm... is everything, okay?" She teetered over to flop down in the chair next to Marrok, as if the length of Ramona's legs made it difficult for her to balance. The fairy topped Scarlett by at least eight inches, so the new taller body must have been confounding her.

Marrok found himself smiling. "You doing something new with your hair, Ramona? You're looking a little... different today."

Scarlett ignored him. "What kind of trouble is he in?" She demanded, still focused on Dr. White. "Because, I *know* that he's a complete and utter jackass, but... I think he deserves another chance."

Ohhhh... she was here to *protect* him.

Despite himself, Marrok's heart turned over. It was stupid as hell to risk herself to try and help someone like him, but it was just about the *nicest* thing anyone had ever done for him. She'd apparently been serious about her All For One speech. That was... adorable. Even in her ridiculous Ramona costume, he could think of six hundred different things he wanted to do to her body to say thanks.

Scarlett adjusted her lab coat again and kept up her persuasive speech to Dr. White. "Tossing Marrok in the dungeon at this point in his treatment will just undo all the hard work I've put into making him less horrible."

"Oh, I don't mind doing hard, *hard* work with you, Doc." Marrok assured her.

The glare was the same, but Ramona's flat gray eyes lacked the punch-to-the-stomach purity of Scarlett's crystalline blue gaze. As much fun as it was to torment her about the disguise, he really didn't like looking at his True Love and not seeing his True Love. He missed the cherubic redhead scowling at him. Letty's curvy little body was much more enjoyable to mentally undress.

"Don't worry, Ramona." Dr. White said coldly. "Mr. Wolf isn't in trouble. I was just enlisting his help in finding that damn glass slipper."

Marrok felt Letty still.

He shot her a lazy smile. "Yeah... It seems that Scarlett's been holding out on us, Doc. You got any idea where she might have stashed Cindy's shoe?"

Gray eyes flashed to his again, this time wide and a little scared. "No! No, I have no idea where Scarlett put that slipper. In fact, I'm not convinced she has it, at all."

"Oh, she has it. The question is how do we get her to talk?" Dr. White drummed her fingernails on the desktop. Each one was painted in silver polish, so they shone like small mirrors. Marrok could see his own image reflected in them like a funhouse. God, that was creepy.

"I can get Scarlett to tell me about the shoe." He said with just the right amount of arrogance to *really* piss her off.

Sure enough, Letty's fear faded into irritation. "I highly doubt that."

"Oh please." He rolled his eyes. "You've seen how she lusts after me, right? It'll be simple."

"I've seen nothing of the kind!"

"Mr. Wolf is known for his prowess with women." Dr. White said with something less than clinical detachment. "That's why we're having this little meeting. He's going to use his legendary abilities for the side of Good. The best looking man in the Four Kingdom's can certainly fuck on command. It's the only thing wolves are good for."

Marrok stared back at her expressionlessly.

Even creepier than Dr. White's nails and the heartless carcasses on the walls was the way she would leer at him. She entertained herself with the male patients. Marrok knew that and unfortunately her come-ons towards him were getting more and more blatant.

He couldn't even look at Letty, ashamed that she was seeing this.

All his life, his looks had drawn attention he didn't necessarily want. He'd grown up alone, after his parents had been killed by some punk kid named Peter. Marrok barely remembered them. He'd been on his own and trying to survive when he was drafted into Wolfball. It was participation or death.

And, too many times, "participation" meant some woman he didn't want touching him because she'd made a deal with his beloved coach. At the beginning, he'd been at the mercy of everyone bigger and meaner. Now, he was strong enough to defend himself physically, but that didn't mean as much inside the WUB Club. The power structure was different and people would always try to prey on someone they saw as weaker than themselves.

He would never escape what he was. He was resigned to that.

Scarlett wasn't.

"You can't ask Marrok to sleep with someone to further your own plans." She snapped. "It's immoral and unethical. Besides, we have rules about the patients engaging in sexual activity. It's in chapter three of the handbook."

Marrok's mouth curved. Both at her heartfelt defense of his honor and because she'd actually read the stupid handbook they handed out to the inmates. If she kept it up, he was just going to die from her terminal adorableness.

"Well, there are rules and then there are *rules*." Dr. White chuckled like she hadn't just used the exact same phrasing five minutes before. "I mean, the man isn't called the *Big* Bad Wolf for nothing. If he seduces that troublesome ugly stepsister and solves our problems, it's just nature taking its course."

Marrok's small smile faded. "She's not ugly." He reiterated firmly. "While the doctors are messing with Letty's records, maybe we should recheck what exactly she *is*, because there's no way she's an..."

"She's Bad." Scarlett interrupted. "*That's* what she is. Very, very Bad."

He looked over at her in frustration.

She made a "shut-up" sort of face at him.

"Well, whatever she is, I can seduce her, Dr.

White." He kept his attention on Letty. "I'll just need constant access to her. Oh, and there can't be a lot of guards around. The girl will never get naked with an audience. At least, not yet. I'll need some privacy to get the job done."

Scarlett's mouth parted as she realized that he'd just cleared the way for them to operate without dwarf surveillance. He saw her eyes light up with excited understanding.

No Baddie could ever look so delightfully delighted.

"Of course." Dr. White agreed. "Do whatever you want with her. Just remember that we're on a schedule here and…" The intercom on her desk buzzed and she reached over to hit it. "Yes?"

"Dr. White? The cameras are all down and the security office is burning. We think it was the fire imps, again. The dwarves say they need you."

"Oh for God's sake… I have to do *everything* around here." Dr. White got to her feet and went stalking towards the door. "See him back to the craft room, Ramona." As she passed, she ran her mirrored talons across the width of Marrok's shoulder. "I'll be expecting a detailed update later, Wolf." She leaned down closer to his ear. "*Very* detailed."

Marrok shifted out from under her touch, stifling a cringe. He didn't like being pawed at, especially not in front of his True Love. He hadn't been interested in Dr. White *before* he found Letty, so he sure as shit wasn't interested now. Wolves were loyal to their True Loves. Always. Something else Good folk could never wrap their brains around.

One day, Dr. White was going to stop with the "subtle" and start with the demands. It was a big reason why he tried to play nice at the WUB Club and not draw her attention. He wasn't going to do what the person in charge of assigning electroshock therapy *wanted* him to do. That wasn't a great spot to be in.

Scarlett's eyes narrowed. Her head whipped around to look at him as Dr. White swept from the room. "She's sexually harassing you!" She said with righteous indignation.

Marrok's jaw ticked. "Yeah, well, I'm just an irresistible guy."

"It's not a joke." Scarlett had been openly hostile to him for weeks, mostly because he'd been trying to get a rise out of her. Now, her hostility faded and she gazed at him with genuine concern. "Does she treat you that way all the time?"

"A lot of people treat me that way." He said flatly.

"People just expect you to sleep with them, because you're good looking?"

"People expect me to sleep with them, because they think I'll trade sex for whatever it is they're offering. Buying yourself a player for the night is just part of the wonderful game of Wolfball."

"That's not a game."

Why would this girl be the only one to understand that? Not even Marrok could explain his hatred of the age-old process. Good folk were constantly angered and confused by his resistance. Most of his Badness arrests were directly related to his refusal to submit. But, even knowing that it would just mean more pain and trouble, he'd never willingly sold himself. Maybe, on some level, he'd been imagining this exact conversation with his True Love. He'd wanted to be able to look her in the eye and tell the truth.

He met her gaze. "You were right earlier. I never wanted to be a part of those stupid games. A lot of us don't. They force the wolves into it. Out there is worse than in here for me. No matter where I go, I'm caged. At least here, I don't get attacked or pawed at as much."

"You're supposed to be safe in this hospital, though. Instead, Dr. White is using her position to exploit you. You shouldn't have to put up with being threatened, Marrok."

"I have never touched that woman." It was important that she know that. "I won't sleep with Snow White, no matter how many times she offers me a better room, or a shortened sentence, or a..."

"Of course you won't!" Letty interrupted as if that was obvious.

Even Marrok had questioned why he bothered to resist Dr. White. He could've been out of here months ago if he just submitted. He'd done far worse things, but he'd never been able to bring himself to even consider it. Scarlett clearly never doubted he'd make the pointlessly moral choice, though.

He wasn't sure what to make of that.

"I'm sorry." Scarlett continued. "I didn't know how hard it was for you. No wonder you want to escape from the hospital *and* from Wolfball."

He didn't want Letty to know about any of this. It would be hard for someone so clean to ever fully comprehend what it meant to feel dirty. "I never considered escaping until you came along." He said honestly.

Maybe it took someone Good to have that much optimism. To think they could stage a jailbreak and make things better. Baddies were used to losing. They just sat behind bars and endured. The WUB Club didn't have breakouts because none of the inmates had enough hope to even try for freedom. It was why the staff was so complacent and arrogant.

Aside from Trevelyan, no one had ever escaped. And even the dragon had been convinced he'd be killed in his jailbreak attempt. He just hadn't cared. Trevelyan had reached the point where he'd rather die trying than stay imprisoned. No doubt he'd been shocked when he actually got away. That was so different than Letty's boundless faith.

"Well, we're going to get out of here, okay?" Scarlett leaned forward and gently took hold of his hand. It was quite possibly the first time in his life that he'd been touched with nothing but caring. "It isn't your fault." She said sincerely. "Don't worry. I'll make sure you're safe."

No one had ever said that to him before.

Marrok folded his fingers around her palm, not sure how to respond. What she'd said was ludicrous. It was the exact kind of bullshit he'd normally scoff at, but he was actually touched by her words. He'd been a provoking jackass to Scarlett every day since they'd met. He was twice her size and a thousand times more ruthless, but she was promising to keep him safe. And she *meant* it.

Jesus, this girl was Good.

He looked into her wrong-colored eyes, saw the soul deep purity of his recklessly kindhearted True Love, and he... believed.

He believed every crazy story she'd ever told in share circle. Believed all the loony claims about Cinderella stealing the prince. Believed that shoeless bitch was the *actual* ugly stepsister. Believed that Letty had been set-up.

"That glass slipper doesn't belong to Cinderella, does it?" He asked quietly.

She slowly shook her head.

Marrok believed her. Believed *all* of it.

...He just didn't care.

Marrok had waited too long to find Scarlett to ever give her up. Maybe she wasn't exactly how he'd pictured his True Love, but there was something very appealing about the girl. The mix of the soft and the tyrannical charmed him.

More importantly, she reached out to offer him comfort when there was absolutely nothing in it for her. He'd never imagined having a True Love that nice. He'd never even *liked* nice before, but he liked it now. Every selfish, criminally inclined, biologically driven instinct in his body told him to do whatever it took to keep Scarlett.

And for a guy serving time in a psych ward for Baddies "whatever it took" was a pretty broad mandate.

"The shoe will prove Cinderella isn't the real princess?" He persisted. "That's why she wants it? To destroy the evidence?"

Charming wanted to marry a foot. At least that's how it seemed to Marrok.

Some fairy godmother had given him the glass slipper right before that infamous costume ball a couple months back and told him it would only fit his destined princess. If Cinderella had somehow tricked that nimrod and the shoe didn't actually fit her, she'd be out of the castle on her ass.

"That slipper will blow Cindy right out of the water." Scarlett confirmed with visible satisfaction. "It doesn't fit her and I can prove it. Once Charming sees that she's an imposter, it's all over for that twisted nymphomaniac."

"Does she really fuck those mice?"

"They're *rats* and yes she does. I'll be telling Charming about that, too."

"You really think he'll believe you? Even with the shoe?"

"Yes." There was absolute conviction in Scarlett's tone. "Charming is under some kind of spell, but I know we can get through to him. We grew up together. Dru and I wouldn't even be in here if he'd been able to prevent it."

Unfortunately, Marrok believed that too. Why wouldn't the Prince of Blondness want Letty? Especially, if they had a history. Which meant *Marrok's* True Love was Charming's destined bride.

Fuck.

Marrok and Cinderella were actually on the same side in this. That shoe couldn't see the light of day. He had to find it and make sure that Scarlett didn't show it to Charming. Otherwise, the closest Marrok would ever get to Letty was chasing after Charming's ridiculous pumpkin-shaped coach.

"That's why we need to escape." Scarlett continued earnestly. "Once I get the glass slipper, everything will be the way it's *supposed* to be."

Marrok smiled and thanked the Lord he was unrepentantly evil. "Oh, absolutely it will." He agreed. "I'll make sure everything works out how it should. No matter what I have to do."

Chapter Five

Scarlett's delusions about her stepsister grow more elaborate and perverse. I can't even speculate on what kind of damaged mind would concoct such twisted tales about our beautiful Cinderella.

Psychiatric case notes of Dr. Ramona Fae

Cinderella slapped her dressmaker, knocking the woman to the ground. "You stupid cow! You call this a wedding gown. I wouldn't wear this to clean out a sewer!" She gave the embroidered silk a vicious yank, tearing the fabric from her body. Pearls scattered as threads ripped, destroying days of work. The round gems scattered around the bedroom, bouncing on the marble floor.

The goblin seamstress desperately tried to gather up them up, again. "But, your highness, we made it exactly to your specifications."

"Bullshit! It's a rag. Is that what you want me to wear when I become princess of the Westlands? *Rags?*" Her eyes narrowed. "You're mocking me, aren't you?" She gave the woman another shove. Like most of the castle's servants, the dressmaker was a Bad folk, so *of course* she'd be a deceitful bitch. "You're *mocking* me!"

"No! Your highness, I swear I..."

"Isn't it enough that I suffered all my life?" Cinderella's eyes filled with misty tears. "That I've worked and slaved every day, with nothing but my gentle nature to get me through? Now, you don't even want me to have a dress on my special day. You *want* me to be a laughingstock!"

"But your highness, the greatest designers in the Four Kingdoms worked to create this dress for you. It's the most expensive and beautiful..."

"Mice!" Cinderella shrieked, cutting her off. Instantly, the double doors to her golden bedroom were thrown open and her gang of rodents marched in.

Since moving into the castle, she'd given all the human-sized mice blue palace uniforms and made them guards. They were now in every vital position within the Westlands, answerable only to her. They were her only defense against dissidents in her new kingdom; all the naysayers and whiners and assholes who were working against her. Agitators were everywhere.

She *knew* it.

Everywhere she looked she saw smirking and judgment; heard whispers and snickering. Her men were making sure all those enemies were punished. Unlike Charming's dickless guards, her men weren't afraid to get the job *done*.

It was gratifying to see the goblin's eyes widen in panic as the mice bore down on her. You had to show the Baddies who was boss.

"Wait!" The woman scrambled to her feet. "I didn't do anything! Don't let the rats..." She trailed off with a scream as two of them seized her arms and dragged her from the room.

"They're *mice*." Cinderella shrieked after her. Why did *every*one want to belittle *everything* she had? What had she done to make the entire world turn against her? Why was she soooooo unappreciated?

"Your highness?" Gustav, her top mouse, stepped into the room and closed the door, lowering his eyes respectfully. Because, why *wouldn't* you address a future princess in a deferential and obedient way? Was it really so much to ask that she be given just the *tiniest* bit of reverence? "May I speak with you?"

"Yes." She decided, because she was a gracious and giving person, goddamn it.

"We had another call from the Wicked, Ugly and Bad Prison." Gustav was taller than she was, with the long nose, red eyes, and sharp teeth of a mouse. *Not* a rat. She would never surround herself with *rats*. He was a *mouse*. "Dr. White says she may have had a breakthrough with finding your glass slipper."

Cinderella's lips pressed together, trying to hold back a fit of totally justifiable swearing. Everything in her life came down to a *fucking shoe!* This was all Scarlett's fault. Her stepsister was the most petty and uncooperative bitch in the world. "What *kind* of breakthrough? Does she have my slipper or not?"

"Thus far? Not."

Cinderella's hands clenched around Snow White's invisible neck, a strangled sound of frustration in her throat. "How hard is it to just beat some information out of someone? Huh?! It's like that slut of a doctor is *trying* to make this difficult!"

Maybe she was. Maybe Scarlett had gotten to her.

Cinderella's eyes narrowed in consideration.

Everyone was against her.

"Once again, your highness, I would be happy to question Scarlett for you. I know I could get her to..."

"I *told* you that won't work!" She tore off her veil and threw it at him. "Charming would find out if I had Letty tortured by my men! He's so pathetically *Good.*"

Sometimes he would look at her and Cinderella sensed that Charming didn't want her at all. Even with the spell convincing him that she was the one who fit that glass slipper, he looked mildly repulsed with his destined bride. He'd seize any opportunity to leave her.

It wasn't *fair*.

Cinderella's lower lip trembled in self-pity. "Letty would've already gotten word to Charming, if she wasn't safely locked away. He's *always* liked her and Dru better than me. He'd be getting them out of the WUB Club, right now, if he could." His disloyalty made her hate him, but Charming was the only way to the crown. "Do you *want* my future husband to think I'm some kind of monster? *Do you?!*"

"Of course not, your highness. I seek only to make your life perfect."

"How can it be perfect when everyone wants to see me fail?" Cinderella wiped at her eyes. She was under attack from every direction. "I need that shoe! Why won't Scarlett just give it to me? How did she even smuggle it out of the Westlands?"

"I don't know, but we searched everywhere and it's definitely not in this kingdom."

"She's so duplicitous." Cindy sniffed back more tears. "And I can't find a single black-market godmother to make me another one. It was mystically patented or some fucking thing. What am I supposed to do if Scarlett somehow gets free and shows everyone the truth?"

"We could just kill her, your majesty."

"You think that hasn't occurred to me?! But, you heard her shouting when they dragged her away. She said she sent the shoe to some friend of hers, who will take it straight to Charming if anything happens to her or Dru. He's already fighting the spell. That could tip him over the edge into remembering."

"Do you believe her?"

Cinderella couldn't take the chance. Not with the

rumors about Scarlett's family. "*First*, I need to find that shoe and get through the wedding." Once she was officially a princess not even Letty could fuck things up. "*Then*, I can kill her."

"We'll locate the glass slipper soon, your majesty."

Cinderella's eyes instantly dried. "You'd better." She turned back to the mirror and made sure her makeup wasn't running. Thankfully, she still looked fairest of them all.

Her golden hair was tied up in a neat bun; her tiara was big and sparkly. Really, she was the most beautiful woman in the Four Kingdoms. Her head tilted. Maybe this dress wasn't *so* bad, after all.

"How do I look?" She demanded.

"Perfect, your majesty."

Of course she did. Cinderella smirked at her reflection. Charming was lucky to have her instead of some ugly stepsister. If he knew the truth he'd be *thanking* her. Any man would be thrilled to touch her.

She was the *real* princess.

Cinderella lifted her hands to cup her breasts, singing a cheerful song as she stroked her own nipples through the bodice of the dress. Her stress level was high, thanks to everyone being so endlessly cruel to her. She could use some release and there was one surefire way to achieve it.

"How long do we have before the cake tasting?" She asked in a sultry tone.

Gustav met her eyes in the mirror, already anticipating what she wanted. His whole demeanor changed, trained to perform his role whenever she asked. If he didn't, there would be hell to pay.

"Enough time for you to do some chores, wench."

He said harshly.

She gave a shiver of pure lust. "Yes, sir." She went to gather the supplies, her body already humming.

Cleaning was the only thing that ever turned her on, but, to make the experience *truly* erotic, she needed her mice guard watching. She was so pristine and important. A true princess. Subjugating herself in front of lesser beings was just delightfully twisted. She loved the feeling of being submissive to something as useless and ugly as these rodents. It completely violated the natural status quo.

It was so wrong.

So… hot.

At least once a day, Cinderella was on her knees in front of her men, cleaning the floor and panting for release, so she kept her scrub brush and bucket close at hand. The stupid palace maids didn't understand that. She was always screaming at them to stay out of her room and let her do the cleaning herself.

She soooooo enjoyed chore time.

Kneeling in her wedding dress, she looked up at Gustav and waited for his orders. It had better be something really depraved or she'd make him suffer later.

Luckily, he knew what was expected of him. That was the benefit of properly training your pets. "I'm going to come on the floor." He began unbuttoning his pants and she nearly purred. "Clean it with your dress. I want you to remember how dirty you are on your farce of a wedding day."

Her eyes grew heavy as she watched him work a hand over his erection. "I'm a princess." She whispered, her eyes on the swollen flesh. "You can't treat me this way."

"You're nothing but a cleaning wench." His eyes

glowed as he rubbed himself harder and faster. "You're only good for scrubbing up my leavings. And your work had better be spotless or next time I'll make you wash it with your tongue."

"You wouldn't dare. Not again."

"Again and again, until you learn to do your chores properly."

She licked her lips in anticipation. "Couldn't you just come in my mouth, sir? It would save me so much time."

Occasionally, he allowed that, but only when some of the other men were there to see her lower herself. The sexual humiliation got her off. Especially when he refused to let her come. Gustav didn't relish chore time the way some of the men did, so he often got creative about carrying it out. Sometimes, he'd order her to give him a blowjob and then leave her aching, while the other guards laughed at her frustrated cries.

It was no wonder he was her favorite.

"Beg me and I'll consider it, wench."

"Please, sir." Cinderella whimpered as she saw he was getting close. "Please let me suck you. Don't make me scrub your seed from the floor."

"You don't deserve the taste of my cock." Gustav's head tilted back, the tendons of his neck straining. "Remember, I want it all spotless or you'll be sorry. The men like to see me punish your disobedience."

Oh yes... And she liked to be punished.

The degradation of someone like *her* at the mercy of these low creatures...

She gave a shudder as he came all over the marble. It was a euphoric release for her to see the sticky mess and know she had to clean it. She almost wanted to do a bad job of it so he'd make her do it again, this time with her mouth and with the others all watching her shame. God, she needed this after the day she was having.

"Now, do your chores, wench."

"Thank you, sir." She panted and started scrubbing.

Chapter Six

Benji must build his confidence!
Why is the big oaf too stupid to see that?

Psychiatric case notes of Dr. Ramona Fae

"You aren't rotting in the basement." Avenant didn't seem thrilled by the news. "I didn't expect Dr. White to be smart enough to see through Scarlett's pitiful Ramona disguise, but I thought at *least* she'd toss the wolf into the pit for some torture." He sighed. "Every day in this place is another opportunity for disappointment."

Marrok flicked him off.

Scarlett ignored them. She sat down beside Drusilla at the arts and crafts table. It was macaroni necklace day, so her sister was carefully stringing brightly painted noodles, a distant expression on her face. They'd drugged her, again. Usually, she and Dru had different craft times and it was disheartening to see her sister struggle with even these simple tasks. Drusilla's eyes were unfocused and glassy, all her attention on choosing just the right blue rigatoni. It was going to take her awhile, since she couldn't focus enough to thread the yarn through the hole.

Scarlett had to get Drusilla out of the WUB Club before it killed her.

She reached over to gently touch her sister's wrist, helping Dru hold the pasta in the correct position, and then glanced over at Esmeralda. The witch was still disguised as Scarlett, so it was kind of disconcerting to look at her own face with someone else wearing it.

"How long can you keep this spell up, Ez?"

If Ramona's Esmeralda mask disappeared, this whole plan would fall apart really quick. When the doctor woke up in the dungeon and started ranting that she was really Ramona, chances were the guards would just ignore her. If she actually *looked* like Ramona, though, her story would have a *bit* more credibility.

"I can keep the glamours up until tomorrow, maybe." Esmeralda already had three pasta necklaces looped around her neck. All of them were painted black. "Anything more than that, I'll have to use more power and it'll set off the magic alarms."

So they had a day.

Scarlett let out a long breath. Okay. She could do this. She wasn't sure *how* yet, but her grandmother would expect her to take charge and think of something. Villainy was in her blood, no matter what Marrok might think.

"Well, we have Ramona's keys." Scarlett told the group, trying to sound positive. "We just need to find a way to use them to get all of us out of here."

The seven of them were crowded around one of the craft room's repurposed picnic tables. The gloomy space was about half the size of an average school cafeteria and painted in a particularly lifeless shade of prison gray. Add in the bars on the windows, and the fact that the only two "crafts" the inmates were allowed to make were edible jewelry and cotton balls glued into the shape of white rabbits, and Scarlett had never felt particularly inspired by the room.

Right now, though, she needed some creativity. *Fast*.

Benji crunched his way through a handful of dry noodles. "Well, you look like Ramona, Scarlett. You can just walk right out the front door. Maybe you could tell the guards we're all going on a fieldtrip and just take us with you when you go."

"A fieldtrip?!" Rumpelstiltskin hissed incredulously. "There are never any *fieldtrips* around here except to the dungeon." He gave his scalp an agitated itch, smearing yellow paint in his hair. "As soon as we try to leave the grounds, we'll be gassed." His eyes went up to the stained acoustical tiles of the ceiling, already scanning for the telltale clouds of purple smoke.

Marrok was staring at Esmeralda. "I just cannot get used to looking at you looking like Letty." He frowned like the witch's Scarlett façade annoyed him for some reason. "You two need to switch faces again, because it's creeping me out."

"Focus." Scarlett ordered.

"Will Ramona's keys access the weapons locker in the front security office?" Avenant inquired. He thoughtfully added a red rigatoni to his necklace and studied it for a beat. Changing his mind, he switched it to a green one. For some reason, he always took craft time seriously. "If we could get into that, we could acquire some guns and force our way out of here."

Rumpelstiltskin and Esmeralda looked intrigued by that idea.

"We're not using guns." Scarlett snapped. "I told you when we bombed the security cameras, we're doing this so no one gets hurt."

"Except for Dr. Ramona." Benji reminded her guilelessly. "You hit her in the head with that chair. That probably hurt a lot."

"Fine. New rule: Hitting with chairs is okay. Guns are *not*." Scarlett looked over at Marrok. "I don't want to kill anybody." She insisted, already anticipating his eye roll.

Instead, he nodded. "Shooting our way out the front door won't work. It's not just *getting* out, it's *staying* out." He leaned forward, his body very close to hers. For some reason, it made her heart speed up. "We have two options: We need to slip away quietly, so they don't have the flying monkeys on our ass right from the jump, *or* we need to leave so big that they'll be distracted."

The monkeys were the best trackers in the Four Kingdoms. As soon as Dr. White found them missing, those flying bastards would be hunting for them. Marrok was right. They needed to be very careful not to raise any alarm bells *or* they needed to set off every single alarm there was and slip away in the confusion. Otherwise, the escape would be all over before it even began.

Scarlett winced a bit, both at the idea of being tracked by winged chimps and because she was suddenly noticing Marrok's stunning profile. Why did he have to be so handsome?

She seriously *was* going insane and it was all his fault.

"Right." She cleared her throat. "Well, no matter what, we have to go tonight, when it's dark. Everyone on board with that?"

"How?" Esmeralda asked. "We'll be locked in our rooms."

"It's too bad Charming isn't here to help us plan." Dru mused hazily. "He could get us out. He's very smart, Letty."

"Charming is under a spell." Scarlett told her. "But, I know he's doing everything he can."

Marrok shot her a brooding look. "Yeah, he's really come through for you so far."

"He's *under a spell*." She insisted. "Like that other prince was when the mermaid gave up her voice to win his heart and what's-her-name tried to take her place by hypnotizing him."

"Oh Jesus, you *bought* that story?"

"The point is, Charming is *trying*." There wasn't a doubt in Scarlett's mind, but she didn't have time to wait for him to get things done. "Even when he isn't enspelled, it's hard for him to get through the bureaucracy of the Westlands, though."

"That's why I banished all bureaucrats, lawyers, politicians, and sports stars from my kingdom." Avenant agreed. "They all want to steal my power." He looked pointedly at Marrok. "*Especially,* the sports stars."

"And that plan worked out *great* for you." Marrok drawled. "How's the view from your lofty throne? Oh wait... better ask the *new* ruler of the Northlands."

"Ask quickly, because that usurper won't be sitting on my throne for long."

Scarlett ignored the bickering. "What's important is Charming's on our side and working to free us."

"Sure he is." Marrok refocused his snark on her. "Which is why he's organizing a dream wedding with your mortal enemy. I guess it's all part of his master plan."

"He doesn't *want* to marry Cinderella." Scarlett was starting to get annoyed. "He's been brainwashed! He'll be thrilled when we show up to save him. Believe me."

"Oh, I *do* believe you." Marrok assured her. "But, he's still an asshole."

"He is not! Charming is a deeply noble man."

Dru nodded. "And handsome, right Letty?"

"Of course." Although, it was hard to call any

man handsome when she was looking at Marrok. The wolf just reset the bar. Charming was studious and clean-cut and... kinda vanilla when compared to the jackass currently glowering at her.

Where had *that* thought come from?

Scarlett cleared her throat and refocused on Esmeralda. "Anyway, like I was saying, we can use Ramona's keys to get out. I'll unlock your cells tonight and we'll all go together."

"And we're just supposed to believe that you'll come and save us?" Avenant scoffed.

Marrok looked over at him. "We all know she will." He said with flat certainty. "You and I would leave everyone else to rot, but she's not like us."

"I'm not Good." Scarlett insisted.

Avenant glanced at her skeptically and then looked back to Marrok. "Even if I buy she's one of them -- Even if I accept that she'll let us out of our rooms tonight-- *then* what do we do? How do we get *free?*"

Scarlett had no clue.

She opened her mouth to say something vague and reassuring, only to hesitate when one of the craft room nurses meandered by.

"Everything okay, Dr. Ramona?" The heavyset elf named Harriet asked without much interest. She looked as bored and hopeless as most of the inmates. The WUB Club staff showed up every day to work at a place where people were sent to be forgotten and decay. Not surprisingly, they weren't a joyful lot.

Scarlett tried to look professional and calm as she smiled at the woman. "Yes, thank you. I'm just bonding with my favorite share circle."

Rumpelstiltskin slid down in his seat, trying to disappear.

Harriet shrugged like she didn't see why anyone would bother with any of them. Then, her gaze fell on Marrok. She preened a bit. "If you don't want to waste your time with these nuts, Wolf, I could probably find you something more… interesting to do in the back room."

Scarlett's eyes narrowed at the nurse. "He's fine right where he is." She snapped.

Jesus, did *everyone* try to proposition the guy? The corruption at the WUB Club was sickening. They were supposed to be helping to rehabilitate Marrok, instead they were using their positions to exploit him. Scarlett had spent every day of her incarceration irritated at the wolf, but now she was starting to see him in a whole new light. His amazing looks made him a victim in this place.

And even when he got outside, he wouldn't be free. Not if he went back to his old life of playing Wolfball for the Eastlands. The wolves were virtual slaves no matter where they went, especially the ones who brought in money for their teams.

Why was there no place for them to go and be safe?

Marrok's gaze stayed on Scarlett, not even glancing Harriet's way. "I'm fine here." He agreed simply.

The nurse didn't appreciate the rejection. Her mouth thinned. "Suit yourself." She looked down at Benji's half-eaten necklace and scowled. "Do we have to go through this every other day? Stop eating all our craft supplies, fatty!"

Benji swallowed the skein of yarn he was chewing on. "Sorry." He whispered.

Harriet made a disgusted face. "The next time I catch you, you'll be spending craft time in the library." She went marching off to another table to break-up a shouting match over which looked prettier: penne or garganelli.

Marrok's jaw ticked.

Benji looked down at the tabletop, close to tears.

"Well, we could at least kill *her*, right?" Avenant looked around the group with new enthusiasm. "Who was that pussy who robbed from the rich and gave to the poor and everyone *praised* him for his thievery? Well, ridding craft time of that woman would be the same principle. On the surface it's a crime, but it's really for the greater good. The only moral choice." He nodded eagerly, agreeing with his own argument. "Shall we vote on it?"

"I vote yes." Esmeralda muttered. "I hate that fucking bitch." She reached over to pet Benji's furry arm comfortingly.

Rumpelstiltskin sat up straighter and scowled down at the yarn in his hand. "Back home I could spin this into gold and make *real* jewelry." He said randomly.

Scarlett didn't even hear them, her mind racing with a new idea. The WUB Club was designed to be a miserable hole, but the library was the very worst spot outside the cells in the basement. It was a dank, moldy, rarely used room full of decades old magazines and "scientific" treatises that explained why Baddies were genetically inferior. Every single book in the place was a manifesto of hate and Good folk superiority.

No one went to the library. Even crossing the threshold was a punishment. And its unbarred windows overlooked the western side of the property. All that lay beyond the dirty glass was the vast Lake of Forgetting and the Enchanted Forest on the opposite shore.

...The endless, creepy, maze-like woods that could hide *anyone*.

Letty's eyes narrowed in deep consideration. It might be possible to get outside the hospital through the library windows. From there, they could make it to the lake... but the water was poisoned. If even a single drop touched your skin, you'd develop permanent amnesia. You ended up just sitting down on the shore and waiting for the guards to come and hustle you back inside, your entire life a complete blank.

The Lake of Forgetting worked even better than a wall, because it curved around the entire side of the WUB Club. Several hundred acres of black water, especially enspelled to keep Baddies in.

But, then, no Baddie had ever been quite as motivated as Scarlett was to get *out*. If she could cross the lake and get to the forest, not even the flying monkeys could find her.

"Benji?" She looked over at him and smiled. "Being a bridge ogre, I'll bet you know a lot about boats..."

***

"This will never work." Rumpelstiltskin looked like he was about to hyperventilate. "We're going to be gassed for sure. This whole day has been a bad idea, but this is just..."

"Shut-up." Avenant ordered. "We all know we're doomed, but whining about it won't help. Just quietly resign yourself to death."

Scarlett did her best to disregard the negativity. "Benji, sweetie, you look fabulous. Don't worry, at all. I know that this is going to be fine. I have total faith in you."

He swallowed so hard his throat clicked. "But,

Letty…"

"The key is to think 'I can do this. I can do this. I can do this.'" She pointed at her temple. "The power of positive thoughts can create positive action."

"Oh my God, you just quoted Dr. Ramona." Marrok shook his head. "You really do need to get out of here, Red. Psychobabble rots the brain and you have such an *adorable* one."

She spared him an irritated look and he grinned at her.

It was difficult to stay perpetually annoyed at the handsomest man in the Four Kingdoms, but Marrok did his very best to make it possible. Or at least he had until today. Suddenly, he was teasing instead of mocking; smiling at her like he wanted her to smile back. It was so much harder to hate him when he was being playful.

She really wished he'd stop it.

Considering the fact people apparently preyed on his looks, she was doing her best not to stare at him, but it was difficult when he was so damn gorgeous and flirty.

She forced her eyes away from Marrok's brilliant smile and focused on Benji, again. The poor guy was terrified, his body shaking in fear. The whole plan would fall apart if he couldn't do his part.

"Benji, I believe in you." She gripped his shoulders and tried to exude confidence. "When you walk out there, what are you going to think to yourself?"

"I can do this?" He guessed.

"Again."

"I can do this." He repeated in a slightly louder voice.

"One more time."

"I can *do* this."

"Yes, you can!" She gave him a helpful shove

towards the door. "Go get 'em, tiger."

"He can't do this." Avenant said sourly as Benji teetered towards the front office. "No way in hell will anyone believe he's Ramona."

The disguise was a little harder to pull off with a bridge ogre than it had been with Esmeralda and Scarlett. Ez could give Benji Ramona's size and shape, but he was still a lumbering blue giant underneath the glamour. He walked with a heavy stride, there was no telling what he might blurt out in panic if he was questioned, and he was nervously munching on a clipboard.

Still, he could find them a boat. Scarlett couldn't think of another way to get them all across the lake and, without crossing the lake, she had no idea how they were going to escape.

Beside her, Esmeralda watched Benji approach the security door that kept the prisoners out of the WUB Club's foyer. The witch was now disguised as Benji. At this rate, poor Ez would have no idea what she was supposed to look like by the end of the day. "I hope I got everything right on his hair." She muttered to herself.

Benji clomped his way to the security door and swiped Ramona's ID badge in front of the lock. He held Ramona's keycard like it was trying to escape his grasp, his fingers visibly trembling.

"You can do it, Benji!" Drusilla called loudly, still bleary from the drugs.

Scarlett winced at her sister's volume, as everyone else made desperate "Shhhh!" sounds.

Benji cringed at the delirious support. When the door buzzed open, he trooped out into the front office, looking like he was headed for the gallows. The dwarf guard behind the check-in desk glanced up as "Ramona" went by. He gave a disinterested nod in Benji's direction and then went back to texting on his phone.

That was it.

No sirens. No interrogation. No flying monkeys swooping down.

Benji blinked like he couldn't believe the disguise was actually working. Still braced for the other shoe to drop, he just stood there for moment, waiting to get caught. When no one came rushing in with stun guns, he finally looked over his shoulder at the rest of them. From the blank expression on his face, Scarlett surmised that he'd never imagined getting this far and now he'd forgotten what he was supposed to do next.

Scarlett made a desperate "go, go, go!" motion with her hand, waving him towards the outside door.

Benji jolted out of his frozen shock. "Right!" He mouthed. Nodding vigorously, he all but ran out the door and towards the parking lot. The outside door swung shut behind him as he disappeared into the sunlight, fleeing the hospital.

He was free.

There was a moment of stunned silence as the other six digested his success.

"Holy shit." Marrok slowly shook his head. "That was amazing, Red." His mouth curved like he was proud of her and he looked at Avenant. "I *told* you Letty would pull it off. You owe me five gold coins, ya prick."

She'd done it! Her plan had worked. At least, this part of it.

Scarlett bent over, her hands on her knees, and tried to remember how to breathe.

Later that night, Benji would return with a boat. They'd sneak out through the library and meet him at the lakeshore. Fifteen minutes later, she'd be in the Enchanted Forest, headed for her grandmother's house

and redemption. It was all going to work…
So long as Benji actually came *back* to the prison now that he was finally unshackled from its bleak walls. Which he totally would. She was sure of it.
"We'll never see that ogre, again." Rumpelstiltskin predicted with a sigh.

Chapter Seven

Wolves are bred to fight and fuck. I always bear that in mind, because it's pointless to try and deal with them like they're thinking beings. They are just beautiful animals.

Psychiatric case notes of Dr. Ramona Fae

Scarlett measured the window with a string of several dozen uncooked noodles. "So, if each ziti is approximately an inch, we should all be able to fit through these windows with no problem." She looked over at Marrok. "That was another reason it had to be Benji who went to get the boat. No way would an eight foot bridge ogre squeeze out a window. He might've gotten stranded in here."

Marrok nodded like he gave a shit whether or not Benji came with them. "That was definitely a concern of mine." He deadpanned.

Thanks to Dr. White's seduction mandate, he and Letty were alone in the library, although it was hard to see the mildewing interior as a particularly romantic setting. The mostly empty shelves were tipped at odd angles, only two light bulbs worked in the entire large room, and the steady dripping sound of water was coming from somewhere overhead. He was fairly sure the Good folk only called it a "library" to taunt the inmates. It was no wonder the place was deserted.

But, on the other hand, there was definitely an upside to being the only two people in the space, regardless of how rank it was. Marrok tipped his head to admire his True Love's posterior as she balanced on a chair.

Thank God she was back in her own body again. He'd missed it.

"So now the only problem is how we get the window open." Still standing on the seat of the chair, she dropped the skein of yard and freezer bag full of pasta to the floor and turned her attention to the lock. "Damn it, everything else here is a rusty mess, but of *course* this would be brand new." She turned to look at him. "Can you pick it?"

"Yeah, but it wouldn't stop the alarm from going off." He nodded to the wires attached to the frame.

Scarlett frowned at it, her expression thoughtful. "Breaking the glass would make too much noise. Maybe we could cut it."

"The craft room has safety scissors." Marrok suggested helpfully.

It was so gratifying to have those blue eyes glaring at him, again. The color was a magic all its own. He was definitely going to veto any more body-switch plans.

"Are you going to help or not?" She demanded.

He endeavored to look innocent. "I *am* helping." He moved behind her and "helpfully" laid a hand on her "EVIL" t-shirt. "Here let me steady you." His palm slipped under the hem of her top and his thumb brushed the soft skin of her lower back.

She batted him away.

Marrok chuckled, delighted with the girl. In the most perverse way possible, he liked that she was so prickly. His looks didn't matter to her, at all. He never even had to try with most women, but Letty was so hard to impress.

Unless your name was Charming, anyway.

His smile faded. "Are you in love with that prince?" He demanded before he could stop himself.

"What?" She shot him a distracted frown and climbed down from the chair. "Is it really so hard for you to concentrate and take this seriously?"

"Red, you wouldn't *believe* how seriously I'm taking this."

The more he thought about the situation, the more complications Marrok saw in being bound to this girl. Damn if he wasn't growing... attached to the little do-Gooder, though. He'd be keeping his True Love no matter what, but he was starting to want to keep *Letty*.

"As a matter of fact, I *don't* believe you're taking it seriously." She adjusted the t-shirt back into place and poked a finger into his chest. "This escape has to go off *perfectly*. Any mistakes will get us caught and tossed in the dungeon. Is that what you want?"

Her lecturing tone completely turned him on. "No, I want something different."

Scarlett missed the seduction in his voice. Against the odds, the woman was turning out to be one hell of a criminal mastermind. But, she clearly couldn't decipher Marrok's *blindingly obvious* hints that he wanted to ravish her.

"I wish I knew more about how Trevelyan pulled off *his* escape." She continued, her very sexy brain consumed with unsexy thoughts. "Ez says you two shared a cell."

Well, *that* brought down the mood...

"Back when my counts of Badness were in the single digits, Trevelyan and I were locked up together." Marrok allowed. "By the time he left, we weren't exactly friends." He delivered that massive understatement in a calm tone, but Scarlett still squinted over at him.

"There's a difference between 'not being friends' and being 'mortal enemies.'" She pointed out suspiciously. "Why am I guessing you two were the later?"

"Because you're a not-so-evil genius?" He shook his head. "Seriously, investigating Trevelyan won't help us get out of here. Trust me."

"He didn't tell you anything?"

"Nothing helpful. Unless you need a rundown of insults and death threats to use against me. He was screaming those pretty loud on that last day."

She made a face. "It's like you *try* to make everyone hate you. It's the only explanation."

"Sad part is I don't have to try that hard."

She sighed in resignation. "So, what did you do to piss off the dragon?"

No sense in lying. "I didn't help him escape."

Her eyebrows drew together. "Trevelyan wanted you to escape *with* him?"

"Yep."

"And you refused?

"Yep."

"Why?"

"I was getting out in ten months." Wolfball season ensured that Marrok got paroled every spring, no matter his sentence. "Didn't seem worth the risk."

"Right now, you only have *six months* left and you've agreed to come with me."

He shrugged. "With you, it's always worth the risk."

Scarlett frowned at him in confusion.

It amazed Marrok that he was the only one who noticed how pretty this girl was. Her relentless demands and shiny hair created such an appealing package. It just went to show that people would believe whatever you told them. Tell them that the naked emperor guy from a couple kingdoms over was wearing clothes and everyone agreed. Tell them that Scarlett was the ugly stepsister and that's what they saw.

People were idiots.

Marrok shifted closer to her, smiling as her eyes went wide in surprise.

Letty was so out of her league that she didn't even notice he'd cornered her, until her back hit the window sill. Whatever Prince Useless did with his royal days, it must have been edited for television material. Charming certainly hadn't taught this girl very much. Marrok could've had Letty's pants off in less than a second and she was completely oblivious to the danger.

"What are you doing?" Scarlett blinked, still not getting it. "Is this part of the pretend seduction thing?"

"Yep." Marrok lied. He could see her pulse hammering in her neck as he dipped his head even closer to hers. "Just play along." He advised quietly. "Otherwise you'll give us away."

"To who?" She sounded out of breath. "We're the only ones in here."

He made his voice grave. "Spies are everywhere, baby."

"What?" She gazed up at him, looking baffled and distrustful and sexy as hell. "I don't think that..." His lips brushed against hers and she trailed off with a gasp.

God, he'd never heard anything hotter.

Marrok's hand came up to touch her jaw, making sure she couldn't slip away. Not that she was trying to move. In fact, Scarlett was so befuddled that she froze for a beat. He sensed the gears in her clever little mind whirring, trying to figure out what had just happened.

Allowing her to think too much would be a very bad idea. The last thing he wanted was Letty talking herself out of this before he'd gotten a chance to convince her.

Luckily, he could be pretty damn convincing.

Marrok suckled her lower lip and she jolted. "That's it." He whispered. "Let me in, baby." His mouth opened against hers, seeking entrance... and she hesitantly responded.

Scarlett softened against him, her lips parting. She'd tried to hold out, but she wasn't immune to him. Thank God. Marrok was on fire for her. He must have been out of his mind to ever think he'd prefer some aggressive she-wolf to this girl in bed. Nothing could feel better than the slow melting of her tension. He felt her lean closer to him. Her hand came up to rest on his shoulder and Marrok groaned, deepening the kiss.

Christ, she was sweet.

True Loves were usually sexually attracted to each other. God knew, Marrok had wanted to rip Letty's clothes off from the moment they'd met. But, she was a Good folk. It had been impossible to know for sure that she'd feel the same way. Except, now she was kissing him back, and her body was pressing against his, and Marrok knew he could make her want him.

Triumph filled him.

Marrok had waited so long to find his True Love, he'd thought she'd never arrive. To have her in his arms was better than he'd ever imagined. He lifted her up so Letty was sitting on the windowsill, his mouth never leaving hers. His fingers tangled in her flame-colored hair and he stepped between her legs. While she was off balance, he was going to race forward as far as she'd let him. That would make it easier to lure her even farther along the next time.

Strategy was all part and parcel of being a Baddie.

She drew in a surprised breath as she felt the hard length of his arousal pressing up against her. Marrok managed a soothing sound, even as his free hand found her hip. He tugged her closer and she gave a small whimper that made him see stars. Holy *shit*, this girl was perfect. The addictive little sounds she made and the way she smelled and the feel of her skin.

Why the fuck had he ever questioned having Letty as his True Love? No one else would *ever* do now that he'd tasted her. This woman was...

Marrok's predatory instincts suddenly lit-up.

Someone else had entered the library. He knew without even turning around that it was Dower, one of the other wolves locked up in the WUB Club. One of his old team mates from Wolfball.

Shit.

Marrok pulled away from Scarlett, irritated that he couldn't take the time to admire her flushed face and dazed eyes. "Hold that thought, Red." He lifted her down from the windowsill, and smoothed a hand over her hair. "I gotta take care of something, real quick."

Her flustered gaze wasn't meeting his. She looked completely astonished and he could already tell she was going to do her best to deny everything. "I don't know what just happened," she blurted out, "but it was a mistake and..." She stopped short, finally spotting Dower over Marrok's shoulder.

Marrok arched a brow at her. "Told ya. Spies." He turned to see the other wolf moving closer, blocking the exit.

Dower was a large, bearded scumbag with a long list of gruesome crimes. The guy was hyper-focused on being Big Wolf on Campus and he randomly hated

Marrok.

Well, maybe not "randomly."

Marrok never did play well with others. He'd showed Dower up at Wolfball countless times, put his head through a TV camera, and may have been responsible for the jagged scar on Dow's forearm where his hand had been reattached. It was hard to keep track. The "game" was usually kill or be killed, so all the wolves inflicted life-threatening violence on each other just to survive the rounds. Half the time, it was impossible to know who was who out there. No one cared about sides. Just about survival.

Marrok surreptitiously moved his body so he was between the other man and Letty. "First time in the library, Dow? I never took you for a reader."

That wasn't technically true. Dower wasn't an idiot, which made him all the more dangerous. The guy had shaggy black hair and a pair of unsettling ice-blue eyes that saw far too much. He was as big as Marrok, in their human-forms. Unlike Marrok, though, he was eager to team up with other players, on and off the field. He usually traveled in a pack. Marrok didn't sense anyone else lurking, but they wouldn't be far behind Dower.

Dow drew in a deep and exaggerated sniff. "Fuuuuck, Marrok. You cornered yourself a prize." He smirked at Scarlett. "I *thought* there was something weird about you, honey, but now I can smell it. What's a Good girl like you, doing in a place like this?"

"I'm not Good." Letty objected righteously. "Why does everyone keep saying...?"

Marrok cut her off. Wolves could scent the truth, even if she couldn't. "The Good folk have no idea what she is." His eyes stayed on Dower. This whole situation had "pain in the ass" written all over it. "All of them live their lives in the dark, so it's not surprising they'd occasionally misplace one of their own."

"Well, do they have any idea what she's *planning?*" Dower taunted. "Because, I couldn't help but overhear Little *Miss-Placed* mention something about an escape." He arched a brow at Scarlett. "Doesn't seem like a Good folk would be plotting something like that, but the hypocrisy of you assholes never ceases to amaze me."

"I'm. not. Good." She pointedly spaced each word. "And we're not planning any escape." Her voice was too high. "That's ridiculous. You *completely* misunderstood our conversation."

Dower gave a snort. "Yeah, I'm sure you're in here for the educational opportunities." He gestured around the dank library with a contemptuous wave of his giant palm. "Oh and for sucking face with Marrok."

"Yes!" Her expression lit up. "Of course! That's right. We're here for *sex*." Lying didn't come easily to Scarlett, but Marrok gave her points for enthusiasm. She beamed, visibly thrilled with how quickly she'd come up with a cover story. "Yes. Obviously. This is where Marrok and I have our assignations."

She'd just used the word "assignations." The girl was simply adorable.

Dower fixed Marrok with a skeptical look. "You expect me to buy that you're only in here to get blowjobs from a fake ugly stepsister?"

"She's not ugly." Marrok said mildly.

"I'm not fake!" Scarlett protested at the same time.

"Well, whatever she is, I *know* she's plotting an escape. And if she's getting you out, I'm going, too." Dower decided. "I'm here for life, because of that fucking championship game." Popularly known as the "championship massacre." Even by Wolfball standards it had been a bloodbath. "I got nothing to lose by making a break for it. Either I'm in on the plan or I'll be telling Dr. White about your little 'assignation.'" He sneered at Marrok. "And, just so ya know, I think it's disgusting that you'd ever willingly touch one of *them*."

"Oh come on…" Marrok leaned back, so his hand was on the chair that Scarlett had been standing on, and flashed a man-to-man smile. "You've never wanted to dirty-up a Goodie just for fun?"

"No! Because, I'm not a fucking pervert." Dower declared passionately, although a jury of his peers had disagreed on that score. "Bad enough when they pay the coach and we *have* to touch them, but to *choose* one is just twisted."

"Bullshit. We all have fantasies. Besides, you know that every one of those Goody-Goods is *dying* for something between her legs more interesting than beige tapioca. Those knight-in-shining-armor pussies probably screw the poor girls with their metal pants on."

Scarlett whacked his shoulder in annoyance.

Dower couldn't have been more invested in this philosophical debate. "Look, there's *them* and there's *us*." He made an emphatic hand gesture that indicated one side versus another. "Good and Bad shouldn't mix." He glanced at Letty. "No matter how many Good broads need to be fucked by real men."

She made a face at him. "Then, *you'll* certainly be out of luck."

Marrok shrugged. "I don't 'mix' with Letty, so much as I bend her over that table and take her from behind while she begs me to spank her." He nodded towards the table beside Dower.

Scarlett's mouth dropped open and Marrok

almost smiled. If she was going to invent a torrid affair as their alibi, she really needed to work on not looking so shocked when he added some spicy details. The table thing had just come right off the top of his head, but now he was sort of intrigued by it, if he did say so himself.

Dower was, too. His gaze slid up and down Letty's body, like he was picturing Marrok's story playing out and not finding the idea "disgusting," at all.

Marrok arched a brow. "Don't knock it 'til you try it, Dow." He made it sound like an offer, his tone clearly suggesting that the other man could share Letty's lush curves. Marrok would see him dead first, but Dower didn't know that. "You know the Good ones love to be Bad."

Dower's puritanical bitching aside, he suddenly wasn't so outraged over the notion of fraternizing with Good folk outside of work. Not when there was a chance his dick could have an "assignation" right that moment. His eyes drifted over to the table with a speculative expression on his face.

...Which was just what Marrok had been waiting for.

His hand tightened on the back of the chair, his body already in motion. Hefting it up, he slammed it right into the side of Dower's head. The solid wood legs cracked against the other man's skull, knocking Dow to the ground. Marrok briefly saw the guy's enraged expression and then he brought the chair down two more times making sure Dow was unconscious.

Marrok glanced over at Scarlett who was gaping down at Dower. "No killing people, just beating them with chairs." He reminded her. "See? I paid attention to your rules."

She slowly raised her eyes to his. "You are an

annoying jackass." She said sincerely. "But, right now, I think you're awesome."

Marrok's mouth curved, happy to have impressed her. "Wanna try out the table for real?"

"No." Scarlett crouched down next to Dower. "We need to tie him up." She looked back over at the skein of green yard. "Do you think that would hold him?"

Marrok made a skeptical face. "No." It wasn't like they had any better options lying around in the library, though, and Dow was down for the count. "More importantly, we need to stash him somewhere so nobody stumbles across him."

"Like where?"

"Closet? Bathroom?" He jerked a thumb towards the bookshelves. "Or we could dump him back in the stacks. I doubt anyone's going to look for him in here."

Letty debated that. "How long do you think he'll be out cold?"

Considering the beating Marrok had just given him? "Hours."

"Alright." She nodded. "We'll be out of here tonight. So if we can just keep him out of sight until then, everything will be fine." She frowned at Dow's unconscious form. "We have bigger issues to deal with, right now."

"I agree. We should get back to making out."

That got her attention. "I told you, that was a mistake!"

"No, it wasn't. I knew exactly what I was doing."

"Oh, I'm sure you *did*." She stood up and crossed her arms over her chest. "But whatever it is you're up to, I'm not falling for it. You're not tricking me, not distracting me, not *pretending* to pretend to seduce me..."

"Did it feel like I was pretending to pretend?"

"...It's not happening, Marrok!" She continued like she didn't even hear him. "I have no idea what you'd hoped to accomplish..."

"Really? You couldn't figure it out? Because, I wasn't being real subtle about my master plan when I had my tongue in your mouth."

Letty kept going. "...but, I am soooo onto you. I understand that because you're so," she hesitated, "*incredibly* handsome..."

Marrok grinned. He didn't want her *just* wanting him for his looks, but --honestly-- what else did he have to offer a woman? Letty finding him attractive was a huge step in the right direction.

Her eyes narrowed. "...that you're used to women being drawn to you and being blinded by your charm. But, I am not an idiot. Men who look like you do not come on to ugly stepsisters. Not without an agenda."

"You're not ugly."

"What do you *want?*" She demanded. "Just tell me why you kissed me."

"Basically, it seemed like a good first step to getting you naked."

Letty stared up at him in frustration. "And why do you want *that?*"

"Why do I want you *naked?*" He repeated incredulously. Was she kidding?

"Yes. The truth."

What could he say that wouldn't make her mad? Now did not seem like the ideal time to mention the fact that she was his True Love. Or that he spent every share circle fantasizing about her body tied to his bed. What would Letty want to hear? "Because, I think it would be fun?" He tried.

"*Fun?!* We have to hide Dower, disable the alarms, hope that Ramona stays locked up in the basement, outsmart all the guards, pray that Benji comes back, and do about a thousand other things or we're never getting out of here... And you want to have *fun?*"

"I'm always having fun when you're around, Red." The girl was a constant source of new and surprising ideas. "We'd just be having *more* fun if we were having sex."

"You're unbelievable. You could have any woman in here and you turn them all down, but you're flirting with *me?*"

"Yeah."

"Why?"

"You're the one I want."

"*Why?*"

God, that was just her favorite word. He hadn't faced an interrogation like this since his last arrest. Marrok tried to come up with an explanation that she'd believe, but that wouldn't scare her away. No Good girl would be thrilled to be bound to a wolf. What could he tell her? The very first thing that came to mind made him sound like a pansy, but it was completely true.

"Because, you reached out and held my hand."

She looked mystified by that response. "No one's ever held your hand before?"

"No. That's not what they want from me."

"I don't want anything from you, besides your help." She said it like she had a pretty good idea what was usually demanded of him. "I promise I'll get you out of here, no matter what. You don't have to sleep with me."

"I *want* to sleep with you." He'd never had to actually seduce a woman before, but it was coming naturally. "There's something real between us, baby. A connection. It's been there from the beginning. Can you feel it, too?"

Blue eyes met his and she gave a hesitant nod.

Marrok's mouth curved.

She quickly rallied. "But, that doesn't mean I'm going to fall into bed with you. I *know* that something else is going on here, so you might as well just tell me what it is and..." Before Letty could continue her newest argument as to why everything he said was a lie, the room went dark. One of the light bulbs overhead blew out, plunging the library into deeper gloom.

Marrok and Scarlett both looked up.

"Great." He muttered, although, on the plus side, it did abruptly stop Letty's questions. She fell totally silent. He glanced over at his contrary little True Love, surprised that she'd given up her inquisition before beating him with a phonebook. "You okay?"

Letty was staring up at the ceiling with the same faraway expression that she always got when she'd been struck by a new and surprising idea. "I know how to disable the alarms." She whispered.

Chapter Eight

Rumpelstiltskin is tedious to listen to, be around, and write about. But, for a few extra food rations, he'll make *amazing* jewelry out of straw. I've already finished my holiday shopping!

Psychiatric case notes of Dr. Ramona Fae

"So we have two choices." Scarlett leaned across the table, her eyes intent. She'd corralled Avenant, Ez, Marrok, and Rumpelstiltskin in the dining hall and was doing her best to appear inconspicuous. All around them, motley groups of inmates ate the same small portions of porridge they were given for every meal. "Listen to both options before you start yelling, alright?"

"I don't make any promises." Avenant informed her seriously. From the careful way he was speaking, it was clear that he'd been given his nightly dosage of meds and was trying to fight through them.

Esmeralda rolled her eyes at him and finished off her runny gruel. "I think I'm even hungrier in this body." She patted her stomach, which was still disguised as *Benji's* stomach. Given the paltry food rations in the WUB Club, everyone was usually starving. It was another way to keep the patients weak and demoralized.

"We'll eat when we get out of here." Scarlett assured her. "Anyway, I used Ramona's keys to steal her tablet and did a little bit of internet research on how this place was constructed."

"I helped." Marrok put in.

"You played solitaire." Scarlett corrected.

"They have the plans for this place online?"

Avenant rolled his eyes. "Typical. Crimes only happen because the Good folk make it so damn easy."

"Yeah, the WUB Club homepage helpfully explained how secure everything is and the details were a good starting point for my research." Even then, it had taken Scarlett the better part of the afternoon to find out what she needed to know.

Things would've no doubt gone faster if not for Marrok being there. It was hard to concentrate on anything when he was lounging a few feet away, looking beautiful and wild and perfect. He was deliberately trying to be appealing and it worked, damn him. As if he wasn't distracting enough *before*, now he had to go and prove that he was the best kisser in the world. It just wasn't fair.

That jackass was up to something. Kissing her like that made no sense. Why would he want her when he could have anyone? He *had* to have some ulterior motive, but Scarlett couldn't figure out what it was. Marrok seemed committed to the escape, so she doubted that he was trying to undermine her plans. And, since he was obviously planning to leave the WUB Club with the rest of the group, it also didn't seem likely that he was playing along with Dr. White's plan to seduce Scarlett out of the glass slipper.

So what was his game?

Aside from making her insane with desire and general irritation.

He caught her frowning at him and shined a typically stellar grin.

Scarlett made a face at him and refocused on the group. They were all there except for Benji, who'd already escaped, and Dru. Cindy made sure Letty and Dru were kept on separate schedules as much as possible, so

Drusilla ate at the second dining time. Given how drugged her sister was, poor Dru wouldn't have much to contribute to the discussion, anyway.

"So, I've come up with a plan." Letty lowered her voice. "We have to cut the power."

Rumpelstiltskin swallowed. "To... the building?"

"Yep." She didn't see a way around it. "And, like I said, there are two ways to do that. Option one: Someone's got to stay behind."

Instantly, there was an outcry around the cafeteria table.

"Fuck that." Rumpelstiltskin and Avenant chorused.

"I'm not staying here!" Esmeralda yelped.

"I vote we leave Avenant." Marrok said at the same time.

Scarlett made an irritated "Shh!" sound at all of them. "I said no yelling until you hear me out." She reiterated. God, they just could *not* follow directions. "We're not getting out of here if the power is on, so we have to disable it. Period. Now, we can sabotage the system in the utility room, without too much trouble." Scarlett had total confidence in her crew's abilities to destroy. "The problem is there's a backup system. Fifteen seconds after we lose the primary power, the backup will kick-in and lock everything down. All the doors will seal tight."

"So?" Rumpelstiltskin demanded.

"So, no way will the person who cuts the power be able to make it to the library. They will be trapped behind all the automatically locked doors."

Silence.

"What's the other option?" Esmeralda finally asked.

"We take out the backup power, *too*. If it can't come on, none of the doors will be able to electronically lock. Ten minutes to midnight, we blow everything and all six of us escape through the library window in the confusion."

"I like this plan better." Avenant decided. "Let's go with option B."

"Just wait." Scarlett held up a hand. "If we cut the backup power, *none of the doors will lock.* Think about that. We will have literally opened up the cells of everyone in the WUB Club. We will be escaping at the same time that everyone else is suddenly running around here free. Some of them will probably escape, too."

"I can live with that." Esmeralda shrugged and pushed away her tray. "A lot of people in here are political prisoners, just like us." She'd obviously been thinking about Scarlett's speech about justice for Bad folk. She tapped an agitated blue finger against the tabletop. "We *all* deserve to go free."

Scarlett wasn't willing to go *that* far. "I wouldn't say *all*, but..."

Avenant cut her off. "I'm still liking the plan." He opened his cardboard carton of milk. "Granted, the others will be benefiting from our hard work, but, if anyone else gets away, the flying monkeys will have to split their resources to follow them. It'll give us more time."

"*Whose* hard work?" Marrok challenged. "Certainly not yours. What have *you* contributed?"

"I add much needed class to this consortium."

Scarlett ignored that, too. "Alright, so even if we're okay with the freeing *everybody* aspect of things, there's a bigger problem." She continued. "The backup system is in the boiler room and the boiler room is in the basement."

"The dungeon?!" Rumpelstiltskin paled. "No *way!* No *way* am I going down there."

Esmeralda looked over at Avenant's tray. "Are you going to eat your porridge?"

"Yes."

She sighed. "The first thing I'm doing when we get out of here is have a big spicy taco."

"We're not *getting* out of here." Rumpelstiltskin sounded frantic. "Not if we have to go down in the dungeon!"

"You'd rather one of us stay locked in here?" Marrok retorted. "You volunteering?"

"I'm not leaving anyone behind." More cynically, Scarlett was also pretty sure nobody in the group was willing to fall on their sword for the others. Baddies weren't into self-sacrifice, so Plan A was doomed. "That's why I'm voting that we go with the basement option."

Avenant gave a "told ya so" wave of his elegant palm.

"I'm not going down there!" Rumpelstiltskin insisted.

"I didn't say *you* had to do it." Scarlett retorted. "I'm saying one of us will have to sneak into the dungeon and…"

Marrok laid a hand on her arm, forestalling her words. Scarlett glanced over at him in surprise and saw that his attention was fixed on a pack of men stalking across the cafeteria towards them. Dower's cronies were looking for him and conducting a table-by-table search. Terrified inmates shrunk down in their seats as the four hulking wolves demanded answers from them.

…And now the pack's eyes had fallen on Marrok.

"Oh no." Scarlett glanced over at him and tried

not to panic. "Now what?"

Topaz eyes glowed. "Just don't say anything. You suck at lying."

Her grandmother was always saying the same thing.

"What are we lying about?" Esmeralda turned to look at the wolves. "Wait, did we have something to do with Dower going missing?"

Scarlett winced. "Kinda."

"Am I supposed to know who Dower is?" Avenant inquired. "Because, I don't."

"He's the guy Marrok and I left tied up in the library." Scarlett tried not to stare at the wolves bearing down on them. "I think his men have noticed he's gone."

Rumpelstiltskin groaned and scurried under the table to hide.

"Fellas." Marrok leaned back in his chair like he didn't have a care in the world and casually smiled as the other wolves surrounded their table. "Did you want something?"

"Where the fuck is Dow?" Richardson, the biggest of the men, snarled.

Avenant shrugged. "I still have no idea who that is. The rabble just becomes a blur of faces and whining." He drank from his paper carton and sighed. "And why do we never have *chocolate* milk?"

"This has your paw-prints all over it, Marrok." Richardson loomed over him. "You've *always* had it in for Dow."

"We have religious differences." Marrok allowed. "I want him to rot in hell and he disagrees."

"Where *is* he?!" Richardson bellowed. His beefy hand seized Marrok by the shirtfront and hefted him out of the chair. "Tell me, you son of a bitch!"

"Good news, Red." Marrok's gaze slid over to hers for half-a-second before sighting on Richardson's fuming face. "I don't think we'll have to *sneak* into the dungeon, after all." His skull slammed forward, crushing the bridge of Richardson's nose.

Scarlett's eyes went wide as all hell broke loose.

She shouted Marrok's name in panic as the other wolves surged forward to attack him. He went careening backwards into the table, sending trays and chairs in every direction. The fight was six against one.

"No!" Scarlett leapt forward to try and help him, although she had no idea what good she could do. The wolves were all trained fighters and double her size. She just knew she couldn't stand by and watch Marrok get hurt.

Avenant leapt to his feet to avoid flying globs of porridge. "Oh for God's sake, it's like dealing with children."

Forgetting that she was now housed in the body of an eight foot ogre, Esmeralda tried to scramble out of the fray. She climbed up on one of the mismatched wooden benches along the wall, only to hit her head on the ceiling. She grabbed her skull, cursing in the forgotten language of witches. Thankfully, everyone was too busy to notice.

The room descended into chaos as fighting broke out everywhere simultaneously. The cafeteria attendants desperately tried to restore order as all the aggrieved inmates took this golden opportunity to attack each other. Trolls and monsters and sorcerers and enchanted beings of every sort threw food, and plastic silverware, and punches. The emergency siren sounded a continuing loop of high-pitched sound.

"Marrok!" Scarlett grabbed one of the wolves by

his blond ponytail, wrenching him away. "Stop! Leave him alone!"

The blond wolf turned with a snarl of fury. He drew his hand back and punched her.

Punched her!

Scarlett doubled over in surprise and pain, her eyes watering. No one had ever hit her before. It hurt! The guy prepared to strike her again and she wasn't sure what to...

Marrok tackled the guy with a manic roar. He launched himself at the blond wolf's midsection, dragging him to the ground. The greatest player in Wolfball took down his enemy like the other guy was a sack of flour. They hit the floor hard enough to send them both sliding ten feet across the room. Marrok was already on top and beating him.

"Son-of-a-*bitch!*" He slammed his fist into the other man's face, looking incensed. *"You just hit my True Love!"*

Scarlett's eyebrows soared.

Hang on, *what* did he say? Had she heard that wrong over all the noise?

The guy tried to break free of Marrok's attack, still fixated on Scarlett. He was a Wolfball player, too, and he seemed to think his best chance of survival was to get to Scarlett and use her as a shield against Marrok. The sport was brutal and basically without rules, so it was probably instinctive to use an opponent's weakness against him.

The guy struggled to reach her, his hands clawing on the linoleum for purchase. Scarlett was too surprised to move... but she didn't have to. He wasn't getting close to her, anyway. Marrok wrenched him back, catching him in a chokehold. The other wolf flailed around like a fish on a hook. Scarlett just stood there breathing hard, knowing she was safe from the man.

Marrok was protecting her.

"What the hell?" Richardson grabbed Scarlett's arm and dragged her closer. "You're Marrok's True Love?" He got right in her face, breathing deep. "Holy shit, you're *Good?!*"

"No, I'm..." Her protest ended with a cry as he yanked her around. Her back was against his front, his hand at her throat.

"Marrok!" He bellowed. "You ready to tell me where Dower is, now?" His sharpened nails dug into her skin and Scarlett flinched.

Marrok froze. His normally sardonic face was deadly serious as he slowly released the other wolf and stood up. The blond guy was now unconscious. "Let her go." The tone was ice cold.

"Fuck you. Where's Dow?"

"Let her *go*." This time it was an order.

"You want her back, you tell me what I want to know." Richardson dipped his head to sniff at her hair. "And I'm betting you want her back *bad*. Christ, I hate her kind, but they always smell so damn... Good." He smirked at the pun.

Marrok's eyes narrowed.

"Don't you tell him anything." Scarlett warned, her attention on Marrok. Dow knew too much. If he was released, the whole plan was ruined.

"Shut-up!" Richardson screamed. "Marrok is going to tell me what I want to know or his woman will be headless in about three seconds..."

He broke off abruptly and Scarlett felt the impact of something right through his body. Then, Richardson was toppling over on top of her, his whole form going limp. She heard Marrok swearing viciously as she was dragged to the dirty floor.

She looked up and saw Avenant standing there, one of the metal cafeteria trays in his hands.

"I have no idea why hitting people when their backs are turned has such a bad reputation. I've always found it most effective." Casually dropping the makeshift weapon, he sat back down and resumed drinking his milk.

"Letty!" Marrok raced over to crouch down next to her. "Are you okay?" He pulled her free of Richardson's unconscious weight, helping her up. "Are you hurt?" His palm caressed her bruised cheek, scanning for more injuries.

Her heart flipped over in her chest at his gentle touch. "No, I'm…"

The swinging doors to the cafeteria burst open and the dwarf guards came charging in dressed in full SWAT gear. They began hitting patients with their riot sticks and screaming orders. People who'd had nothing to do with the fight were beaten to the ground.

At least two dozen inmates shouted, "They did it!" in panicked unison. Fingers pointed at Scarlett and Marrok.

"Okay." Letty swallowed hard as the guard closed in. She quickly tossed Avenant Ramona's key and started desperately whispering instructions. "Let yourselves out of your cells tonight. Remember, Benji will be back at midnight. You guys take out the primary power ten minutes before that. We'll do the backup. Then, we'll meet in the library. *Make sure everyone is there.*"

"Do what now?" Avenant asked with a frown. It was impossible to know if he was hazy from the drugs or just not listening.

Letty wanted to shake him. "Pay attention! If you forget any of this, we're screwed!"

Marrok sighed as they were surrounded by armed dwarves. "In case you hadn't noticed, Red, I think we're *already* screwed."

Chapter Nine

We intercepted more letters intended for Prince Charming today.
Scarlett is still determined to contact him.
I've upped her medication.
Again.

Psychiatric case notes of Dr. Ramona Fae

Cinderella barely resisted the urge to push the wedding cake onto the floor.

She imagined smashing the hideous pink rosettes against the black and white tiles, her too-big feet jumping up and down on the stupid sparkly monogram. Then she'd rub the simpering baker's face in the mess and have her mice beat him with the dorky cake topper of a couple dancing.

She asked for so little. Demanded nothing more than her due as a princess. And, her disloyal subjects rewarded her restraint and kindness by giving her even *less*. They *wanted* her wedding to be an embarrassing farce. They *wanted* her to suffer.

Either that or they were trying to make her snap.

Maybe this was all a plan to incite her. To make her lose her temper in front of Charming. Well, provoking her wouldn't work. Cinderella had spent years crafting her perfect image and she wasn't about to lose it in front of her groom. Even under a spell, Charming was suspicious of her. So outwardly she would keep her cool and smile through the constant attacks. She would show them all she was a *real* princess. Sweet and benevolent and serene.

...Even though she wanted to kill every single

asshole out to ruin her wedding.

Even the two shuddering climaxes she'd had from scrubbing at Gustav's feet couldn't make up for this. Her gaze slashed over to Charming, trying to gauge his reaction to the grotesque monstrosity of a cake. *Surely* he saw it was a direct insult to his gentle bride. Not even someone as blandly, blindly *Good* as the prince could miss this outrage.

"It's gorgeous, Antonio." He told the fuck-wad baker. "You're really outdone yourself."

Cinderella wished a house would fall on his head.

Charming was a blond Adonis of a man, with sunshine hair and rich chocolaty eyes. But, his good looks were squandered on someone so sickeningly... earnest.

Charming favored tailored slacks and turtleneck sweaters. With his wire rim glasses and constant intellectual chatter, he always seemed more like a college professor than royalty. He liked to have boring discussions about philosophy and social justice with Scarlett. But did he ever want to do anything that Cindy enjoyed? Of course not. The *one time* Cindy had convinced him to go to the hairdresser with her, he'd seem bored.

And now *this*.

Antonio grinned, *obviously* laughing that his disrespectful slight against Cinderella was going unpunished. Like all Baddies, he was stupid and worthless and scheming. "I did my best to make the cake perfect for you and our princess, majesty." He simpered.

Charming gave the furry idiot a pat on his arm and glanced down at Cinderella. "Didn't he do an incredible job?" He prompted when she remained silent.

Somehow she found it in her to hide her hatred. It felt like spikes were being driven into her cheeks, but she even managed a smile. "Well... I know he tried his best."

Antonio's face fell.

Charming looked annoyed at *her* for some reason. "Can I speak with you for a moment?"

He drew her to the other side of the royal kitchen. Everyone thought he was *such* a gentleman, but really he was just weak. The thought of being married to someone so weak was repulsive.

"The staff just wants to please you." He said in a disapproving tone. "Can't you try harder to...?"

She cut him off. "That *thing*," she pointed to the cake with a wild gesture of her hand, "is a blight on baked goods! I wouldn't feed it to a pig, let alone present it to a royal princess. You *must* see that!"

He looked confused by what was painfully obvious to anyone with eyes. "It's *beautiful*, Cindy. Probably the most beautiful cake I've ever seen."

The man was either blind or stupid.

"Bullshit! That fucking tree ogre probably got his dirty green hairs all over the frosting!"

"Antonio is the best baker in the Westlands."

Tears burned Cinderella's eyes. Why was everything so impossibly hard? Why couldn't she have *one* nice thing? "I just want our wedding to be perfect. Don't you want that? Do you *want* the other kingdoms to mock us?"

"Of course I want the wedding to be perfect." Charming agreed, but his voice wasn't enthusiastic. If her bitch of a stepsister was here, he'd probably be *thrilled* to get her an adequate cake. He'd make sure every detail was up to standards. "But, I don't see that necessitates treating people so..."

"They aren't people!" She interrupted. "They're

servants. They're Bad folk. If you can't control their disrespect, I'll do it myself!"

"You're being irrational."

"And you're being a pussy!" She shrieked. "You've resented me ever since the ball!" The spell couldn't make him love her. It just muddled his mind, so he thought she was the one who'd fit the shoe. Still, *anyone* should be thrilled to have her for a bride. "You blame me for what happened to Letty and Dru, even though I was the victim!"

"The girls wouldn't intentionally harm you." He said. "They wouldn't harm anyone. Under the law, I can't get them out of that prison yet, but I *know* there has to have been a mistake."

"The wizard-judge said they were probably plotting my death! You've heard the rumors about their mother's family and *still* all you care about is setting them free."

"That has nothing to do with…"

She started sobbing. "If it was up to you, I'd be dead. That's what you *really* want!"

"That's not true."

"It is! You're taking their side over mine! *Admit it*."

"I just know the judge was wrong. I know Letty. I know Dru. If they'd been able to have a real trial and they weren't carted off before I could talk to them…"

"Bad folk don't deserve trials! It's in the Westlands' constitution!"

"Well, I'm in the process of changing that law." He retorted. They'd had this argument before. "Once I do, I can force the courts to reexamine their case and we can find out what *really* happened at that ball."

"I already told you what happened." She hissed.

"Don't you believe me?"

He paused for a moment too long. "Of course I do."

"You're lying!"

"I just think you must have mistaken some of the facts. I can't imagine Scarlett coming at you with a hatchet."

"Well, she *did*." Jesus, was it really so hard to imagine Letty as an attempted axe murderer? Cinderella could picture it so clearly that she almost believed it had happened herself. It wasn't a lie so much as a preemptive strike. She'd just accused her stepsister of something before Letty had a *chance* to ruin her. How did he not see it? "And what kind of prince doubts his bride's word?" It was *infuriating* that he didn't trust her.

Charming arched a brow. "Scarlett was in a gown, at the palace, attending the ball, when she allegedly attacked you."

"So?"

"So, where on earth did she get a hatchet?"

Silence.

Cinderella glowered up at him. "You and I had sex that night in the garden." She finally spat out. "You know we did. *I'm* your True Love. You'd better get used to it and let this drop, or you're never going to touch me, again. You can go fuck those Baddies you love so much."

Charming slowly shook his head and that familiar look of disgust passed over his face. He tried to hide it, but it was always there just under the surface. Charming wanted nothing to do with her. "I know you're supposed to be my True Love. And the glass slipper says you're my destined princess. I'm trying to respect all that. But, don't fight me about getting Letty and Dru out of jail, because it *will* happen."

Cinderella was too angry to even speak. Prince or not, he was *such* a whiny loser.

Turning on her heel, she headed for the door. Sooner or later, Charming would discover the truth. Cinderella had placed hundreds of calls to the idiot she'd bought the spell from, hoping for some way to ramp up Charming's dosage, but there was no answer. Typical of a Bad folk to be so totally unprofessional.

But, honestly, it wouldn't matter anyway. There was no way Cinderella could keep him in the dark forever, especially not if he was determined to get to Letty. The spell would break if he uncovered the truth and Scarlett would do anything to destroy Cinderella's life. She'd tell him *everything* just as soon as she could.

So there was only one thing for a real princess to do.

After all, Cinderella needed Charming to *get* the crown, but she didn't need him to *keep* it. Come her wedding night, his royal righteousness was a dead man.

Chapter Ten

Marrok begins to show signs of sexual interest in Scarlett.
This can only be further proof of his masochistic leanings.

Psychiatric case notes of Dr. Ramona Fae

The basement was even more dank and moldy than the rest of the WUB Club. It was the oldest part of the facility and a dungeon in the literal sense of the word. Stone walls. Thick doors. No windows. It was a place that no one ever escaped from and that nobody *ever* wanted to go.

Except Scarlett.

She was exactly where she wanted to be.

Mostly.

She was locked in an eight-by-eight cell, with nothing but a bucket and a "mattress" made of hay. That wasn't really helping the plan. But, she *was* in the basement. She just had to find a way to make it to the boiler room and everything would be fine.

Or rather *they* needed to find a way to make it to the boiler room.

The guards had dumped Marrok in the cell with her, no doubt as part of Dr. White's ongoing seduction scheme. The wolf took up a lot of space in the cramped cell. Scarlett was doing her best not to look at him, but it was hard. Even in the darkness, she could see the glowing gold of his eyes.

He sat with his back against the wall and watched her pace. "You wanna talk about it?"

"No." She didn't even have to ask what "it" was.

"'Cause you seem a little tense."

"Of course I'm tense. I'm thinking about our escape."

"You're thinking about *me*."

"Don't be such a narcissist."

"Baby," he watched her with something like compassion, "it'll be alright. Being my True Love isn't the end of the world. I *know* you could do better, but --I swear-- I can be a loyal husband to you. You can trust me."

He was determined to talk about it. Fine. "You might *think* I'm your True Love, but there's been a mistake." She'd been rehearsing the perfect calm words in her head. "It's just not real."

"Uh-huh." Marrok sounded like he was humoring her, now. "You understand that wolves are biologically programmed to identify their True Loves, right? It's like arguing that I've 'made a mistake' about blinking or swallowing. It's *automatic*. I have no control of it."

"So... if you *could* control it you would?" Scarlett translated, annoyance derailing her prepared speech. A familiar feeling of uncertainty filled her. A sense that she was a complete letdown to someone else. "You're disappointed to have me as a True Love?" She paused. "I mean, disappointed to *think* that I'm your True Love. Because, I'm not."

"I'm not disappointed. I'm just *surprised*. I was expecting someone more... evil."

Scarlett refused to be hurt by that answer. All her life, she'd heard similar complaints from her grandmother. Letty wasn't good enough to be Good or bad enough to be Bad. On some level, she knew that.

So what *was* she?

"I honestly have no idea what to do with you."

Marrok continued. "Most True Loves just meet, recognize each other, have sex a bunch of times, and plan a honeymoon crime spree. You're much more challenging."

"Breaking out of here *is* a crime." Scarlett defended. "And --you make a good point-- Bad folk *do* know their True Loves right off. So, *if* we were bound, I'd feel this too and I *don't.*"

Was that true? Even as she said it, Letty wasn't sure. She definitely felt *something* with Marrok. She had right from the start. A... connection.

Shit.

Marrok shrugged. "You're Good. Good folk have no way of sensing their True Loves before the wedding night. It's one of your major problems as a group, because how the hell can you be sure you married the right person until it's too late?"

"I'm not Good and I'm not your True Love! You say these things about me that just aren't true. I know you *think* they're true, but they're *not.*"

"Because of Charming?"

"Because of many things. The first one being, you and I are not compatible. You are handsome and famous and..."

"Bullshit. That's not what this is about. You're just afraid of me."

"I am not!"

"Prove it."

She hesitated. "Prove it how?"

"Come here and let me show you that you're mine." His tone was pure temptation.

"Forget it!" When True Loves slept together, it was supposed to be more *explosive* than between ordinary people. Scarlett wasn't sure she believed that, but she also wasn't willing to test the theory for herself...

Although it would explain why kissing Marrok had been so incredible.

Shit.

"Obviously, sex would be *your* solution, but I'm interested in more important things." She tried to ignore the traitorous part of her body that was deeply interested in seeing just how "explosive" it would be with him. Her alleged True Love was amazing, astonishingly, addictively gorgeous. She found herself just gazing at him for a beat, imagining... Bad things.

"I can be about more than just sex." He told her.

"I know you *can*, but you seem to resist it."

"I'm not the one resisting." He dropped his voice. "Come on. I promise it'll be fun."

Shit!

Scarlett forced herself to glance away from the pretty. "No! Look, if we're True Loves --and I'm not saying we are-- but *if* we were somehow bound to each other, obviously we'd have to," she made a frustrated hand gesture, "undo this."

Marrok's expression became unreadable. "Ya think so?"

"Yes! It would be the only option."

"We'd both have to agree in order to break a True Love bond."

"Right." She nodded, feeling desperate. What in the world would she do with the handsomest, Baddest man in the Four Kingdoms as her True Love? ...Besides ravish him. Shit, shit, *shit!* "We could both just agree to break it." It was a fairly simple legal process.

"No, we couldn't."

"Yes, we could! We'd need to go before a wizard and sign a sacred scroll, but..."

"Let me rephrase: I *won't* agree." Marrok

stipulated flatly. "It will never. fucking. happen." He carefully spaced each word. "I will stay in this cell and die, before I part with you."

Scarlett blinked. "You're kidding."

"Do I sound like I'm kidding?"

No, he didn't. Marrok sounded more serious than she'd ever heard him. Scarlett stared at him, feeling lost. "Why? You don't want *me*." He could have anyone.

"I've done every crazy thing you've asked, because I want you! *You're* the one who isn't happy about the True Love thing, not me. As far as I'm concerned, you and I are *married* already." He snorted. "But that kinda puts a kink in your plans to be Mrs. Prince Charming, doesn't it? Is that the problem?"

"You have no idea what you're talking about."

"Don't I?"

"*No.*"

He arched a brow. "So you gonna give up on that glass slipper, then?"

"Oh my God!" Scarlett threw her hands up. "I am so sick of that dumb slipper!"

"Then, give it to Cinderella and let her keep that asshole prince. I know he's got a castle and a hell of a pumpkin patch, but he's not your True Love. I don't give a shit if your foot fit his shiny shoe, you don't belong with Charming."

Scarlett ran a hand through her hair. "You don't understand."

"Red, I'm the only one who *does* understand." He arched a brow. "Believe me. I was surprised by this, too. Good/Bad pairings don't happen very often. I certainly didn't think one would happen to *me*. You're freaking out about it and I can relate. Take some time to adjust and…"

She cut him off. "Maybe I'm freaking out because

we're locked in this stupid cell." She gestured to the algae covered rock walls. "Just concentrate on escaping and not this crazy theory of yours, alright?"

Marrok sighed. "I'll get us out of here, if you promise to think about what I've said."

Like she could think about anything else. Scarlett crossed her arms over her chest. "You know how to get us out of this cell? Seriously?"

"Yep."

"How?"

"I need to whisper it in your ear." He explained gravely. "Spies, again."

She cast a skeptical look around the tiny room. "You think spies are hiding in here? Where? In the bucket?"

"Can't be too careful." He crooked a finger, beckoning her closer. "Come here. I promise it'll only hurt for a second."

She firmed her jaw. "*Fine.*" Marrok was still sitting on the floor, so she marched over and crouched down in front of him. "What's your brilliant plan?" She asked in an exaggerated stage-whisper.

Marrok leaned forward and caught hold of her wrist. "Closer, baby. They'll hear." He tugged her towards him and somehow she wound up straddling his lap.

It was all his doing. She'd *hardly* moved at all.

Scarlett let out a shaky sigh as she found herself pressed against him. God, he felt wonderful between her thighs. She started mentally listing all the reasons why this was a terrible idea. "So, tell me about your plan." She said, trying not to notice how stunning he was in close-up.

"I'd rather *show* you my plan." His teeth nipped

her lobe and she jolted.

"I said no sex."

"Making out isn't sex. It's innocent fun."

Scarlett's eyes drifted closed as his tongue touched her ear. "You're such a jackass."

"I really am." He pulled her down so she was seated firmly against his huge erection. "Christ, very, very soon, I'm going to taste every inch of your skin until I'm drunk on you."

Scarlett swallowed. "Your real problem is your lack of confidence."

"My real problem is my lack of *you*." His lips found her throat. "I'm working on fixing it."

"That is the stupidest line..." She trailed off with a gasp as his mouth trailed along her skin. "You're not even *trying* to concentrate on our getaway, are you?"

"Sure, I am. You just make it hard. You make *me* hard." He kissed her jaw. "And it doesn't count as a stupid line if it's true."

Scarlett instinctively undulated against him, because it *was* true. He was so big and so... "Oh God." Marrok angled her hips with his hands so he was pressed against a *really* pleasant spot. Even through two pairs of sweat pants, she could feel the heat of him. "I'm not having sex with you in a dungeon." She warned breathlessly.

"So you've said."

"Because I really mean it."

Marrok's mouth curved at her weak tone. "How about when we get out of the dungeon?"

"We'd have to actually *get* out of the dungeon first, and it doesn't seem to be happening."

"That didn't sound like a 'no.'"

Oh shit...

He was moving against her and she was losing track of why she should be stopping it. Marrok shifted her again and Scarlett sighed in surrender. It had been a miserable day… month… longer. It felt like heaven to be held by this man. Her body was burning for him.

"When's the last time you came really hard, baby?" He rocked her against him more firmly.

"I don't know." She bit her lower lip and, despite herself, hoped he was about to offer to fix that. "A long time."

He liked that answer. "Not since you've been in here?"

"No! Of course not." He should know that. Since she'd arrived in the WUB Club, Marrok had consumed all her non-escape specific attention. Even when she was busily hating him, she was still focused on the wolf. "Who would I sleep with in this place besides you?"

He smiled at that phrasing. "Yourself?"

"Oh." She blinked. "No, there are cameras in all the rooms." Or there *had* been before they torched the security office.

"I didn't let that stop me from having a real nice time fantasizing about *you*."

She swallowed. "I guess I'm more particular about having an audience."

"Well, luckily, I make a really *good* audience." He tugged the drawstring tie of her sweatpants loose, his gaze locked on hers.

Scarlett stared back at him, her breathing getting choppier as she understood what he wanted. "I can't!" But, Christ, it was so temptingly Bad.

"I consider you the brains of the operation, Red, but I'm going to have to disagree with you on that one." He leaned forward to brush his lips against hers. His tongue slipped into her mouth and her desire spiked even higher. "I bet you *can*."

"Not in front of anyone..." She trailed off with a whimper as he caught hold of her wrist, drawing it down.

"Don't worry." He crooned. "Even Good girls can be a little wicked with their True Loves."

"I wish you'd stop saying that."

"But, it's true. You're mine."

Scarlett hesitated, her brows coming together. She'd meant calling her Good. In that moment, it hadn't even occurred to her to object about the True Love thing. Before she could figure out what that meant, his hand led hers past the waistband of her pants and between her legs.

She gasped as his fingers spread over hers, pressing her hand against her own weeping core. "I can't." She protested. "I need..." She tried to think, passion clouding her brain. She was still certain she couldn't pull this off herself, but she had to have relief. "You do it." She offered frantically. "You do it for me."

He let out a hissing breath as she spread her legs wider. "Oh, I *will*, baby." He kissed her again, more wild than before. "Later. Right now, I want you to show me." He moved his hand on top of hers, guiding her motions. "That's it. Nice and deep."

Oh *God*, it felt sooo good and... Bad. How else would it feel with this man?

There was no way to fight the tidal wave of desire that swamped her system. Christ, what had he done to her? Scarlett's eyes closed tight and her forehead dropped forward onto his shoulder. She began rotating her hand herself, her body growing languid.

"That's my Good girl." He kept his fingers over hers, but he was no longer directing them. He was just feeling her move. "You like that?" He nuzzled her hair.

She nodded against his chest, more turned on than she'd ever been.

"Tell me how it feels."

"Tight."

"Oh, I know you're going to be tight."

"No, I mean..." She licked her lower lip. "Everything feels so hot and tight. I need..."

"Not yet, baby. Let me watch for a minute."

She swallowed hard and did what he wanted. For a long moment, she just sat on his lap and let him watch her. In the quiet room, all she heard was their mixed breathing and the rustle of their clothes. She'd never experienced anything so erotic. Her free hand came up to grip his shirtfront, hanging on, trying to postpone the inevitable. Her eyes opened, sightless and desperate, her fingers moving faster. There was no way she could last for much longer.

"*Marrok.*"

He didn't take pity on her suffering. "I like hearing you cry my name. You thinking about me?"

"Y-yes." She said on a shudder. Technically, he'd only touched her hand, but he might as well have been lodged tightly inside of her. It was all him.

"Every time I come, I'm thinking about you, Letty."

She moaned, so close.

"Six weeks and you didn't let me near you. It was just me and my fist. Maybe I like seeing the tables turn."

"I'm sure... you like seeing... a lot... of things, right now."

"You are a very pretty sight." He murmured.

Scarlett raised her eyes to his and saw his expression was tight with desire. "Please." She begged.

"Please what? Tell me what you want."

"Touch me." Although it nearly killed her, she slipped her palm from under his. His skin grazed her swollen flesh and her whole body arched. "*Oh*." Her hips moved on his hand, needing him deeper. "Please touch me, Marrok."

"Fuck yes." His fingers pressed inside of her, stretching her. He brushed against some magical place and whispered, "Come for me, baby."

She was so starved for him that was all it took. Scarlett's eyes went wide as she... exploded. "Marrok!"

Her whole body shook with warm, wet convulsions, her mind going blank with pleasure. Scarlett processed golden eyes watching her, drinking in her ecstasy as she climaxed. His hungry, triumphant expression just pushed her higher. It felt better than anything she'd ever felt. She cried out, glorying in it, riding his palm all the way through the aftershocks. After a timeless moment, she slumped against him, replete and struggling to breathe.

"Beautiful." He murmured into her ear, cuddling her closer.

Letty blinked back a sudden rush of tears. No one had ever called her beautiful. As reality returned, she began to feel confused and unsure. What had just happened? She'd never done anything like that before. It was wrong.

Except, maybe she really *was* going crazy, because this man just felt... right.

"They were totally justified in locking you up." She tilted her head to look at him. "You really are dangerous."

"Never to you." His thumb came up to brush against the bruise the blond wolf had left on her cheek and his face grew serious. "I'm sorry, Letty. I never expected a wolf to hit a woman."

"It wasn't your fault." Scarlett glanced away, off-balance by how gentle he was with her.

Why was it so easy to be with a man who'd annoyed her every day she'd known him? Marrok hadn't even had to try hard to talk her into it. She'd been eager and willing and she'd wanted him. She *still* wanted him. What was wrong with her? They'd just been talking about Charming. Now, Marrok probably thought she was like all the skanky women who hit on him because he was so attractive.

She shouldn't be doing this.

Scarlett cleared her throat and moved away from him, straightening her clothes. "So, are you ready to explain your plan for getting us out of this cell?" She asked, not meeting his eyes.

Marrok sighed and reluctantly released her. "Back to business?"

She gave a jerky nod.

"You think it'll be that easy?"

"*Yes.*" It had to be. This couldn't happen. Not this way. Whatever was going on she could control it.

"Alright." Marrok sounded amused. "Well, my plan is simple." He arched a brow. "I'm going to seduce you."

Chapter Eleven

Drusilla had a lot to say in our private session today. As usual, none of it made any sense.

Psychiatric case notes of Dr. Ramona Fae

The dwarf guard opened the cell door and stood silhouetted on the threshold. "Which one of you says you wanna see Dr. White?"

"That would be me." Marrok stood up and dusted his hands together. "Is she ready to meet with me?"

"Yep."

"Excellent. I think she'll be pleased with the progress of my mission." He looked over at Letty who was standing against the opposite side of the cell. "So long, Red. It was fun."

It was hard to know if her look of extreme aggravation was part of the act or genuine.

Scarlett was busily panicking over their PG-rated tryst, no doubt trying to figure out where she'd gone wrong in her Good little life that she'd landed in the arms of a wolf. The woman had started freaking out seconds after her mouthwatering orgasm against his hand.

Thank God he hadn't gone with his first instinct to take her against the wall or she probably would've fainted. If he pushed her too fast, Letty might go back to her plan to break the True Love bond.

And Marrok had been totally serious earlier. He'd never, *ever* agree to that.

He needed to tread very carefully and coax her

into this, because he was more determined than ever to keep this woman. Luckily, Scarlett's own instincts were working in his favor. Her body knew she belonged to him. She responded to his touch even better than he'd imagined. Soft and sweet and perfect. She'd looked up at him with dazed blue eyes and Marrok had seen exactly how it was supposed to be. He just had to convince Letty to see it, too.

...And escape from the insane asylum.

His plan on that front was fairly straightforward. Dr. White was expecting him to seduce Scarlett and bring her information about the glass slipper. So why not send word that he'd been successful? It was a guaranteed door opener. Snow White was eager for any scrap of information, no matter what the hour.

Although, the doctor had no clue how hard it was to seduce Scarlett or she'd know it was a trap. Marrok had never worked harder in his life... Or been so sexually frustrated.

"What time is it?" Scarlett asked the dwarf.

He flashed her a distracted look. "Eleven forty."

Marrok saw Scarlett stifle a wince. Timing had been a problem in a place with no clocks or windows, so they were cutting it close to the ten-to-midnight deadline.

The dwarf stepped into the room to motion Marrok forward with a "hurry up" gesture. "Dr. White isn't happy to be dragged out of bed at this hour, so this had better be important, Wolf."

"Oh, it is." Marrok assured him, sauntering forward. "I'm going to tell her how this woman right here is really a unicorn."

"What?" The dwarf's tone was a mixture of amazement and doubt. He automatically looked over at Scarlett, scanning for hooves and a horn.

The second his attention left Marrok, Marrok moved. He seized the guy by the front of his uniform, dragging him forward. He slapped a palm over the dwarf's mouth, so he couldn't cry out, and slammed the guy's head into the stone wall. The guard's unconscious body slumped to the floor. That was simple. Marrok dragged him further into the cell, dumping him on the hay mattress.

"You sure do knock out a lot of people." Scarlett observed.

"Only under your peace-loving orders, Red."

She made a face at him. "Let's just find the boiler room." She hurried over to peer out into the hall. At this time of night, the WUB Club worked on a skeleton crew, so it was empty. "Alright, this way." She started off with a determined stride.

Marrok grabbed the guard's keys and weapons, then followed her. He locked the cell door behind them, trapping the guy inside, and jogged a few steps to catch up with his indomitable True Love. The girl was always plowing ahead with her new and interesting ideas. Marrok was immune to being inspired and even he was almost inspired. "Do you know where the boiler room is?"

"Basically."

"Basically?"

"Well, I know it's down here somewhere." She looked around the endless rows of doors and gray stone. "Maybe we should split up to find it."

Leave Letty alone with bastards so rotten they were locked in the basement of a prison? Yeah... that wasn't going to happen. "No. We do this together."

"Are you worried about me?" She sounded almost confused by the idea.

"I'm worried about *me*. There are scary people down here."

She shot him a glare, not believing his careless lie. "If we don't cut the backup power in the next ten minutes, we'll be stuck here forever. You get that, right?"

"You're assuming that Avenant and the others can cut the main power on time." Something Marrok wasn't *at all* convinced about. "And that Benji shows up with the boat. And that the rest of this crazy plan actually works. Chances are we're going to be stuck, anyway."

"I don't think so." She said with a sad and adorable faith in their fellow criminals. "I think that they'll…"

"Scarlett!" Dr. Ramona suddenly shrieked. "You *bitch!* I'll get you for this!"

Letty and Marrok whirled around and saw Esmeralda's fake face scowling at them through the small barred window of a cell door.

"I know you're the one who put the group up to this!" Ramona tried to squeeze her hand through the bars and grab at Scarlett. "None of the others have the brains to pull off something so twisted and cruel."

"I think she just insulted me." Marrok looked down at Scarlett. "That doesn't show empathy for my ego-construct."

"If it makes you feel any better, I think you're capable of unimaginably cruel and twisted things." Letty assured him.

"You'll never get away with this!" Ramona screeched with clichéd mania. "Whatever you have planned, it will all be over when I get my real face back. I'll tell them *everything* about that infamous ball!"

Scarlett paled. "You don't know…"

Ramona cut her off. "Drusilla told me *plent*y in

our private sessions. Things I doubt you want anyone to find out about that night. Things I bet you've kept secret from *him*." She looked towards Marrok, her eyes wild. "Did she tell you about Charming and sex in the garden?"

He cringed and glanced at Letty. "Please *don't* tell me about that." It was the last thing Marrok ever wanted to hear. Scarlett touching Charming was the stuff of his nightmares. Her soft body opening to another man, panting Charming's name with those sweet little sounds...

Fuck.

Scarlett's jaw firmed as she stepped closer to Ramona's cell. "Tell whoever you want." She hissed. "Everyone will find out soon enough." Turning on her heel, Letty started off again, but Marrok could see she was shaken.

"It's all over, Scarlett!" Ramona gripped the bars of the small window and rattled the cell door. "You know it is! There's no way you can win!"

"She's a terrible doctor." Letty muttered, pretending to ignore Ramona's rant.

Marrok sighed. "Baby, whatever happened between you and that asshole, I don't care." Actually he cared *a lot*, but there was nothing he could do about it. Besides, he fully planned to keep her away from Charming for the rest of forever after, so he could cope as long as he didn't dwell on the visuals. And if that didn't work, he could always just kill the guy. Either way, he didn't like seeing her upset. "You don't have to tell me anything."

"That's a relief, because I don't plan to." She retorted, still out of sorts. "What happened at that ball is..." She stopped short, her eyes falling on a door down the hall.

The words "Boiler Room: Stay Out!!!" were painted on the wooden surface.

"Thank God." Scarlett raced forward. She tried to open the door, but found it locked.

"Here." Marrok handed her the guard's keys and she wrenched open the door.

The boiler room looked like a boiler room. There was equipment and pipes and a stack of brooms, mops and gardening equipment leaning in the corner.

Scarlett immediately headed for a utility panel on the wall. "I think that's it." Thick cables came out of the top of the gray box. "If we sever the connection here, the backup system won't be able to switch on." She hesitated. "Well, according to my internet search on 'how to cut power to a building.'"

"Sounds reliable to me." Marrok arched a brow. "Did it say *how* to sever it?"

"I was sort of skimming." She stepped forward to squint at the switches and wires. "Any thoughts?"

"None that won't get us fried."

"Damn it! We have to..."

The lights blinked out.

All over the WUB Club, the electricity went off. Machines shut down. Computers went dark. Magic inhibiting anklets stopped working.

Avenant and the others must have cut the main power supply.

"Oh no!" Scarlett stared up at the ceiling. "They're early!"

"I told you they'd fuck it up." Given the mental limitations of the rest of the group, it was pretty much a given. Marrok hated to agree with Ramona, but the doctor had a point. Without Scarlett standing over their shoulders and directing them, they were like headless geese.

And not the semi-intelligent golden-egg laying

geese. The regular stupid kind.

"We have fifteen seconds." Scarlett said desperately. "Otherwise everything will shut down. We have to sever the backup system..." She trailed off with a squeak as Marrok grabbed an axe from the stack of tools in the corner. "What are you doing? Don't! You're going to be electrocuted!"

"I know." Marrok agreed with an irritated sigh and slammed the blade into the thick cables protruding from the box. A shower of sparks flew into the air.

Scarlett shouted his name in panic and Marrok went flying across the room.

With the magic inhibiting ankle bracelet disabled, he could shift into his wolf-form. To Marrok and most of his kind, the wolf was their natural state. Being locked away from the other half of himself had been the worst part of the WUB Club. It had been months, but changing was so natural to him that he didn't even have to think about it.

Marrok hit the wall with a sickening thud, his body already in mid-transition. The wolf-form was larger and more resilient than his human side. It was why Wolfball could be so brutal. His instincts took over and, by the time he fell to the ground, he was fully a wolf. He lay there for a second, stunned and in agony, but alive.

...And the backup electrical system was destroyed.

Scarlett gaped down at him.

Marrok knew what she was seeing. The wolf was a huge bipedal creature, covered in a thick layer of constantly moving fog. Neither human nor animal, it existed in between the two. The black smoke took the place of fur. Beneath it lurked a monster of fangs and muscle and glowing yellow eyes.

Wolves were massively strong and closer to their primitive instincts. Yet, their human brains could still function. Marrok and his kind inspired more gruesome stories than any other monsters in the Four Kingdoms. And there was some truly terrifying competition on that score.

Scarlett eyed him nervously. "Marrok? Are you okay?"

"Yes." His voice was deeper than usual, filled with rumbling darkness. "It's alright." He got to his feet, bracing himself against the wall. "I won't harm you. I'd never harm you."

The wolf knew this woman straight down to the bone.

She stepped forward. "I'm not frightened, dummy." Her small fingers reached through the black fog of his wolf-form and caught hold of his arm, steadying him. "I meant are *you* okay. Are you hurt?"

Freed from the constraints of the magic inhibitor, the wolf was wild for her. Marrok had never doubted that she was his True Love. Not from the first moment he saw her. But, now everything in him was *screaming* that she was the one. The wolf wanted to pin her to the ground and just *take*.

She was his.

"I'll be fine." Marrok got out. His powers were already fixing the damage to his body. He just needed to stop his rioting emotions. All he wanted was to drag Letty closer and not let go. "Just give me a minute."

She stared up at him and smiled. "You did it, you know." She nodded towards the smoldering utility panel. "You really did it! The power's off!"

As much as he liked impressing her, they weren't out of there, yet. "We have to go."

Doors all over the WUB Club had just opened and Marrok wasn't the only Baddie whose powers were now unleashed. They had to get to the library. Shaking off the pain in his still healing body, he herded Letty towards the door.

Prisoners were already making their way into the hall, trying to figure out what had happened. Their cell doors had been automatically opened and now they were looking around in confusion. Inmates of the WUB Club were beaten down enough that they didn't instantly rush for freedom, but, fairly quickly, Marrok could see some of their faces changing from shock to crafty speculation.

The worst offenders in the place suddenly had their powers back and were free to wreak havoc on the Good folk who'd caged them.

This wasn't going to be pretty.

Swearing under his breath, Marrok hustled Scarlett forward. He wanted to get as far as possible before the surprise wore off and all hell broke loose. "Stay beside me." He warned. "No matter what happens, you stay *right beside me*."

Ahead of him, he saw a Cheshire cat named Kit walk out of her cell. The pink fur of her coat was matted and dirty from living in the prison's squalid conditions, but she was still sane enough to know a golden opportunity when she saw one. Kit looked right at him and gave a creepy, too-wide smile. "Thanks for the assist, Wolf."

"Believe me, we didn't do this for you."

She smirked. "I've been in there for four years, two months and a day, so I don't really care *why* you did it. I'm just happy you *did*. In repayment for my freedom, I'll give you a word of advice." The Cheshire cats were the mystics of the Four Kingdoms, often speaking in riddles and prophesy, liberally mixed with "I know something you don't know" smugness. Kit's gaze held his, green eye swirling with secrets. "Beware the Jabberwocky, my son."

What did that psycho have to do with anything?

The Jabberwocky was the most infamous Baddie in the Four Kingdoms. No one had ever even seen him, but his reputation for viciousness and criminal insanity was the stuff of legends. He controlled a whole gang of thugs called the Lollypop Guild, who'd mete out his harsh vengeance with candy colored hammers. No way did Marrok want to piss that freak off.

"Is the Jabberwocky in here with us?" He demanded.

Kit just gave a feline shrug and vanished. Her toothy grin was the last part of her to disappear. She was the first Baddie to escape the WUB Club, but she wouldn't be the last.

"Gee, I'm sure glad we just set *her* free." Scarlett cleared her throat. "Um... Didn't Kit behead the Queen of Hearts with a croquet mallet?"

Marrok nodded. "If it makes you feel any better, the forensic evidence under the rosebushes should've been ruled inconclusive at trial. A lot of skeletons could've been wearing a crown."

Scarlett was running to keep up with him as they headed for the stairs. "A crown with a heart on it?"

"Now you sound like that whiny judge." Marrok dragged her through the growing crowd. Still in his wolf-form, no one did more than glare at Marrok as he shoved them aside.

Being the Baddest Bad guy in the joint had its privileges.

Unless the Jabberwocky was in there, not much could slow Marrok down.

"We have to find Drusilla." Scarlett pushed back a

handful of spectacularly shiny hair. "I can't leave without my sister."

"I know." Given Letty's softhearted tendencies, she wouldn't want to leave without *any* of her ragtag crew. "Don't worry. They'll meet us in the library." Baddies understood the importance of self-preservation. He fully expected them to be ready and waiting to go.

If they hadn't left already.

A who's-who of the criminal elite were also heading for the exit: Hansel and Gretel the serial-killing conjoined twins. The man-eating Ugly Duckling. Miss Muffet, the Arachnid Queen, and dozens of others. They were all rapidly adjusting to their change in circumstances and reclaiming their "normal" lives… Which meant people were about to die.

Fights were already breaking out among the inmates. Powers began charging the air. Angry words mixed with maniacal laughter.

From the corner of his eye, Marrok saw a dwarf guard scramble into an empty cell and slam the door shut behind him. Hopefully, the staff would stay out of the way for the next fifteen minutes or so. For their own good, all the guards and doctors and nurses who'd tormented and imprisoned the Bad folk needed to hide.

The lunatics had taken over the asylum.

Chapter Twelve

Before his escape, Trevelyan opened up in our private sessions, revealing a deep anger towards Marrok. It seems the two of them had a falling out, and the dragon feels betrayed.
What kind of idiot would betray a dragon?

Psychiatric case notes of Dr. Ramona Fae

If the dungeon had been madness, the main hospital floor was complete anarchy.

Scarlett stayed glued to Marrok's side as he fought their way through the throng. His massive and intimidating wolf-self shielded her from the blasts of magic and fights and random rampaging. She'd never seen him play Wolfball, but she suddenly understood why he'd dominated the field. Even criminally insane people took one look at him and stayed back.

Scarlett herself wasn't afraid of him, at all.

Intellectually, she knew Marrok was fearsome looking, but the black tendrils of mist were oddly attractive to her. His perfect face was still partially visible in the wolf, the angles harsher and shadowed. He was beautiful. She felt safe beside him, even in the midst of the chaos.

A gnome with a long wart-covered nose threw a chair through the window of Dr. White's office, glass flying everywhere. Instantly, more inmates were forcing the door open and scrambling inside. Papers were ripped from file cabinets and trophy cases full of psychiatric awards were toppled to the ground. The sound of magic mirrors smashing joined the chorus of shouting and assorted noise.

Scarlett couldn't say she felt bad about the destruction.

Dr. White ruled the WUB Club like her own personal fiefdom, mistreating and exploiting the inmates she was supposed to help. The woman was no doubt planning to help Cinderella kill her as soon as Scarlett handed over the slipper. Plus, she'd pawed at Marrok, making him uncomfortable and ashamed. For that alone, the doctor deserved everything coming to her at the hands of the mob.

Letty hated Snow White.

That *had* to prove she was Bad, right?

"*Shit.*" Marrok skidded to a halt so fast that Scarlett bumped into him.

Ahead of them, some chortling fire imps had torched the floor. Flames were blocking the entire hallway, licking up the walls. There was no way anyone was getting through that... and it was the best route to the library.

"Shit!" Scarlett agreed, looking around desperately. "We'll have to go through the recreation room." They didn't have a choice.

Marrok quickly changed directions and headed the other way. "This whole thing would be a lot easier without the other felons getting in our way."

Scarlett had to agree. She'd had no idea so many people were actually housed in the WUB Club. With the electricity gone and their powers unleashed, there were countless unstable people looking for payback on their oppressors. Most of them were just rioting for the fun of it, but a few were intent on getting free.

The new path led Marrok and Letty passed the front door to the WUB Club where Benji had escaped earlier. As Scarlett watched, a red goblin dashed past the security door and was summarily shot down by a dwarf guard barricaded behind the check-in desk.

Letty cringed in horror. "Oh God!"

On autopilot, the goblin rushed forward a few more steps before his body collapsed into an awkward heap. At least five other dead and dying inmates were lying around him. The guard quickly reloaded, randomly firing at everything he saw.

"I *was* going to suggest we just walk out the front door." Marrok shook his head. "I've reconsidered."

"All the weapons are right there in the security office." Scarlett felt terrible about the carnage and the waste. "That's the *worst* way to get out."

"Crazy people aren't known for their planning skills." Marrok jerked at thumb at tiny Thumbelina who was trying to rip the iron bars off a window with her bare hands.

Scarlett would've suggested that she head for the library, but Thumbelina was a venomous monster who was better off locked up. No one wanted a repeat of the Neverland massacre. Her blood feud with Tinkerbelle had orphaned thousands.

It was difficult to see in the unlit hall. Scarlett tripped over a mattress someone had pulled from their room and abandoned. She hit the ground and instantly tried to cover her head, afraid that she'd be trampled by the crowd.

Marrok grabbed her. He swept her up like she was no heavier than a Wolfball, not even breaking his stride.

She clutched hold of his shoulders as he lifted her into his arms. "I'm okay. I can walk."

Although, it *was* interesting to touch the dark fog

that covered him. It felt cool and tickly against her skin. There were whispers that wolves made love in this form and it heightened the pleasure. She had the wrong and random thought that it would be fascinating to kiss him and test the theory for herself.

Marrok ignored Scarlett's prompting to put her down. He carried her right into the rec room, where a leprechaun was busily stealing the TV. The little guy carted it off, the plug dragging on the floor behind him. God only knew what he intended to do with it.

Two seconds after they crossed the threshold, Marrok's body went tense. He gave a growl of pure hate, his head swiveling towards the opposite side of the room. Scarlett couldn't see anything, but she sensed that they weren't alone.

"Did you really think *yarn* could hold me?" Dower taunted.

He stepped from the darkness, blocking the door to the library. Several other wolves were by his side. Scarlett recognized that two of them were Richardson and the blond guy who'd punched her. They were all in wolf-form, their skin shifting like low-hanging fog.

"Why don't we avoid the pointless bloodshed and you just tell me how this escape plan is gonna work?" Dow continued. "So far, I'm mighty impressed with your True Love's strategic plotting. Maybe she's not so Good, after all."

Scarlett wished she could take that as a compliment. "You can't come with us. Even if we wanted you to, there just isn't room for so many people."

"Well, we'll just have to thin the herd, then." He smirked at Marrok. "I'm pretty sure I know where to start."

Marrok slowly set Letty back on her feet and

nudged her behind him. "Wait here for a minute, Red."

She caught hold of his wrist. "Don't do anything crazy." She whispered. "There are five of them and only two of us."

"Yeah, but I'm really fucking pissed." He launched himself --not at Dow-- but at the henchman who'd hit her in the cafeteria.

Apparently, he still wasn't over that.

Scarlett cringed as Marrok tackled his enemy and slammed him into the ground. It was like watching a lion take down a gazelle. No wasted moves or feigned mercy, just flashes of teeth and snarls of fury. Marrok ripped into the blond guy, his body a fluid and deadly weapon.

The other man didn't even try to fight back. Instead, he gave a shriek of terror and tried to claw his way back to his cronies for help. No one was eager to lend a hand. The wolves seemed far more interested in watching Marrok tear him apart. For a heartbeat of time, everyone just stared at the graceful ballet of death

"Do those two have a history I don't know about?" Dow asked conversationally.

Richardson nodded. "Tober punched Marrok's woman."

"Ooohhhh, that explains it." Dower snorted. "Jesus, what kind of wolf hits a girl?"

"Marrok!" Scarlett shook off her surprised daze and started for him. "Don't kill him! I'm alright. Really. Let's just *go*."

He didn't give any indication that he'd heard that. He was intent on destroying the man who'd struck her. Scarlett appreciated the thought, but they didn't have time for any of this. Especially since the other wolves weren't going to let Marrok and Tober have all the fun. They began to wade into the fray and Marrok turned to attack them, too.

His next target was Richardson, the guy who'd held her in front of his body until Avenant bashed his head with the cafeteria tray. Marrok clearly hadn't forgotten about that, either.

"Stop!" Richardson's eyes reflected genuine terror as he hit the ground with Marrok's hands around his throat. "I didn't hurt her! I didn't hurt her!"

Dower tried to pull Marrok away, only to wind-up flat on his back with a bleeding nose. Marrok didn't even have to stop his attack on Richardson to strike him down.

Marrok was outnumbered and Scarlett still knew he was going to win.

Or he *would've* if the bombs hadn't started detonating.

With the power off, the guards couldn't automatically release the sleeping gas from the ceiling vents, but they could use the handheld smoke grenades stockpiled for emergencies. Loud blasts and flashes of light came from the hall, followed by frightened screams. The horrible purple vapors started pouring through the door of the rec room.

Breathing in the poison meant a mystical sleep that could last for decades.

"Marrok!" Scarlett started for him. "We gotta go! We gotta go!"

"Fuck!" He threw one of the wolves aside, sending the smaller man's body into a stack of orange chairs. "Move!" He reached out to grab her arm, yanking her forward. He was moving so fast, her feet barely touched the floor. They ran for the opposite side of the room. Marrok all but tossed her through the door, keeping her ahead of him and both of them ahead of the smoke.

Dower was right behind them.

Scarlett and Marrok kept going towards the library. Dow stopped long enough to slam the door shut behind him, ignoring the pounding and frantic cries of the other wolves.

"What are you doing?" She shouted as he locked his friends in the rec room.

"You want the smoke to get in here?!" He roared back. "Better them than me."

If Letty could've reached Dow, she would've punched him herself. "You *asshole!*"

"Hey, at least I didn't knock 'em over the head with a chair and tie them up, princess!" Dower raced after them. "Can we get out this way? Is that why you were in the library before? Is that our escape route?"

"You're not coming." Marrok bit off.

"The hell you say! I got as much of a right to get out of here as anyone!" He followed them right into the library.

Scarlett decided to just ignore him. She had bigger things on her mind.

Up ahead of her, she could see Esmeralda sitting on a short dust-covered bookcase. The witch was back to looking like herself and painting her nails with her magic. She tapped each finger with another, shifting the color from green to black.

"There's nothing else you could be doing?" Scarlett snapped.

"You said to wait here, so I'm waiting." Ez retorted. "Geez, I was beginning to think I was the only one who remembered the plan."

Scarlett looked around, her heart rate spiking even higher. "You're the only one here? Where are Dru and the others?"

Esmeralda shrugged.

Scarlett turned stricken eyes towards Marrok.

"I knew they'd screw this up." He muttered. "I told ya so."

"I can't leave without my sister." Letty whispered.

"I know." One palm touched her cheek, reassuring her. "It'll be okay, baby."

Scarlett stared up at him. She didn't believe that Marrok was her True Love. Not really. He couldn't be. Why would an ugly stepsister get the handsomest man in the Four Kingdoms? But, he was always so gentle with her. Always trying to protect her or help with her plans. It was impossible not to want this man.

Underneath the snarkiness and villainy, Marrok was actually... Good.

He really was.

She looked into his eyes and realized something very, very important. Good folk were also Bad and Bad folk were also Good. Nobody was all one thing or the other. Maybe that's why everyone always had such a hard time figuring out what she was. Society liked to brand people, trying to quantify them, but hearts and minds were so much more complicated than arbitrary designations.

Everybody was both Good *and* Bad.

This plan wasn't just about bringing down Cindy. This was about ripping down all the boxes and letting Good folk and Bad folk just be... *folks*. No more labels. There needed to be a place where everyone was welcomed and had a voice. It was the only way they'd ever have peace in the Four Kingdoms. The only way the prejudice and hatred would stop.

Scarlett stood on tiptoe and brushed her lips

against Marrok's. Sure enough the misty black edges of his wolf-form felt magical against her mouth. The kiss only lasted a second, but it sent desire shooting through her whole system.

Golden eyes gleamed with hunger as she pulled back and smiled at him. "You keep going, alright?" She reached up to touch his hand, which was still on her cheek. No matter what else happened, she wanted him to escape from this place. "I have to go back for Drusilla."

"No. *I'll* find Dru." Marrok gestured to the window. "You get down to the lake and I'll meet you there."

Was he joking? "I'm not going anywhere."

"Yes, you fucking *are!* If I have to, I will drop you out that window myself."

Letty scowled at him. She took it all back. The man was a nightmare.

"Whoever's not here gets left behind!" Dower proclaimed. Picking up on the key parts of the plan, he headed for the closest window. "We gotta get out of here!" He smashed in the large pane with his elbow.

Esmeralda squinted. "Since when is Dow coming? Did I miss a meeting?"

Dower disregarded that and used an ancient copy of everyone's favorite manifesto of intolerance *No Good Bad Folk* to knock the remaining glass from the window.

"There's no way I'm leaving!" Scarlett poked a finger into Marrok's chest. "Forget it! This was *my* plan and I'll see it through!"

"See it through from the goddamn boat!"

"There's a boat?" Dower heaved himself through the opening he'd created. "Thank Christ. That was going to be my next question. No way could we swim the Lake of Forgetting."

"There is no *we*." Esmeralda snapped. "*You're* not part of the Tuesday share circle."

Scarlett kept her eyes on Marrok. "I won't leave." She repeated in quieter voice. "Not without you and my sister."

He made a frustrated sound. "You are a crazy, stubborn, impossible…"

The door to the library swung open, interrupting his string of helpless complaints. Avenant came strolling in, dragging an unconscious Drusilla with him. "I'm having a terrible night." He announced to no one in particular. "You wouldn't believe the…"

Scarlett cut him off, dashing for Dru. "What happened to my sister?!"

"The gas, of course. It's everywhere."

"Oh God." Scarlett looked down at her sleeping sister and tried to stay calm. Dru was still alive. It was just a sleeping curse. It could be cured. She would be okay.

…But it was hard not to panic.

Marrok snatched Dru away from Avenant, carrying her towards the window. "Dower!" He bellowed. "Help me get her out or you're not setting foot on our boat!

"Who is that new man?" Avenant frowned at Dower and then over at Esmeralda. "He's not part of our share circle."

"I know! I told them that. They're not listening."

"I'm helping. That means I go, too." Dower dropped to the ground outside and turned back to assist Marrok in lifting Dru through the window. Catching her shoulders, he pulled her out of the library and into the moonlit night. "See? *Helping*." He carted her towards the lakeshore.

Scarlett did a quick head count. "We're still missing Rumpelstiltskin."

"He's probably dead." Avenant shrugged without a drop of caring and headed for the window. "He'd want us to save ourselves."

"I sincerely doubt that."

"You're probably right. Trolls are selfish beings." Avenant shoved past Marrok and climbed out into the yard. "God, I missed the cold air." He drew in a deep breath. A frigid breeze was blowing across the desolate hospital grounds, no doubt reminding the ex-prince of the Northlands.

Esmeralda looked less pleased about the whole situation. "I can't believe I'm about to get on a boat." She'd apparently looted the nurses' snack supply in preparation for the trip. A stolen backpack full of candy bars and chips was looped around her shoulders. "Witches and water don't mix."

"No one mixes with this water." Avenant called back. "It causes permanent amnesia."

"Yeah, but it'll also cause me to melt." Esmeralda followed Avenant out.

Scarlett and Marrok were the last two in the library.

"Baby, it's gotta be close to midnight. We're out of time."

She shook her head as he backtracked to grab her arm. "I told Rumpelstiltskin that we'd *all* make it out."

"We can't help him." Marrok insisted, tugging her towards the window. "You heard Avenant. The gas is everywhere. We leave now or we're not leaving."

"But, I promised him that... Hey!" Scarlett ended her protest in a yelp as Marrok lifted her off the ground again and unceremoniously passed her through the window. "Wait a second!" She shouted as she was dropped outside. "You can't do that! *I'm* in charge of this plan!"

"Consider it a mutiny." Marrok easily pulled himself through the opening and landed beside her. "Leaving the troll behind isn't on you. It's all *me*. Okay? There's nothing you can do to stop me from dragging your ass to that boat."

He was trying to make her feel better about abandoning Rumpelstiltskin. Trying to alleviate her guilt and take all the blame.

Scarlett gave up being annoyed at him. There was nothing either of them could do about this. Not with the clock ticking and the gas filling the halls. She allowed Marrok to hustle her towards the lakeshore. "I know that we don't have a choice. I just feel like I'm letting him down."

"Well, I wouldn't feel *too* badly about it." Avenant called sourly from the darkness up ahead.

Scarlett and Marrok stopped short. In front of them, Snow White and a dozen dwarf guards stood with Rumpelstiltskin at their side.

"See, Doctor White?" The troll said. "I *told* you they were planning an escape."

Chapter Thirteen

Sometimes I think Esmeralda is getting worse instead of better. I've taken to carrying a water pistol with me to our private sessions, just in case I need to melt her.

Psychiatric case notes of Dr. Ramona Fae

"You fucking little worm." Marrok's gaze fixed on Rumpelstiltskin. "You'd better hope I don't live through this."

"Blow me, Wolf! You and Letty were trying to get me killed with this stupid plan. Instead, I cut a side deal that's going to get me out of here. You'd have done the same thing if you were smart enough to think of it!"

Scarlett didn't have time to be angry at him. She was too busy trying to think of a way out of this mess.

To her right, the vast lake stretched out in the darkness. On the opposite shore, she could make out the winking lights of distant villages. All they had to do was get across the water and she'd have a clear shot at the Enchanted Forest. They were too close to freedom to just give up.

Especially since Benji had actually returned for them.

The bridge ogre was back to looking like himself and being held at gunpoint by two of the guards. Dower must have handed him Dru, because Benji was cradling her limp body against his chest. A fishing boat was tied up to the hospital's small dock, just waiting for their escape.

There *had* to be a way.

"Did you really think you'd get away with it?" Dr. White arched a brow at Scarlett. "Oh I'll admit, you got much further than I ever would've guessed, but you're a *Bad folk*, you stupid twit. Your kind never wins."

"I don't believe in Good folk and Bad folk, anymore." Scarlett said honestly. "I think we're all the same."

Dr. White and the dwarves scoffed at that idea. Even the other members of the Tuesday share circle squinted at her like she'd lost her mind.

Dower snorted. "Your woman is crazy, Marrok."

Despite the circumstances, Marrok's mouth curved. "I know." He kept his body between Scarlett and Dr. White. "I think she's adorable."

"I'm disappointed in you, Wolf." Dr. White took a step closer to him. Her words were taunting, but her face was tight with anger. "I thought we had a deal, but instead you tried to play me. For what? For *her?*" She pointed at Scarlett. "Why? What could an ugly stepsister offer you that I didn't?"

"Well, first off, she's not a psychotic bitch."

Esmeralda gave a nervous laugh at Marrok's wiseass response.

One of the guards whacked her in the head with a gun.

Dr. White stopped directly in front of Marrok, one hand trailing down the chest of his wolf-form. "You're such a beautiful brute." She murmured. "You just need training." She glanced over at the guards. "Take them all to the dungeon. Except the wolf. He and I have some things to discuss *privately*."

Scarlett's eyes widened in horror. "No!"

"The only way you're going to get me into bed is if you kill me first." Marrok told the doctor flatly.

"Don't think I won't." Snow White hissed.

"*I'll* fuck you, Dr. White!" Dower volunteered.

The dwarf guards moved forward to grab Marrok's arms. He shoved them away. The rest of the escapees were standing there with their hands up, already sure they were beaten. But not the wolf. Scarlett watched him begin his losing battle and felt something shift deep inside of her.

Marrok was going to fight.

Bad, Good, ugly, beautiful, wicked, charming... All those labels meant nothing. She wasn't sure who they applied to or why they mattered. She just abruptly knew that she and Marrok were alike in so many ways. Ways that were so much more important than the designations on their rap sheets or their reflections in the mirror.

They were partners.

"I'll tell you where the glass slipper is." Letty blurted out.

Marrok's head snapped around to stare at her.

Scarlett kept her attention on Dr. White. "I'll give you whatever you want. Just don't hurt him."

"That's more like it." Dr. White smirked and motioned the guards back. "Where is the shoe?" She demanded coldly, stalking towards Letty.

Scarlett edged towards the lake. "First, you have to promise to help my sister. The gas knocked her out. I want Dru up and awake..."

"Yes, fine." Dr. White waved that aside. "Where's the shoe?"

"Do you promise to help Drusilla receive True Love's kiss? That's the only thing that can save her." She took another step sideways. "Can I trust you?"

Dr. White followed her. "I don't see how you have much *choice* but to trust me."

"I have a choice." Scarlett retorted. "Because, you want the glass slipper and, unless my sister is safe, we don't have a deal."

"Well, then I'll just have to *question* the wolf about it, won't I?"

"You touch him and you're *never* going to get it." Scarlett spared a quick look down, gauging the distance to the edge of the lake. Her eyes flicked back up to meet Marrok's and she saw realization dawn. The two of them could communicate without words.

He shifted to give her more room.

"Do you think you can threaten me?" Dr. White scoffed. "You're *nothing*."

Letty refocused on Snow White and did her damnedest to piss the woman off. "I must be *something*, since Marrok's chosen me over everything you've tried. He wants *me*. Not you."

"Do you think I care what that oaf *wants*. He'll do as he's told."

"He hasn't so far." Satisfaction filled her, because it was true. "You've threatened him and bribed him and imprisoned him and tried to make him feel small, and he's *still* fighting you. Because, he's a better person than you will *ever* be."

Marrok stared at her, a strange expression on his face.

"He's just a wolf!"

"He's *my* wolf. And he'd rather stay locked in a dungeon than touch you. He told me so." Scarlett arched a brow and got really mean about it. "Then, we laughed at how utterly pathetic you are."

"Oh shit." Dower muttered. "I don't think she should be saying that."

"You smug little bitch!" Dr. White gave Letty a

shove. "Do you really think he *wants* to be with you? Huh?! Look at him! He's just stuck with your ugly ass because you're his True Love and animals are stupidly loyal."

"She's not ugly." Marrok put in quietly.

Dr. White turned to give him a venomous look. She opened her mouth to spit out some withering insult, but she never got the chance. Scarlett used Snow White's momentary distraction to seize her arm. She spun the doctor around, wrenching her towards the Lake of Forgetting. Snow White stumbled forward a single step. Just six extra inches. But that was enough. Dr. White automatically tried to catch her balance...

...And wound up standing ankle deep in the water.

As Scarlett watched, the doctor's eyes went blank, her mind fading into mystical amnesia. Snow White had no memory of what had just happened, or of who she was, or of anything else. Scarlett had just... erased her.

No one moved.

"My God." Marrok finally said in something close to awe. "This is why I'm yours, Letty. Because you are fucking amazing."

"Open fire!" One of the guards shrieked.

Marrok threw himself at Scarlett, shoving her to the ground as bullets erupted. She hit the cold grass, shielded by his body.

Snow White turned towards the noise, like she had no idea what was going on. Benji moved to protect Dru. Avenant rolled his eyes and reluctantly ducked. Rumpelstiltskin ran back towards the hospital in blind panic. Dower desperately scrambled towards the boat.

For a moment, Letty thought they were all going

to die. That it would be a replay of all the times Good folk had mowed down Baddies with impunity.

Only this time it finally occurred to Esmeralda that Bad folk could strike back.

Her magic was so much stronger than the guns. The witch looked towards the guards and her powers melted the bullets in midair. The metal projectiles liquefied, pooling to the ground. At almost the same instant, she lifted a palm and blasted out a pulse of green energy. It looked like a mixture of lightening and birds in flight as it arced over the dying grass. The guards were blown backwards, toppling off their feet.

Esmeralda seemed stunned when her attack worked. If it wasn't for Marrok and Scarlett's example, she probably wouldn't even have tried. Bad folk were so used to losing that she seemed downright confused by her easy victory.

The dwarves were no less flabbergasted. They began radioing for reinforcements, screaming for someone to bring more weapons. Not even magic could combat everything in their arsenal.

"Go!" Marrok roared. He pulled Scarlett up by the back of her shirt, propelling her towards the boat. The rickety wooden dock swayed under her feet as they ran. He lifted her over the side of the fishing boat and quickly followed her aboard.

Dower was already working to untie the ropes so they could launch. "We gotta get outta here! How do you drive a boat?!"

"Benji!" Letty called. "Come start this thing!"

Benji handed Dru's unconscious body to Avenant as they all clambered onto the deck. "Hang on." The weight of his giant form sent the hull sinking a foot deeper in the water.

"Weren't we supposed to be escaping *quietly?*" Avenant demanded.

"Where am I?" Snow White called blankly from shore. "Should I be coming with you?"

"No!" Half of them bellowed back.

Benji got the engine started and spun the boat's wheel, trying to get them out on the water. More guards were racing across the dismal lawn, headed for the lake. They were loaded down with an impressive array of guns, already siting on the boat.

"Uh-oh." Scarlett hit the deck and grabbed Marrok's hand, pulling him down beside her. "Tell me that isn't a rocket launcher."

"That looks like a rocket launcher." He told her anyway.

"Why the hell do they have *rocket launchers?!* The hospital doesn't have the cash to heat the rooms, but they have the budget to buy rocket launchers?!"

"Faster, Benji!" Esmeralda screamed.

Scarlett squeezed her eyes shut and knew they weren't going to make it. The guards were going to sink the boat. The boat was going to sink into the water. The water was going to erase their memories. Without memories, they weren't going to even exist. Everything about them was about to be eradicated and there wasn't a damn thing they could do about it.

And, even knowing how it was about to end, if Letty had to do it all over, she'd make the *exact* same choices again. If she was going to die today, at least she was going to die fighting.

Still, that didn't make her feel any better when she felt an explosion rock the side of the boat.

Scarlett saw the bright flare as the weapon fired and heard the shrieking whine of it streaking through the air. Then the hull was shuddering beneath her and she could smell smoke as something caught fire. She looked at the distant shore and knew it was still too far away.

Dower cursed. "We're all gonna drown! Why did I let you talk me into this?"

"We're not lucky enough to drown." Marrok shot back. Scarlett could see the wheels in his head turning and coming up empty. They really were out of good options. "We're not going to make it to the other side of this lake, Red." He finally said.

"I know."

"We either go back," Marrok continued, "or we go in the water. Your choice, baby."

Either way was pretty much a death sentence.

She craned her neck to look over the railing and back towards the WUB Club. Benji had the engine going full speed, so they were out of range of the dwarves' weapons, now. They'd built enough distance that the concrete walls of the hospital looked smaller. She wanted it to fade away completely. Going back would mean never leaving, again. She'd be locked-up and watched even closer this time.

On the other hand, touching the water meant losing everything that made her Scarlett. She'd either sink to the bottom and die with no clue as to who she was, or she'd be fished out by the guards and spent the rest of her life in a fog. She'd still be in the WUB Club, she just wouldn't be *her*, anymore.

Scarlett blew out a long breath. "I think we have to go back."

"You sure?"

"No. But, if I'm going to be stuck in that pit, I at least want to remember the expression on Ramona's face when I hit her with that chair."

Marrok started laughing, the sound of it wild and free.

Scarlett found herself grinning in response. No, she didn't want to forget *any* of this. Hell, they'd escaped once. They could do it, again.

Maybe.

"I'm not going back." Avenant shook his head, standing by the stern. The cold air blew through his long blond hair, the white strands reflecting the moonlight like icicles. "You *are* crazy, Scarlett! We're a few hundred yards from *never* going back and you want to go back?!"

"We're sinking, you idiot!" Esmeralda shouted. "*You* might be better with a personality reboot, but most of us *like* having our memories. *And I like not melting!*"

"*I'm not going back!*"

"Letty!" Benji cried. "What do we do? I have to know right now!"

Scarlett cursed, still not wanting to say the words that would return them to their imprisonment. Logical or not, it wasn't in her nature to give up. She frantically tried to think of a miracle. There *had* to be a way.

"Keep going!" Avenant insisted.

Dower leaned over the edge to look at the depths of the lake. He obviously had no idea how to swim and was terrified by the dark waves. "Unless you guys can walk on water, we only have like two minutes before…"

Avenant's eyes narrowed. "Wait." His head whipped around to look at Scarlett. "I *can* walk on water."

Marrok snorted, looking aggravated about this entire situation. "I don't even want to *think* about the theological implications of…"

"Ice, you moron!" Avenant interrupted. "My powers are back, so I can freeze the lake."

Scarlett and Marrok exchanged a glance.

"This is why we put up with him through all those meetings, isn't it?" He surmised.

She gave an excited nod and looked over at Avenant. "Do it!" She'd *known* there had to be a way! "Benji?" She staggered to her feet. "Stop the boat so the ice can form around us."

"Hang on." Dower held up his palms, his tone anxious. "Let's think about this. What if we fall through the ice? What if we drown?"

"I know how to freeze a lake, interloper." Avenant cracked his knuckles as Benji cut the engine and the boat slowed.

Extending a hand, Avenant gave his fingers a complicated wave. Almost instantly a rush of cold air washed over the water like a cyclone. The arctic blast was filled with magic. Not just physically freezing, but drawing on the powers of ice and snow and deadly cold winter. Letty had never felt anything like it.

Maybe Avenant really *was* the rightful Prince of the Northlands.

Scarlett ducked back down beside Marrok, staying out of the worst of the blizzard. "How long will this take?" She had to raise her voice to be heard over the howling wind.

"For someone of my abilities?" Avenant glanced at her with an arrogant arch of his brows. "It's already done."

"You're kidding?" She blinked and then poked her head up to look out over the frozen lake. He wasn't kidding. As far as she could see there was nothing but beautiful, frosty, solid ice. Scarlett barely suppressed her victorious fist pump.

Tuesday share circle for the win!

"Everybody get overboard." She ordered. "We're hiking straight across the ice."

Avenant gave a slanting smile. "Admit it, peasants... Could the usurper wearing my crown have pulled *that* off?"

Chapter Fourteen

So much of the patients' acting out comes from envy. They know they can never experience the pure and noble life that Good Folk do. They are doomed to wickedness.

Psychiatric case notes of Dr. Ramona Fae

Cinderella was on her knees, cleaning the already spotless floor of her bedroom. Naked and panting from desire, she ground the bristles of her scrub brush into the tile and tried to improve her dark mood.

Charming had betrayed her.

No one cared about her wedding plans.

They all wanted her to fail.

Cinderella was a princess and they treated her like she was nothing. Her own fiancé would rather have an ugly stepsister. Her wedding was going to look like some redneck prom thanks to everyone else's incompetence. The glass slipper was still lost and, if Charming had his way, Letty and Dru would soon be free.

She needed to be fucked. It was the only thing that might make her feel better. But Jack was making her suffer. Cinderella had been cleaning for an hour, so she was hot and ready, and still he wouldn't give her any relief.

At least *someone* was making an effort to improve her day.

"My boots are dirty, again." He was standing directly behind her, his gaze on her exposed ass as she bent over. "Clean them while you work."

She quickly moved to comply. Any hesitation would be punished. "With my tongue, sir?"

"Not this time." His foot slipped between her legs, pushing her knees farther apart, and he wiped the top of his shoe against her dripping wet core. "Make them spotless."

Oh *God*... She moved her hips against the soft leather of the boot. "Yes, sir." Her forehead dropped to cool marble as she tried to wash them with her body. "May I please come, sir?" She was dying.

"Not until I'm inside of you." Jack said heartlessly.

"No." Cinderella gasped in ecstasy. She hated it when Jack took her, which meant that she loved being forced to do it. He was so rough and he sometimes didn't let her come, at all. His passion always left bruises and the marks delighted her. "No, please don't."

"You will do everything I tell you, wench." He gave her a shove with his boot. "I'm going to fuck you until you learn your place."

"I won't do this." She cried, knowing her resistance would just make it rougher and more enjoyably horrible. Jack liked to punish her when she fought. "I'm a princess. You can't treat me this way."

"Shut-up." Jack gripped her hair, wrenching her head back. "Do as your betters tell you or you'll be sorry, understand?"

She whimpered out a helpless agreement.

He enjoyed humiliating her more than any of the other men did, which meant she only called on Jack for special occasions. He would do unspeakably twisted things to her, laughing as she suffered the indignities. Sometimes he took pictures of the depravity and then he showed them to the other men later. It was so low. So terribly degrading.

When she really needed a pick-me-up, she

needed Jack.

His hands callously fondled her, not for her enjoyment, but for his own. He didn't care what she found pleasurable, which just increased her pleasure. Cinderella struggled against his hold, simply to make him grip her even tighter.

"Do you want me to tie you, again?" Jack shoved her down and got into position, not giving a shit about foreplay. "Do you want all the men to come in here and touch you while you're bound?"

"Oh no, please." She whimpered, hoping it would happen.

Last time the men had taken her, one after another, while Jack taunted her. He'd been completely in control, allowing the unworthy creatures to soil her soft flesh for his own sick enjoyment. Telling them to do whatever they wished to her and forcing her to say thank you to each one as they finished. For hours, she'd been at their sick mercy. After it was all over, Jack had made her lick them all clean as he watched.

She'd been so abused and sore and subjugated.

It had been heaven.

"Then, spread your legs wider."

She acquiesced to his brutal demands. Her favorite part of this game was how sick it was that her pure body was being ravished by dirty men who should never touch her. A princess wouldn't lower herself to fight this monster, though. She'd submit and let him have his wicked way with her. What choice did a poor, mistreated girl have?

Jack smirked and began working his erection. Sometimes he came on her naked form before he took her. Cinderella would need to wash herself for hours to remove the taint of this creature sullying her beautiful skin.

"You'd like me to mark you like this wouldn't you, wench?"

"Yes, sir." She'd love it.

"Too bad. It only matters what *I* like." Jack leaned closer to her ear. "It's time to do your chores." He snarled and moved to crouch behind her. "Don't come until I tell you and I'll try not to hurt you... much."

"Yes, sir." She was going to come at his first painful stroke. She could feel it. Disobeying him would carry a severe sentence and she couldn't wait. "Please, make me do my chores."

"What's your most important chore?"

"Servicing you, sir. I'll do anything you say."

"That's right, you will. And I'm in the mood for something *very* special, wench."

"Oh yes..."

A knock sounded on the bedroom door and Cinderella nearly screamed in frustration.

No, no, no, no, *no!*

Why did people want to ruin *everything* for her?

Swearing out the vilest oaths she knew, Cinderella shoved Jack away and reached up on the bed to grab her pink robe. The men knew better than to bother her during chore time unless it was an emergency, so this had better be good. She yanked the door without bothering to belt her robe. "*What?*" She glowered up at Gustav.

"We've had word from the prison, your highness." His eyes stayed on her face, not looking at her naked breasts or Jack standing there with a delicious leather whip in his hand. Unless she ordered him to, Gustav never participated in chore time. His reluctance just made her use him more. "There's been an escape."

Her eyes narrowed. "An *escape?*"

"Yes, your highness. Scarlett led it. She and Drusilla have broken out."

Because he was the closest hittable object, Cinderella hit him. "How could you let this happen?!" She shrieked. "If Letty is free, it could ruin everything!"

"I know, majesty." He didn't even flinch under her blows. He was used to them. "The flying monkeys are already tracking them, but your stepsister has taken them into the Enchanted Forest."

"So?"

"So, the trackers are afraid to go in there. The woods are filled with men from the Lollypop Guild."

"I don't care if they're filled with *landmines!* Get the monkeys in there to track Scarlett down! It doesn't matter what it takes, I want her dead and I want my glass slipper! *Now.*"

"Of course, majesty." Gustav stepped back, his lip bleeding and his cheek bruised. "Prince Charming is searching for her, too."

"Already?" That was so typical of the asshole.

"He's given word that Scarlett and Drusilla are not to be harmed in the recapture efforts."

"*God*, I hate him." Cinderella's hands fisted, her nails digging into her palms. "All I want is my crown? Is it really so much to ask? But, that stupid simpering fool is determined to ruin *everything*. Tell the monkeys to do *whatever it takes* to stop Scarlett and retrieve my property!"

"We should kill Charming." Jack said as Gustav hurried off to do her bidding.

"*Before* I become the princess? You think I should give up everything I've worked so hard for?" She whirled around to face him. "You want me to stand by and let my hideous stepsister steal my perfect life?! You hate me! Is that it?"

"I worship you, highness." Jack stepped closer to her. "Which is why I know you deserve so much better than that ball-less prince."

"I do deserve more." She agreed with a miserable sniff. "After the wedding, I can be done with him. But, for now, he's the only way I can take my rightful place as princess."

"Kingdoms can be gained in many ways. The Northlands was usurped just last year." His hands found her shoulders, pushing her back to her knees. "Charming's guards are a pack of clowns. We could seize control of the palace in moments and give you everything you want. Especially, with your friend and his magic."

"It wouldn't be the same as marrying Charming and *proving* that I'm the rightful ruler of this pitiful kingdom, though."

And no one would see her in her not-*so*-bad wedding dress.

"Whatever you desire, majesty." He pressed her forward so she was on all fours and positioned himself behind her. "Just know that your loyal men are ever ready to serve you."

She cried out in delicious pain as he slammed into her.

Chapter Fifteen

Scarlett Riding should never be free.

Psychiatric case notes of Dr. Ramona Fae

"Are you sure it's safe to stop here for the night?" Letty ducked under the grasping branches of an ancient tree and looked up at him. "Really, really sure?"

"I'm sure. The flying monkeys will be after us, but the forest will slow them down." Marrok glanced back at her. "We'll be okay for a while."

Very few people ever ventured into the woods. The vegetation in the Enchanted Forest moved of its own accord, attracted to any passersby. The branches would grab victims and drag them towards the gnarled trunks, presumably to eat them.

Marrok wasn't exactly *sure* about that last part, but he also wasn't about to get close enough to test what the plants were up to. As far as he knew, no one else had survived an encounter with them. Better to just assume they were carnivorous and stay away.

The Enchanted Forest was an unsettling place, filled with all kinds of hiding criminals, killer plants, and unknown monsters. The law never penetrated the thick woods, so Badness flourished in the gloom. It was said that just stepping foot inside of it was a death sentence for anyone Good.

It was creepy as hell, but that was actually working in their favor. Not only did it mean no authorities were around to intercept them, but the endless canopy of leaves blocked views from above and the constant shifting of the trees helped to cover tracks on the ground. Wolves could navigate the woods much better than the monkeys could, so that cut way down on their chance of being followed.

Marrok found he *liked* the dense forest surrounding them. It felt... homey.

"We need to stop and figure out what we're doing next." Esmeralda agreed. She dropped her backpack onto the ground and sat down on a fallen log. "I mean, where are we *going?*"

"I'm going back to the Northlands to reclaim my crown."

She flashed Avenant a glower. "And you think it'll just be as easy as walking up to your ex-castle and knocking? If we show our faces in public, we'll be arrested."

"So what do you suggest? That we live here in the foliage like squirrels?"

"I *suggest* that we lay low and stay out of trouble until..."

"No." Letty cut off the witch's words with a shake of her head. "We're not laying low."

"Exactly." Avenant made a "you see?" hand gesture. "We can't usurp the usurper if we're hiding."

"*We?*" Marrok echoed. "*We're* not trekking to the Northlands to get your ass back on that icy throne. *We* have better things to do with our time."

Avenant looked affronted.

"Listen!" Scarlett held up her palms to forestall the argument. "We need to stop Cinderella. That's our only chance. *She'll* be the one sending an army after us. If she's gone, we'll be home free. We all have to focus on exposing her as a fraud."

"Here we go with Cinderella, again." Esmeralda

rolled her eyes. "Did anybody ever tell you you're kind of obsessed?"

"I'm not obsessed! I just know that bitch is dangerous. We have to go to my grandmother's house and get the glass slipper. Once we have that, I can take it to the Westlands and show everyone that it doesn't fit Cindy's evil hoof."

By "everyone" Marrok could only imagine she meant "Charming."

Sure enough she kept talking with a disgusting amount of confidence. "When Cinderella is exposed as a lying bitch, Charming will make sure we all have pardons. I'm sure of it."

"The other princes and I don't always get along." Avenant admitted.

Esmeralda snorted at the massive understatement. "Yeah, didn't Charming try to kill you in a duel or something?"

"He would never do that." Scarlett said instantly.

Marrok's jaw ticked.

"You jackasses do whatever you want." Dow snapped. "I'm outta here." He kept going through the trees. "I can move faster on my own, so don't follow me."

"Who *is* that man?" Avenant demanded.

Marrok watched Dower march off. He didn't like the guy around Scarlett, so he was more than ready to see him go. But, it would probably be better if he just killed Dow. What if he circled back at them? There didn't seem much of a reason for him to stage some kind of ambush, but why take a chance?

"Don't." Scarlett said quietly.

Marrok glanced at her.

"Just let him go. He's not worth getting blood on your hands."

"Red, unlike your handsome prince, I don't mind getting blood on my hands. Good folk like your precious Charming trained me to hurt people. It's my job." But Marrok did as she asked and allowed Dower to disappear into the woods. At least he was gone.

"It's not your job anymore." Scarlett gave him a smile and crouched down to help Benji build a pile of leaves for Drusilla's unconscious body to lie on. "Now you're free. We all are." She looked around at the others. "Maybe for the first time ever, we're *free*. We aren't being told what to do, or that we aren't Good enough, or that someone else is in charge of us. We're finally in control of our own happily ever afters."

Marrok had never really considered having his own happily ever after.

From the looks on Esmeralda and Benji's faces, he surmised they hadn't either.

Even Avenant seemed perplexed by the idea. "What are you suggesting? That we *not* return to our old lives, even if your newest impossible plan somehow works and we're pardoned?"

"I'm suggesting we all have a choice. What do you *want* to do?" Scarlett arched a brow at him. "Do you even know?"

Avenant developed a faraway look and fell silent.

"Alright." Marrok cleared his throat, feeling awkward. It was hard for Bad folk to adjust to Letty's way of thinking. They were used to being oppressed and controlled. The world suddenly seemed huge. "Everybody get a couple hours sleep and we'll keep moving towards Letty's grandma's at dawn. I'll keep watch." The rest of the group was dead on their feet. They needed the rest and he needed to scout the area.

Marrok watched as they all settled down in the

thick grass of the forest floor, looking lost in their own thoughts. In a weird way, he no longer found the share circle so annoying. Well, he still found them annoying, but it was more of a familiar, low-grade annoyance, now. Almost like there were *his* annoyances. He would've liked to make a fire for them, but he couldn't risk the smoke.

Marrok was debating the best direction to try for a stream when he saw Scarlett watching him with a concerned frown. She was the only one not preparing for bed.

He met her eyes. "You okay, Red?"

"You're not leaving, are you?"

He squinted in confusion. "Yeah, I'm going to go look for water."

"But... you'll come back?"

Realization dawned and Marrok somehow kept his temper from erupting at the insanely insulting question. Did Scarlett honestly not understand what having a True Love meant? Did she think he'd *ever* leave her? That he'd just abandon her in the Enchanted Forest with a useless group of still-pretty-annoying idiots and a fuck-load of enemies on her trail? Was she goddamn *serious?*

She looked serious.

Unbelievable.

Too frustrated to even answer her, he went stalking off to find a stream. He could sense one was nearby, which was why he'd picked this spot to stop and rest. But, he wouldn't leave earshot, especially not with Dower wandering around. How could she doubt that?

"Marrok." Letty chased after him, apparently still convinced he was making a run for it. "Wait!" She hurried through the creepy trees and Marrok reluctantly slowed down to let her catch up to him. "Let's talk about this."

"Does it seem like I want to talk, right now?"

"You can't go." She insisted. "Just take a second and think about..."

"I have been with you every step of this plan." He interrupted. "*Every one.*"

"You've been amazing. I couldn't have pulled this off without you. But, the plan's not over yet. We still have a long way to go, but if you give me a little more time..."

Marrok cut her off, again. "How little?" He demanded, spinning around to face her. "How long do you think all this will last?"

She swallowed. "Maybe... two days?" It came out sounding like a question.

"Until that damn wedding." He translated, getting even angrier. "Until I help you break-up Cinderella and Charming, so *you* can have him. After that, I can just go, huh?"

"I can fix everything once I get to him and show him the slipper." She said desperately. "Just stay with me until then."

He pressed the palms of his hands into his eye sockets and let out a humorless laugh. "Christ, if I could, I would walk away, right now. I really would."

Or at least, that's what he wanted to tell himself.

She planned on going back to that stupid prince! Why the fuck should he stick around to see that? The woman had total faith in Charming, who'd let her rot in prison, but she didn't trust Marrok, who'd just helped her escape!

It was his own fault he was so angry and discouraged. As a whole, Baddies tended to be untrusting, solitary creatures, but he was getting so...

attached to Scarlett. Goddamn it, why couldn't she be attached to him *back?* Did he need to steal her a fucking castle? He could do that, but it would take a couple of weeks and she didn't even want to give him *that* much time.

What would he do if she never wanted him?

Why *should* she want him?

Letty stared at him, looking wounded. "Whatever I've done to hurt your feelings, I'm sorry."

"You didn't hurt my feelings." He muttered, even though she had. "That's not what this is about."

"Please stay with me." Scarlett pulled out the big guns. "I need you."

Marrok winced. Had anyone ever said that to him before? He didn't think so. Wolves would chew on poisoned apples before they admitted they needed anyone else, so very few people threw those words around the halls of villainy. He liked hearing them, though. God knew, he needed Scarlett so much it was gutting him, so she might as well reciprocate.

"Just hang on with me for a little while longer." She pressed. "Please."

Marrok sighed, exasperated that he was so damn *attached* to someone who was so damn difficult. He wasn't going anywhere, though, so why were they even arguing about it? "Alright."

"Alright? You'll stay?"

"Well, it's either that or leaving my True Love to die in the forest. Does that seem more in character for The Big Bad Wolf?"

"No." She blinked at his tone. "Of course not. God, *that's* why you're mad! I'm sorry. You're right. It's hard for me to adjust to..." She glanced away. "It's just hard for me, because I *know* I'm not who you would've picked for your True Love, if you had a choice. That's all."

Marrok couldn't argue with that. All his life, he'd had an image in his mind of his True Love and she was not this bossy, crazy, too clever, too Good, believer in happy endings.

"No, you're not who I would've chosen." His mouth curved when she shot him a scowl. She didn't appreciate that easy agreement. "But, I would've chosen *wrong*." He'd been a fucking idiot to have ever doubted fate's reasons for giving him this woman. No one else would *ever* suit him. "You're the right choice. You're the *only* choice. I would never want another."

She watched him appraisingly. "Really?"

"*Really*."

A pause. "Why?"

Jesus, not with all the "whys," again. "Letty…"

She cut him off. "Just tell me the truth." She said in a solemn tone. "Why me? Is it just the True Love bond?"

"No."

"Why then?"

For the first time, Marrok realized she was taking him seriously. Very few people ever took him seriously. He wanted to say the right words, but he had no idea what she needed to hear. Why did she always ask for explanations for things that just *were?* His pulse increased, suddenly afraid that he was going to screw this up. That she'd refuse to believe him.

That she'd walk away.

"Because…" Lost and floundering, he automatically did as she asked and told the truth. "I feel safe with you."

Fuck!

Why did he always say such pansy-assed shit to

her?

Scarlett's expression changed at the admission, though. Shockingly, Marrok saw the exact moment when she started to believe they were True Loves. Blue eyes gazed up at him, amazed and unguarded and a little scared.

"You *are* safe with me." She finally whispered.

Marrok realized he wasn't just "attached" to her. He was crazy in love with this lunatic.

"You're safe with me, too." He promised. "Always."

Scarlett swallowed, looking somehow hypnotized. "I know."

He gave a slow smile.

"Actually, you haven't really seen the *best* me, yet." She blurted out. "I swear, I can be really nice."

"You get any nicer and it's gonna get us both killed, Red."

"I mean, people *like* me. Or they did before Cinderella turned them all against me. I can be likable… But *Bad*. Like you."

"You are nothing like me." He scoffed.

"I am if you give me a chance." She insisted, the words coming out too fast. "Really. I come from a long line of villains. My mother was born Good and it was a grave disappointment to my relatives. She went on to marry Cinderella's father, after my own dad died. She was trying to escape the shame that her non-wickedness brought to my grandmother. But, I've *always* been Bad. All the doctors agreed."

"All the doctors are wrong."

"Well, that's what my grandmother says, but I think it's deeper than that. I think I'm Good *and* Bad. That everyone is. Even you."

"It's adorable that you think that." He arched a brow. "Seriously, baby, Good or Bad, it doesn't affect a damn thing about my feelings for you."

She bit her lower lip. "I'm just saying, you and I... I think we have a lot in common."

He felt a little guilty to have her believe something so wrong. "No, we don't."

"We do! We *think* about things the same way."

"No, baby, we *don't*. Believe me. I think Bad thoughts."

"So do I." She assured him earnestly.

Marrok wasn't even in his wolf-form and he still had the almost overwhelming urge to just eat her up. She was soooooooo sweet it was all he could do not to push her to the ground and just ravish her. He wanted to taste that much innocent, sincere Goodness.

"Maybe you're right and everyone has Good and Bad in them, but they sure don't get both in equal amounts." He shifted closer to her. "My brain is disproportionately evil and yours is disproportionately *not*. Believe me."

She didn't understand the truth. "You're not evil." She took hold of his hand. "You're a wiseass and a fiend, but you are always so gentle with me. Always on my side. You've guarded me and listened to me and helped me. You are the only one here I trust."

Fuck.

Marrok looked down at her fingers touching his and felt his heart crack in two. She said she trusted him... and he felt the perverse desire to prove that her faith in him was justified. The only way to do that was by warning her *not* to trust him. He *had* to protect her from himself. It was his job as her True Love.

Who would look after her, if he didn't?

"Baby, I don't even know how to be gentle." He said honestly. "If I were a Good guy, I really would walk away and leave you. Since I'm not going to do that, you should be the one to leave. I want you very, very much and I'll cheat if that's what it takes to keep you for myself."

She tilted her head. "If you're so wholly Bad, why are you warning me about it?"

"Because," he held up their connected palms, "you're the only one who holds my hand."

She smiled at that answer.

God she was beautiful. "You're my True Love, Scarlett. I know you don't completely believe that yet, but it's true." He shook his head. "There's no one else for me. Even if there was, *you* would still be my choice. I will do very Bad things to keep you for myself."

"Well, you've done your duty and warned me about how horrible you are." She assured him. "All I care about is that you'll stay."

"I told you, as far as I'm concerned, we're married. I will *always* stay with you. You should know that."

Scarlett didn't back away from him as his body brushed against hers. "I do know it." She said softly. "I'm sorry."

Marrok was quiet for a beat, just staring down at her. "What do you think we have in common?" He asked, because he just couldn't help himself.

"Well... we both scored really high on the egomaniacal sections of the psych tests. So, we're leaders, whether or not people *want* our leadership. And we make crazy decisions, because we think we're just a little bit smarter than everyone *telling* us we're crazy."

He shrugged. "Crazy is what you need to escape

from an insane asylum."

"You and I are both fighters." She continued, conceding that point with a nod. "And loyal. When we make a commitment to something, we stick to it. And we're protective of our people." She arched a brow. "And we both suck at pasta crafts."

That made him chuckle.

She grinned back at him. "And sometimes I can just look at you and know what you're thinking. Because, I'm already thinking it. We think *the same*, Marrok. Tell me I'm wrong about that. That you don't sense it, too."

He couldn't, because she was right. "I sense it." He murmured. Like he'd told her in the library, there was a connection between them that went deeper than anything he'd ever felt. "The first time I ever saw you, I knew we… clicked."

"I did, too. Sort of." She wrinkled her nose. "You were right in the dungeon, though. The *first* time I saw you, I was mostly just afraid."

That didn't surprise him. "The fifty convictions for Badness?"

"No. You were just lounging there, being gorgeous and snarky… and I knew you were going to cause me a lot of trouble."

"Not as much trouble as you've caused me." He leaned down to nuzzle her temple. "So, you think I'm gorgeous, huh?"

Her free hand came up to rest on his shoulder. "You know you're gorgeous."

"Something else we have in common, because I think you're pretty damn gorgeous, too, Red." He kissed her neck.

"Ugly stepsisters aren't gorgeous." But she tilted her head to give him access to her throat.

"You're not ugly and you know it." Marrok retorted, turning her words back on her. "God, I am just crazy obsessed with you." He breathed in the scent of her, his lips tracing over her skin. He could think of three dozen ways to get her naked in the next fifteen seconds. Since they were having this little talk, though, they might as well finish it. "...But I don't share."

"Meaning what?" She moved back from him with an outraged scowl.

"We both scored high on the evil IQ tests, too. I think you can figure out what I mean."

"Well, I don't share, either. And you're the one with random girlfriends all over the magazine covers."

"I've got no one but you, Red." He arched a brow. "You've got Charming. And that doesn't work for me."

"I told you, it's complicated."

"I don't give a shit about 'complicated.' One way or another, he's gotta go. You get rid of him or I will."

"No! Don't do anything to Charming." She looked over her shoulder as if worried that someone might overhear them and then lowered her voice. "Look, I'll deal with all that after we get to my grandmother's house."

"You promise?"

"I promise."

Marrok was suspicious at her easy agreement, but he let it go. For now. "That's where the shoe is? At your grandma's?"

"Yes. I sent the glass slipper to her before I was arrested."

"And Cinderella didn't check for it with your family?" It seemed like a fairly obvious place to start the search.

"My grandmother is a difficult woman to find. And to deal with. And, well," Letty made a face, "she's just difficult."

"Right." That sounded promising. "Do you know where Grandma is or do we have to look for her?"

"Oh, I can find her." Scarlett didn't sound enthusiastic about it, though. "She lives in the Enchanted Forest, so I've spent a lot of time at her house. She likes to keep an eye on me, especially since my mom and stepdad died."

"She's probably freaking out about the escape, then." Marrok didn't have a family, but he was pretty sure that's how it worked. "It'll be all over the news. Your grandmother will be worried that you were hurt in the chaos."

"No." Scarlett sighed. "She'll just be annoyed that it took me so long to pull this off."

"She'll be *expecting* you to break out?"

"Of course. I'm sure the only reason she didn't stage a rescue herself is because she's testing me. I'm sort of her heir, so she has high expectations about my Badness."

Considering Scarlett wasn't at all Bad, he could only imagine the pressure the she must be under. "Heir to what?"

She let out a long sigh. "The family business."

Chapter Sixteen

The line between Good and Bad is so clear. Anyone who doubts that has never looked into the eyes of someone wicked, ugly and Bad. Good folk can never fully understand their evil.

Psychiatric case notes of Dr. Ramona Fae

    The cottage had a thatched roof and river stone walls. It sat in a glen full of wildflowers, red curtains in its stained glass windows and a decorative wreath on the arched door. There was even a welcome mat on the steps. Pink. With yellow and green letters, surrounded by cartoon candies.

    Scarlett rolled her eyes. Grandma was not a subtle lady.

    "Jesus." Beside her, Marrok hesitated. He looked at the cozy cottage in something like horror. "This is your grandmother's house?"

    "Kind of."

    He shook his head, his gaze locked on the picture postcard of domestic bliss in front of him. "No one who lives here can be Bad."

    "That's the point." Scarlett glanced over at the others. Benji was carrying Dru, Esmeralda was eating a chocolate bar, and Avenant looked bored. Everything was "normal," then. No sense in exposing them to this mess until she was sure her grandmother wasn't plotting something. "Wait here." She ordered and headed for the house. "Don't worry if you hear yelling. Or gunshots."

    "We won't." Avenant assured her.

    They'd all spent the night in the woods, sleeping

on the ground and hidden in the dense forest. Unlike most of the citizens of the Four Kingdoms, Scarlett wasn't afraid of the shifting trees. She'd lived with them from the time she was a child, so steering clear of their grasping branches was second nature.

It had been much more disconcerting for her to have woken-up beside Marrok.

When they'd fallen asleep, there had been a foot of space between them. Sometime during the night, though, she must have rolled closer to him. Her body and instincts were all telling her that he was the safest place to be. When she opened her eyes in the reedy light of dawn, she'd been pressed against his side and his arms had been protectively wrapped around her. Marrok had been staring down at her and she found herself just... staring back.

It had felt calm and intimate and really, really *right*.

She wasn't exactly sure what to do about that, so she'd jerked away from him and busied herself with getting ready to press on towards her grandmother's house.

Marrok had just smiled like he knew some secret she wasn't in on, yet.

He quickly followed Letty up the cobblestone path towards the cottage. "I don't like this. There has to be another..."

"Sweetie-pie!" Scarlett's grandmother threw open the door and beamed at her. "Well, it's about time you showed up!" Jana Wocknee *looked* like a grandma, with silver hair in a tidy bun and a white apron tied around her ample waist. She gave Scarlett a cheery hug. "I thought maybe I'd have to come and get you myself."

Scarlett rolled her eyes, but she still wrapped her

arms around her grandmother and hugged her back. As much as Jana drove her crazy, she still loved the woman. "I broke out of the worst prison in the Four Kingdoms in less than six weeks, Grandma. A lot of people would say that was pretty impressive."

"Well, they just don't understand your potential the way I do, silly goose." She patted Scarlett's head and looked over at Marrok. "Unless *he's* why you were in there so long. Because --my oh my-- he's even better looking in person. No *wonder* you wanted to stay locked up if The Big Bad Wolf was your cellmate."

"Don't sexually harass him." Scarlett didn't want Marrok to feel uncomfortable, although it was pretty much a given, knowing her grandmother. "He shouldn't have to put up with that on top of everything else you're about to put him through."

"It's a *compliment,* Scarlett. Don't be so touchy." Jana arched a brow at him. "The mug shot of you they're showing on TV is the *real* crime. You must have really pissed *someone* off, dear. All the photos they have to choose from and they pick one that doesn't do you justice."

"Yes, ma'am. They wouldn't let me retake it, either."

Scarlett arched a brow at him. "You asked them to take a *better* mug shot?"

"Well, your grandmother's right. It was a bad picture."

"There's no way you took a bad picture." Letty scoffed. It just wasn't possible. She turned back to Jana. "Obviously, his reputation precedes him, but this is Marrok, Grandma. And yeah, he *was* briefly my cellmate. In a dungeon. We're both fine, though. Thanks for asking."

Jana beamed at him, ignoring Scarlett's pointed remarks. "So nice to meet you, dear. Come in, come in!" She ushered them into the doily-covered living room. "Can I get you some tea?"

"No, thank you. I'm fine." His eyes cut around the snug cottage, wincing at the cutesy furnishings. He quickly rallied, but Scarlett could see that he was growing concerned that she'd tricked him and that her grandmother was really just some sweet little old lady. "You have a very lovely home, ma'am."

"This shithole's just a façade to keep those asshole Goody-Goods away." Jana shut the door and reached for her cigarettes, her entire demeanor changing. "Stupid bastards never look beyond the surface. A couple flowerpots are better than a whole pack of pit bulls when it comes to maintaining some privacy in my business." She sat down on a rocking chair and eyed Marrok knowingly. "So... are you fucking my granddaughter?"

Scarlett sighed.

Marrok visibly relaxed as the atmosphere went from welcoming to confrontational. "Oh, thank God." He cleared his throat. "I mean... no, ma'am. I haven't slept with Letty."

Jana's eyes narrowed. "Why not?"

"She won't let me. Believe me, I've tried."

Jana's gaze flicked over to Scarlett. "Are you out of your mind? You turned down the hottest man in the Four Kingdoms? Have you seen this boy's ass?" She craned her neck to admire it. "Maybe your time in the nuthouse scrambled your brains, Scarlett."

"I wouldn't sleep with a guy just because he's good looking, Grandma."

Marrok glanced over at her and then quickly away.

Scarlett realized she'd just hurt his feelings, again. He seemed determined to take everything she said and misconstrue it. For the handsomest man in the world, he could be amazingly insecure.

Actually, no.

It was *because* Marrok was so handsome that he felt unsure. He was used to no one caring about him as a person. She'd seen the way most people treated him. They only paid attention to his stunning face, so he wouldn't expect Scarlett to want him for anything more than that, either.

"I also wouldn't *kiss* a man just because he's good looking." Scarlett continued pointedly. "Or let him touch me." She shot Marrok a sideways glare, a little annoyed that he needed to be told that she wasn't randomly making out with attractive men just for the hell of it. "*Obviously*, there would have to be more to him than just his beauty. *Obviously*, if I was even *thinking* about sleeping with him, he'd have to have won me over... despite the fact he's a jackass."

His mouth kicked up at one corner, the tension easing from his shoulders. "Obviously." Golden eyes met hers, something warm lighting them.

Her spark of irritation faded and she gave him a smile.

Jana snorted. "He won me over just by standing there and looking pretty."

"If it makes you feel any better, ma'am, Letty's my True Love, so I'll be sleeping with her *very* soon."

Scarlett made a face at how quickly he rallied back to annoying form. "Oh good... Your arrogance has returned."

"I like to think of it as optimism."

"True Love, huh?" Jana leaned back on the floral

print cushions of the rocking chair. "Well, he's certainly a step up from Charming."

Marrok's jaw clenched.

Scarlett winced. "We're here to get the shoe, Grandma. Do you still have it?"

"No, I sold it at my last villainous yard sale." Jana scoffed. "Of *course*, I still have it. What the hell do you think?"

"Knowing you, I'm never sure *what* to think." Her grandmother was perfectly capable of breaking the glass slipper just to make Letty's day more challenging. She loved to setup tests. "If the price was right, I'm sure you would've ransomed the shoe back to Cindy behind my back."

"Oh Scarlett..." Jana drew out the words on a feigned sigh. "That was the *younger* me. I told you before, I'm retiring soon. All the plotting and craziness is behind me. I plan to travel..."

"To that land where you can steal the genie lamp. I saw the maps."

"...to spend time with my dear friends..."

"Your knee breaking thugs, you mean."

"...and to mentor my darling granddaughter as she takes over the family business." Jana finished easily. "It really is time that you assume control of the day-to-day running of things, Scarlett. I'm too old to have so much pressure on me." She gave a weak cough.

"I thought I was too *Good* to be in charge, yet." Scarlett arched a brow. "Remember? We had a whole conversation about how important it was that I prove myself to the men and do some *real* villainy before..."

"And you have!" Jana beamed. "Do you have any idea how many Baddies are now running free because you took out the WUB Club? Everyone is impressed with your callous disregard for the safety of Good civilians. You've made me so proud... even if it did take you *weeks* to pull the jailbreak off."

"That's not what I intended..."

Jana cut her off. "Besides, now you have *him*." She nodded towards Marrok. "And he's *orgasmically* Bad. I watched a whole documentary about his crimes on one of those Sunday night sports programs. Made me horny." She winked at him.

Marrok gave a snort of amusement that he quickly tried to cover when Scarlett frowned at him. "Those shows are all lies." He offered, but he was trying not to smile.

"Oh for God's sake." Scarlett crossed her arms over her chest. "Marrok isn't going to get sucked into your schemes, Grandma. Leave him alone."

Jana turned wounded blue eyes on Marrok. "This business is my granddaughter's heritage. Aren't you going to help her keep it alive for the next generation? Do you have some *better* job lined-up? 'Cause I don't think those limp-dicked Wolfball coaches are going to let you back on the field anytime soon."

"I'm never going back. But, the only thing I'm qualified to do is hurt people, so I'm not sure..."

"Well, what the fuck do you think we do around here, boy? Sell pancakes?" Jana stubbed out her cigarette and lit another one. "Jesus, this is so simple! Are you going to be with Scarlett or not?"

"Yes, I'm going to be with her."

Scarlett's stomach flipped at his certain tone. It wasn't overconfidence or ego talking; Just a deep and unshakable conviction. Marrok really intended to stay with her forever after.

"Well, then you're helping her with the business."

Jana declared. "Scarlett's slow-poking around has delayed my retirement long enough."

Scarlett looked up towards the ceiling and prayed for patience.

"Alright." Marrok shrugged. "Whatever Letty wants."

"She wants to *take over the business*." Jana insisted. "Who else could I get to do it? That airhead Drusilla?"

"Dru is not an airhead!" Scarlett snapped. "She's been suffering so much and you haven't even *asked* about her."

"Oh, she's fine." Jana waved a dismissive hand. "You wouldn't let anything happen to that girl." She looked over at Marrok. "Goodness runs in this family like the worst sort of disease. You might have noticed it's infected Letty. She thinks she's the savior of the world."

"She saved me." Marrok said simply. "I knew she would, right from the beginning."

Jana shrugged. "Yeah, at least she's got the guts to offset the moralizing. But, Drusilla's the lamest Baddie since that stupid giant who couldn't even step on the beanstalk kid. No way could Dru run things." She sighed like the saddest woman in the world. "It's an unhappy day when a grandmother realizes that her only hope for a legacy of Badness is her *Good* granddaughter, though"

"Good and Bad are just labels." Scarlett muttered, but no one was listening.

"It's a family tragedy that I have so little wickedness to choose from." Jana lamented. "But, I've done my best to teach Letty wrong from right, so she could take over for me."

"Then, you should be proud." Marrok told her. "Letty is the most amazing woman I've ever met." He sounded like he really believed that.

"Aww. That's sweet." Jana got to her feet. "You know, it wasn't *just* seeing the primetime reenactments of your crime spree that's making me take a chance on you, boy. I've heard how you beat the ever loving shit out of the man who did that." She nodded towards the bruise on Letty's cheek.

"How'd you know...?"

"I have spies everywhere."

"I *knew* there were spies around that prison."

"That's right. And they tell me the other guy is gonna be the only toothless wolf in intensive care."

"Nobody touches my wife." Marrok said without an ounce of pity.

"I like a little bloodlust in a man." Jana stepped closer to him. "I read over your rap sheets, of course, and I approve of your résumé. I really do. So you get a trial run with my granddaughter." She paused. "But, I'm going to be mighty upset if you disappoint me. *Mighty upset.*"

Off in the distance, a coyote howled.

How did she always time that damn thing so perfectly?

Jana smirked at Marrok's "holy shit" expression. "Do we understand each other, boy?"

"Yes, ma'am."

"Oh, you can call me Jana, sweetie. Or Mrs. Wocknee." She reached up to pinch his cheek. "Or even just Jabberwocky."

Marrok paled. "Hang on, *you're*...?"

"You bet your cute ass I am." Her expression went hard. "So, I'm warning you, Wolf. If you do anything underhanded to hurt my granddaughter, I will skin your hide and sell your body for meat. Believe that, because it's true."

"Grandmother, leave him *alone*."

Marrok's eyes stayed on Jana. He looked fascinated to be coming face-to-face with the infamous Jabberwocky. She had singlehandedly built the biggest criminal network in the Four Kingdoms through ruthless intimidation and a total commitment to wickedness. The entire Enchanted Forest was her territory and she was constantly expanding her empire. Most importantly, there wasn't a person in the world who didn't whisper her name with genuine fear and respect.

What Baddie *wouldn't* be impressed?

"I'm sure I'll do underhanded things, ma'am, but they'll be to *keep* Letty, not to hurt her." He gave a pause and, even without the coyote yowl, it was pretty damn effective. "Because, I don't part with what's mine, I don't give a shit who starts threatening me."

Oh, Jana liked that answer.

In fact, given how friendly she was being and the lack of weapons being pulled, it was clear she liked *Marrok*. Letty wasn't surprised. It was pretty much a given that they'd get along like curds and whey. Her grandmother was a huge Wolfball booster. She was already part of Marrok's official fan club.

Literally.

Scarlett sat down on the chintz sofa and prepared to wait out the inevitable flirting and death threats.

"Aren't you a charmer?" Jana giggled in delight and playfully batted his arm. "I knew you would be. *Finally,* Scarlett brings me a real man to intimidate. You wouldn't believe the gutless wonders my granddaughters have dragged home in the past. And don't even get me started on that rat-fucker Charming."

"Cinderella sleeps with those rats, Grandma, not

Charming. I've *told* you that."

The two of them ignored Scarlett's testy correction, basking in their mutual admiration.

"Well, I've never met Charming," Marrok told Jana, "but I completely agree that he's a waste of healthy organs. I expect I'll have to remove most of them very soon."

Jana nodded wisely. "I've had the same thought. Don't bother looking for the brain, though. I don't think it's there."

"Nobody. touches. Charming." Scarlett carefully spaced each word.

They disregarded that, too.

"Would you like some cookies, dear?" Jana herded Marrok over to sit by the fire. "I just baked some shortbread." Her voice sing-songed over the words temptingly.

"Shortbread is my favorite, ma'am." Marrok probably would've said the same thing if she'd offered him cyanide. He couldn't have looked more pleased by Jana's obvious approval.

Scarlett had to wonder if any "meet the family" conversation had ever gone so well for him before. Probably not. The Big Bad Wolf wasn't the average senior citizen's idea of a dream date for her favorite granddaughter. Luckily, Jana Wocknee didn't do "average."

Possibly for the first time in his life, Marrok wasn't the biggest maniac in the room.

"What do you know about the mob presence in Wonderland, boy?" Jana went skipping into the kitchen to gather up some cookies for her new best friend. "I'm thinking of expanding my loansharking into new territories and we'll need to start by taking out the competition over there."

"My understanding is that it's mainly that pussy of a walrus and his little oyster brigade running things in Wonderland. I think we could take them in about a week, if we needed to. Especially if we had a nice garlic butter sauce."

"I do have a taste for seafood." She chuckled. "You know Letty wanted to make some kind of *deal* with him. Why the holy hell would I split my profits with someone I could just kill? The girl gets weird ideas sometimes."

"Letty doesn't like killing people." Marrok said as if she wasn't even in the room. "But, she's definitely a hard ass when it comes to braining people with chairs. I can attest to that. I'd still be in a magic inhibiting manacle, journaling about my feelings, if it wasn't for her violent streak."

He was defending her villainy? Scarlett glanced Marrok's way in surprise.

"And I *know* that she does a better job of being Bad than I could ever do of being Good." He continued. "No one would ever guess she's not one of us. She's got a devious mind and a real talent for creating chaos."

Jana preened. "She gets that from me."

"She also got those big blue eyes from you." Marrok leaned back in his chair, basking in all the grandparental support shining in his direction. "First thing I noticed about her."

"First thing my husband noticed about me was the knife I had pressed to his throat." Jana reminisced. "Yeah, I went to Camelot to steal his big sword from him, but I stayed for his *big sword*. The man fucked like a wicked machine of wickedness."

Great, *this* story, again.

Marrok looked over at Letty. "I love your grandma." He decided.

"I had a feeling you would." Scarlett headed for the door. "I'm going to go tell the others that it's safe to come in. Try not to propose to her while I'm gone."

"Believe me, I'm trying."

Scarlett rolled her eyes and stalked out before they started asking each other for their autographs.

***

"You really should get Letty into bed soon." Jana advised. She headed back over to Marrok, a stack of shortbread on a blue and white plate. "The girl would be a lot less moody if she got laid."

"I'm working on it." Marrok took a cookie and bit it in half. He'd known Scarlett's grandmother for ten minutes and she was already his second favorite person in the world. She was super-famously evil, and being nice to him, and she made a hell of a shortbread. He instantly felt comfortable with the woman. He and Jana spoke the same language. "Letty's skittish of me getting close."

At least, when she was awake.

In her sleep, she'd cuddled closer to him like it was the most natural thing in the world. Marrok had spent half the night just watching her breathe. On her deepest level, Letty knew they were supposed to be together. She just needed a little more time to get used to the idea when she was conscious.

"Well, you're probably the first man Scarlett's met with a testosterone reading, so it's throwing her off balance." Jana sat down across from him. "Was she saying that she already let you kiss her, though?"

"Yes, ma'am."

"That's interesting." Blue eyes narrowed in consideration. "Doesn't seem like Scarlett would screw around on Charming. She's got all those *ethics*." Jana said the word like it meant "lice." "Even though the worthless prick is picking out wedding china with another girl, I'd have thought she have some delusional sense of loyalty to him."

"Letty is *my* True Love. Charming can go blow himself."

"I'm not disagreeing with you, boy, but something's wonky with how it's going down. I know my granddaughter. If she's all set to marry Charming in Cinderbitch's place, why is she staring at you like you're an ice cream cone that she wants to lick up and down?"

"I'm a tasty looking guy."

Even as he said it, though, Marrok's brain was turning over the Jabberwocky's words. Scarlett was loyal straight down to the bone, even towards people who didn't deserve it. When the sleeping gas was flooding the WUB Club, she'd wanted to keep looking for *Rumpelstiltskin*, for Christ's sake. Would someone that Good really ever plan to marry one man and let another one stroke her to orgasm?

Marrok's eyes narrowed.

Come to think of it, Scarlett had come up with a whole lot of excuses to keep Marrok at arm's length. But, she'd never *once* invoked the holy name of Charming as a reason to deny the True Love bond. In fact, she rarely spoke of him, at all. Usually, she just looked uncomfortable when someone brought the piss-ant up.

That *was* wonky.

"She grew up with Charming, right?"

"Yep. It wasn't until this shoe debacle that she showed any interest in marrying that douchebag, though." Jana chewed a cookie. "Until then, the two of them just whined about villains' rights and hugged baby seals or whatever do-Gooders do all day. I'm still not clear on what all happened at that stupid ball. Did she tell you?"

He shook his head. "All I know for sure is Cinderella somehow highjacked that shoe and stole Scarlett's place as Charming's bride. Letty's not going to just let that go. When she sets her mind to something, *nothing* gets in her way."

Jana sighed. "I should've just tossed that glass slipper down a wishing well. Who will take over the family business if Letty's wasting her life as some pointless princess? Granted, she's always been a little too softhearted for this line of work, but she's got the mind for it."

"Scarlett's brilliant." Marrok agreed. "If she takes over, she'll figure out a way to make the business her own."

Jana snorted. "You mean she'll shut down all my most profitable sectors and start building preschools for goblins and trolls."

"That does sound like my Letty."

"Well, no matter what she does, that girl is the best part of my life. My whole hope for the future." She paused meaningfully. "I got no quarrel with you, boy, but no horses or men will be able to reassemble all your broken pieces if you fuck her over. I'm serious about that."

Marrok didn't take offence. Why wouldn't Scarlett's family be protective of her? She was precious and he was a notorious scumbag. Of *course* there would be some grisly warnings. Honestly, he saw Jana's intimidation tactics as a compliment. It showed she took him seriously as a suitor.

"All I want is Letty. She's my life and future, too. I've waited for her too long to ever take her for granted. You have my word."

Jana leaned forward to stare him straight in the eye. "I've got a lot of respect for the fanatical obsession wolves have for their True Loves. You're going to do whatever it takes to keep her happy, right?"

"Yes."

"Even if it means living in the Enchanted Forest?"

"I'll stay here and help her teach trolls to read, or I'll go to the Westlands and overthrow Cinderella, or I'll just live on the lamb for the rest of ever after. It doesn't matter, just so I'm with her." He didn't look away from Jana's appraising gaze. "I am staying with Letty." It was a bald statement of fact.

"So you're going to get rid of Charming, then?" Jana didn't sound terribly upset with the idea. "Good plan. I've got a lot of acreage where we can bury the body."

He sighed. "Honestly, I don't know *what* I'll do if she wants Charming at the end of all this." Marrok didn't even want to think about it.

"You don't *know?*" Jana repeated blankly. "Like, you don't know what weapon you'll use on him or...?"

Marrok cut her off. "Letty held my hand and said she trusted me. Do you know how rare that is for people like us?"

"Of course I do. But..."

"No one has *ever* told me they trusted me before. If I kill Charming, Scarlett will never say that to me, again."

"But, at least you'd have her."

Scarlett's Goodness must have been rubbing off on him, because Marrok wasn't convinced that just having her would be enough. What if he ruined her tiara-filled future and Letty was heartbroken? What if she couldn't forgive him?

What if she never loved him back?

"I have to get her to choose me over Charming." He scraped a palm through his hair. "It has to be her choice. It's the only way I can have *all* of her."

But, what the hell did he have to offer Letty when she could literally have a prince?

"Well, if you want to do it the hard way, you should *definitely* start with getting her into bed." Jana arched a brow. "Charming might have a castle, but if a woman showed up on his mattress, he'd probably think she was a pea. Freaky little 'waiting for the wedding night' tight-wearer."

"Wait. Who told you he was waiting for his wedding night?" Not all Good folk did. Marrok knew that for a grim fact.

"Scarlett did, of course. Well, she implied it. She wrote me about it from that damn hospital, saying that Charming's just soooooo virtuous and how I should stop spreading rumors about him doing Cindy and the rats every night." She snorted. "He probably just couldn't get it up."

Marrok mulled that over. Why had Scarlett lied to her grandmother? Especially since the truth would have won Letty the argument. Charming hadn't waited for his wedding night. Scarlett and the prince had had sex in a garden during that costume ball. She'd said so.

...Actually, no.

His head tilted. *Ramona* had said that in the dungeon. Scarlett herself had refused to talk about it. She hadn't really confirmed or denied a damn thing. Because, she was embarrassed or private or...?

...Or maybe she was hiding something.

Marrok snapped off another piece of cookie and considered his options. "So... where is that glass slipper, now?

Chapter Seventeen

Prince Charming continues to pester me with phone calls, wanting to discuss Scarlett and Drusilla's progress. I begin to worry that he might be in a deep state of denial. Could he really doubt that they are guilty? And, if he does, do we want someone so gullible in charge of a kingdom?

Psychiatric case notes of Dr. Ramona Fae

Cinderella looked down at the man handcuffed before her. "This isn't Scarlett."

"No, majesty. This is Dower." Gustav said seriously, as if it wasn't obvious to *everyone* that the male wolf on the ground was just a *tiny* bit different from a redheaded ugly stepsister. "This is one of Scarlett's friends, though. He escaped with her. The monkeys caught him this morning, near the Enchanted Forest, and turned him over for interrogation."

"I'm not Scarlett's friend!" The wolf named Dower shrieked. He was shackled and kneeling on the floor of the throne room, looking like he'd been attacked by --well-- pissed off monkeys. "I was just in prison with her. I swear, I can't stand that bitch."

"We need to know everything that happened." Charming stepped forward. "Start from the beginning. No. Wait. First tell me if Letty and Dru are alright."

Cinderella exchanged a look with Jack. It infuriated her that the prince had stuck his nose into this. Jack and Gustav could've extracted all the information they needed from the wolf without all this pointless bullshit, but Charming just *had* to be involved. *Had* to stop the mice from doing what needed to be done. *Had* to be underfoot with his tedious morality and busybody ways.

He was such a dope.

"Scarlett's fine." Dower stared up at Charming like the prince was going to save him from further simian violence. If he thought those winged orangutans were mean, wait until the mice got him alone. "Dru was gassed by the purple smoke and is out of it, but she's still alive and all."

Charming frowned in dopy concern.

"Where *are* they?" Cinderella snapped, unwilling to wait for her brain dead fiancé to get to the heart of the matter. She loomed over Dower. "Answer now or you'll be fucking sorry, wolf." She hated wolves. They were such a disgusting, worthless, breed. She gave him a kick, just because she could. "Answer!"

"Jesus!" Charming scowled over at her as Dower crumpled to the ground. "Is that really necessary?"

"*Yes*. If you weren't such a pussy, you'd realize that we need to be tough on Baddies or they'll walk all over the rights of Good folk and..."

"Letty said they were going to her grandmother's house!" Dower cried, cutting her off. "She's looking for a glass slipper!"

Cinderella's eyes slashed over to Jack. "Get him out of here." She hissed.

"Wait!" Charming kept his attention on Dower. "What glass slipper?"

"What fucking glass slipper do you think?!" Dower screeched as the mouse started to drag him towards the dungeon. "Letty says she has Cinderella's shoe, only it's *not* Cinderella's shoe. Letty says she can prove Cinderella is a liar. She says she can prove she's not your bride!"

Well shit.

Charming's head whipped around to face Cinderella, something like triumph filling his expression.

In that second, she knew the prince believed that dirty wolf criminal over her. He believed *Letty* over her. Even through the spell, Charming had *always* sensed that something was wrong. He was *happy* that Cinderella was about to be exposed as a fraud. *Happy* that she wasn't his destined princess. Two days before their beautiful wedding and the son of a bitch was just *looking* for an excuse to leave her at the altar.

"I knew it!" He jabbed a finger at her, his eyes bright with satisfaction. "I *knew* you weren't my True Love!"

Cinderella did what any poor mistreated girl would do when her delicate heart was broken by her handsome prince.

She slugged the bastard.

Her dainty manicured fist slammed into his face, bending the wire rims of his glasses into his nose. Charming stumbled back in shock and pain. Cinderella closed the distance, hitting him again.

Jack dropped his hold on Dower and rushed forward.

"That's all it takes?" She screamed. "The secondhand word of an escaped mental patient is all it takes for you to dump me?!" Jack seized Charming by the arms, holding him still so she could keep hitting him. "I am the most perfect woman in this kingdom and you want a *fucking ugly stepsister instead?!*"

"Oh great." Dower groaned as the mouse wrestled Charming to the ground. "Damn Marrok. This is all *his* fault. *He's* the one who wanted Letty. Not me."

Cinderella's head came around with a snap.

"What?"

"Marrok Wolf! He's the one you want!"

"The Wolfball player?"

"Yes! He's obsessed with Scarlett. *That's* what started this. I didn't even want to leave the hospital. I was a hostage."

The handsomest man in the Four Kingdom's wanted *Letty?* Jesus! The bastard was a mindless animal, but he could probably fuck better than three other men combined. She'd never met Marrok, but Cinderella could certainly imagine all the nasty things someone like him would do to a woman in bed. All the marks and bruises and degradation as he took his fill.

How did Scarlett always get so lucky?

Why was everything in this world so *unfair?!*

"What do you think you're doing?!" Charming roared as Jack cuffed his wrists. "I'm the prince of this kingdom! You can't *do* this!"

"It's already done." Cinderella stood over her fiancé and hated the jackass. "I wanted to do this the *pretty* way, with the cake and the flowers and all the peasants throwing rice at me. But, you couldn't let that happen, could you? You want to ruin *everything* for me."

"You aren't my princess." The spell was failing now that he'd realized the truth. She could see awareness entering Charming's eyes as his memories came rushing back. "The shoe didn't fit you." He breathed in astonishment. "The wolf is right. It wasn't *you!*"

"No, but it *was* me who slaved over the seating chart for our wedding!" God knew, *he'd* been no help at all. Cinderella had tirelessly planned an entire reception and he'd never once said thank you. But somehow *she* was the villain in all this. "I have a hundred and fifty-six lobsters coming in tomorrow, you selfish bastard!"

"You locked up my True Love!" Charming struggled to get free. "You *bitch*."

"She deserved it!"

Goddamn it, why did every little thing in Cinderella's life have to go wrong? Didn't she deserve one special day? Especially, when Letty was being pleasured by The Big Bad Wolf at that very moment? How was it that an *ugly stepsister* got a man like that and all Cinderella got was this pitiful bleating goat? How was that fair?!

She pressed her hands to her temples and bit back a scream of frustration.

When she thought of all the time she'd spent selecting the perfect pink for her color scheme. Her beautiful ice sculptures and a whole fleet of doves couldn't just be *wasted*. Everyone in the Four Kingdoms *needed* to watch her walk down the aisle. She *needed* to bask in the glow of their envy.

Charming's stubbornness was not going to ruin it for her!

"What now, majesty?" Gustav asked.

Jack dragged Charming to his feet. "We should kill him."

"No. He's going to marry me." She couldn't give it up. The royal wedding was her *due!* "I don't care what it takes, get that asshole back here to recast the spell and make Charming forget all this, again."

"Majesty, that won't work. You know that once a spell is broken..."

"Do it, Gustav!"

He obediently bowed his head, but she'd have the other men punish him later. *Strenuously.* No one questioned her orders and got away with it unscathed.

"I'll die before I marry you." Charming spat. "There's only one woman I love."

Cinderella rolled her eyes. "Oh, shut-up."

"This is why Scarlett escaped. She's coming here. She'll set me free and..."

Jack smashed Charming's skull against the wall, which did them all a favor and stopped her groom's blathering. The prince dropped to the ground in an unconscious heap.

"About time." Cinderella looked over at Jack and reached up to fluff her hair. "Now, call the news stations. Tell them their princess has something to say."

Chapter Eighteen

Why does the wolf persist in ignoring my Good advice? He looks right through me during our sessions. Instead, all his attention seems fixed on an ugly stepsister, who throws herself at him in increasingly shameless and disgusting ways.

Psychiatric case notes of Dr. Ramona Fae

Scarlett stepped out of the tub and dried off. She hadn't had a hot shower in six weeks. The water at the WUB Club never rose above "tepid," so it had felt wonderful to stand under the scorching spray and let all her problems wash away.

Except they hadn't *really* been washed anywhere.

Cinderella was still ensconced in the palace, planning to kill Scarlett and Dru and everyone else who might cross her. Until Cindy was gone, no one was safe. Scarlett hated to leave the steamy warmth of the shower, but she had a thousand other things she needed to accomplish if she was going to overthrow her evil stepsister and save the Four Kingdoms.

The bathroom looked exactly the same as it had when Letty was growing up, the walls covered in a hand painted mural of happy bunnies and sunshine. In fact, *everything* in the house looked the same as it had looked ever since Letty could remember. Jana made sure to keep everything familiar and unchanging.

...And camouflaged as the cheery cottage of a sweet little old lady.

Wrapping a robe around herself, Scarlett headed out into her bedroom. The room was decorated in warm yellows and bright blues, with a canopy bed draped with breezy fabric. It was designed to allay suspicions, should anyone come snooping around, but Scarlett had always *liked* the pretty, girly space.

She'd spent most of her life in the Westlands with her mother and stepfather, but Jana's house had always been Letty's home. Luckily, she kept some clothes in the festively painted armoire. She never wanted to see those red sweatpants and "EVIL" shirt again, but she couldn't exactly wear a fuzzy bathrobe on her mission.

She was debating which outfit would be best for infiltrating the palace, when she spotted Marrok. He was sitting on her favorite sunflower-pattered arm chair as if it was the most natural thing in the world.

...In his hand was the glass slipper.

Letty mentally cursed her grandmother. Jana was the only one who could've given it to him. The two of them were like the tag-team from hell.

"What are you doing?" She demanded, afraid to move for fear of what he might do.

"Look at this thing." He held it up with a baffled shake of his head. "What kind of dumbass makes their footwear out of glass? One stubbed toe and you're crippled for life. It's just soooo breakable."

"Put it *down*."

He casually tossed the delicate crystal shoe from palm to palm. "What would happen if I smashed it, do you think? Would Charming believe you about Cinderella being a fraud even without the proof?"

Letty tried to brazen it out. "Of course he would."

"*I* would believe you." Marrok's eyes stayed on hers. "I would always know you were mine. But, I'm going to bet that Charming would need more proof." He pretended to brighten. "Hey, maybe you could tell him something that only the two of you would know. Like maybe... something about that night in the garden. You guys were the only ones there, right? He *has* to remember that."

Scarlett took a determined step forward, only to freeze when he held the glass slipper at arm's length over the hardwood floor.

"Because, God knows, *I* can't get the images of you two together out of my head." He dangled the shoe by one finger. "My True Love and the Prince of the Westlands rolling around in topiary and flowers... It's burned into my skull like acid."

Letty made a sound of extreme annoyance. "Of course, it's all about *you*."

Marrok arched a brow. "You think I'm being conceited, because I don't want my wife sleeping with another man?"

"I think you're an *asshole*, because you're being an asshole." Scarlett corrected. "I mean talk about a double standard! Am I supposed to believe you've kept yourself as virginal as a unicorn all this time?" She didn't even want to imagine the number of women he'd slept with. It would be like counting all the stars in the sky. "You've probably been with every evil beauty queen in the Four Kingdoms."

"I didn't care about them, though. No one else has *ever* meant anything to me. Not the way Charming apparently does to you."

"So, in your world, random hook-ups with *many* people is better than having meaningful relationships with very few?"

"Yes."

"That makes no sense, at all!"

"I've slept with other people." He dropped his eyes. "Sometimes because I wanted to and sometimes, especially when I was younger, because I was forced to."

Her brows drew together at that admission, although it sadly didn't surprise her. Anyone who looked like Marrok would be prey for the monsters of this world, when he wasn't strong enough to defend himself. Nobody would've stepped in to help a wolf or any Bad folk being abused.

Why wasn't there a place where they could be safe?

"If you want, I will postpone the Cinderella thing to help you hunt down and kill anyone who's ever hurt you." She said quietly. "I swear it."

His gaze flicked back up to hers and she still saw uncertainty there. "I just want you to understand that I have been with other people, but I have never loved anyone but you, Letty."

Scarlett felt her lips part in astonishment.

"Maybe you're not ready to feel that way about me, yet." He continued, his eyes intent. "I can accept that. But, it bothers me --*a lot*-- that you would feel that way about someone *else.*"

She had a sudden flash of Marrok telling her that he loved some other woman. That he wanted someone else for his bride. Just the idea of it had Letty wincing.

She felt very... attached to this man.

"Just tell me the truth." He continued intently. "Do you love Charming?"

Scarlett very slowly shook her head.

Marrok sagged forward in relief. "You're sure you don't love him?" He pressed like he still wasn't completely sure. "Really?"

"Really. He's just a friend."

"I don't see you having garden sex with 'just a friend.'"

What could she tell him that wouldn't be a lie? "Well, that was an odd night."

He studied her and she could see his mind working. The man was so damn clever. "So... on this 'odd night,' Charming had sex in the garden?"

"Yes. He did. I swear."

"With *you* or with someone else?"

She faltered, her mind racing. Damn it! Why was he making this so hard?

Marrok's eyes gleamed with satisfaction when she couldn't come up with a quick evasion. "See I *knew* something was off about that story. You were acting too sketchy about it. If it really had been you he slept with, you would've been screaming out the placement of his moles to prove Cinderella was a fake." He made a considering face. "Overall, I'm impressed with how well you kept up the story, though. You can be kinda devious, Red. For a Good Folk."

She appreciated his support of her Badness, but the last thing she needed was him digging into the night of the ball. "Just give me back the shoe."

Marrok wasn't going to let it go. "So, Charming slept with Cinderella. That must have been quite a disappointment for you." He didn't sound particularly sympathetic. "Tell me how it happened. Did she drug him or is he just an idiot? Please say idiot. I have a bet with your grandma."

Scarlett's lips pressed together, refusing to answer him.

He gave the shoe another perilous waggle above the hardwood floor. "Bear in mind, I'm pissed over your lying and holding your glass slipper hostage."

"I haven't lied to you!"

"You let me think you had sex with Charming.

How is that not a lie?"

"It's none of your business who I had sex with, before we even met!"

"I *know* that, so why did you lie about it?"

Scarlett studied him. "You're not going to break that shoe." She finally decided.

He gave the glass slipper a taunting toss in the air. Scarlett's heart went up and down with its assent and fall. Marrok easily caught it and smirked at her. "Are you really willing to bet on me not smashing this thing?"

"Yeah, I am." She kept her gaze on his. "Because, you know that shoe is important to me. If you're my True Love, you're programmed not to do anything that would hurt me."

Marrok hesitated, staring at her.

She arched a brow at him.

"Fuck." He didn't look happy about it, but he stopped threatening shoe-murder. He set the glass slipper on a round side table and made an irritated face. "Feeling pretty smug, aren't you?"

"A little bit. It's your own fault, though. If I believe you love me, then I also believe you're going to do right by me." She shrugged, because it was all very clear. "And I believe you love me."

"Fuck." He muttered again. "I shouldn't have told you that."

"I don't think you had to tell me." Once he said it, she'd realized she'd already known. "You lifted my sister out of that library window before you saved yourself. You shielded me from bullets with your own body. You smile at me differently than you do everyone else." She edged closer to him. "I don't think you're gentle with many people, but you're always gentle with me."

"I don't know how to be gentle." He scoffed.

"Yes, you do."

Had Marrok ever let himself be this vulnerable with anyone else before? He'd told her he loved her, and he wanted her, and about his past. He gave up his silly shoe kidnapping because she asked him to. She could look into his eyes and read his thoughts. The Big Bad Wolf had just given her everything she'd need if she wanted to break his heart.

Luckily, that wasn't what she wanted, at all.

Marrok looked up at her as she stopped in front of the chair. "So, I should let you go off and marry that prince, then?" He demanded. "Even though you don't love him and he slept with Cinderella, and you're supposed to be mine? Is that what someone gentle would do? Because all *I* want to do is kill that asshole."

"Let's just say, if I was insisting on marrying Charming, I think you could talk me out of it without slaughtering the groom."

"What do you mean, '*if*' you were insisting on marrying him? You mean you're *not* insisting on marrying him?"

Risky or not, Scarlett knew what she was going to do. "No." She said simply.

"No?!" He repeated at a roar. "That's all you're going to say? Just *no?*"

She shrugged. "Just no."

"That quick you're done with the idea of being a princess?" He demanded skeptically.

"It's not quick, so much as it's… complicated."

"Complicated, huh? Well, why don't you just break it down for me in small words, then?"

Scarlett braced herself. He took a chance on her and now she'd take one on him. "I'm trusting you, Marrok."

Marrok frowned. "What the hell is that supposed...?" He stopped abruptly as she sat down on his lap. "Christ," he groaned, "if you're trusting me not to touch you, I'm about to let you down." His gaze dipped to the gap in her robe like he just couldn't help himself. "Are you completely naked under there?"

She sent him a grin, feeling how aroused he was. "Completely."

"If this is a distraction, it's a pretty damn effective one." He fiddled with her belt.

She batted his hands away. "You're the one doing the distracting, not me." She reached over to grab the glass slipper and shoved it into his palm. "Here." She shifted sideways so she could rest her bare foot on the armrest of the chair. "Put it on me."

His amusement faded. "I don't want to." He tried to hand the shoe back to her. "I don't want to see you wear that."

"Use your eyes, then. Do you think that little hunk of glass is going to fit my size nines?

Marrok blinked. His gaze went from her toes... to the shoe... and then back again.

Scarlett waited.

"Why, Red... what big feet you have." He finally said.

"Just what every girl longs to hear."

Marrok seemed thrilled, though. More confident now, he tried to wedge the tiny shoe onto her foot, smiling in delight when it didn't fit.

She rolled her eyes. "Ouch." She deadpanned.

"Sorry. I just..." He sounded dazed. "Letty, this isn't your shoe."

"Of course it's not." She didn't understand why it had taken him so long to figure this out. "I couldn't be

Charming's destined princess *and* your True Love, could I?"

"No." He whispered.

"So, if you're right and I'm yours…" She let her voice trail off and gave a "duh" sort of hand gesture.

"I *am* right." His palm came up to caress the side of her face. "You're mine. You're a crazy fucking lunatic, but you're all mine." His forehead leaned forward to rest against hers, like he just wanted to get closer to her. "Did you enjoy tormenting me with the idea of you and Charming or is there some semi-logical reason you didn't tell me this sooner? Because I've been going out of my mind and you know it."

"I know. I'm sorry."

"It was cruel. And not fun-cruel, but actually *mean*-cruel and you're never mean. Why did you lie to me?"

Scarlett swallowed. She really was betting on The Big Bad Wolf.

"I'm trusting you," she repeated, "with something really precious to me."

"You *can* trust me. I am on your side and no one else's. Always."

She sighed and just… told him the truth. "The shoe's not mine or Cindy's. It's Drusilla's."

"Your sister? Charming and *Dru?*"

She nodded and leaned against his chest. It was a relief to finally tell someone. "Her feet are positively tiny. I'm telling you." She let out a long breath. "Seriously, Drusilla is so beaten down. *Everyone* would be coming after her if they knew the truth and she couldn't handle that. So I lied and said I was the destined princess to keep her safe."

"Wait," Marrok still wasn't convinced, "*Drusilla* is

Charming's True Love?"

"Yes. I think Dru must've known for a while, actually."

"Bad folk always know." He sounded baffled. "How in the hell did it happen?"

Letty shrugged. "The night of the ball, we were all in costumes, all trying on the glass slipper in the throne room. But not Dru." She shook her head. "She just waited. When Charming went out into the garden to be alone and brood about the fact that no one at the party fit the shoe, she followed him. That's when she tried on the glass slipper and it fit. Later, Dru told me they had sex and were happy. Everything *should* have been fine."

"Except it wasn't."

"Cindy did something. Some kind of spell or... *something*. She completely hexed Charming, so he forgot what happened, and she passed herself off as his True Love. Dru came running to me, sobbing, just after it happened. I was in Charming's office, checking my email. She still had the shoe on."

"So you took it."

"The glass slipper is the only thing that can blow Cindy's cover." Scarlett gestured to it. "I knew that. I had about two seconds to think of something to keep it out of her hands. So, I shoved it in a box, wrote my grandmother's address on it, and dropped it in a bin of outgoing mail."

"You *mailed* it?"

"It was the only thing I could think to do! I wrapped it in newspaper, first. Anyway, when the rats came barging in to arrest us a few minutes later, they didn't notice. They dragged Dru and me away, but the glass slipper was shipped out of the palace the next morning."

"You're legit *awesome* at plans, you know that?"

She smiled at him. "The glass slipper will prove Dru is the princess." Letty's lips pressed together. "Cindy *knows* I'm going to use it to ruin her. She will hunt me down and kill me if that's what it takes to get it back."

"I'm surprised she hasn't already. Why send you to the WUB Club, at all?"

"I told her I'd set it up so the shoe would be delivered to Charming if Dru or I wound up dead. She believed me. Whatever spell she's using on him, it has to be strong. But, I'm telling you, Charming's smart. He *has* to be sensing something's wrong. Just bringing him the shoe probably wouldn't get through the spell, but if I can get Dru to him, I can *show* him the truth."

Marrok thought for a moment. "How did Cinderella put the whammy on Charming, in the first place? You're right, that's not an easy trick. What kind of powers does she have?"

"She doesn't *have* any powers. I'm sure of it. She must have had help. Probably those damn rats."

"Since when do rats have magic powers?"

"Well, she hired someone, then. What does it matter?"

"Because, before we go after her, it would be good to know if she's hired someone who can vaporize us with magic."

"'Us?'" She repeated. "You'll really help me stop her?"

"What do you think?" His teeth nipped her earlobe.

Letty's eyes drifted shut, instinctively moving against him. "So... you're not upset with me, anymore?"

He nuzzled her temple. "Oh, I'm seriously, *seriously* upset that you lied to me and let me picture you wearing that asshole's ring for so long. But, my annoyance is mitigated by the knowledge that you're *not* wearing his ring."

"It wasn't really a lie."

He ignored the half-hearted denial and went back to untying the sash of her robe. "Besides, I can't possibly stay mad at you when you're half-naked and sitting on my lap."

"I'll remember that for the next time I *don't* lie to you." Her gaze met his as he peeled the terrycloth down her arms. "Charming really isn't an asshole, you know. He's a nice guy, under a spell."

"Christ, you're beautiful." He whispered staring at her naked body. His hands came up to caress her breasts. "On the list of stuff I feel like discussing right now, Charming ranks dead last." All his focus was on massaging the soft globes. "I've got something much more fun on my mind."

Scarlett arched into his hands and tried to concentrate. "Fun or not, we *have* to save Charming. If for no other reason than I need him to wake-up Dru with True Love's kiss."

"Well, seeing as how I hate the guy, you're going to have to make this rescue effort worth my while, Red." His thumbs strummed over her nipples.

"What do you want?" She asked breathlessly.

He gave a wolfish smile.

"You really are Bad." She raised a brow. "You think I'll sleep with you just to convince you to help Charming?"

"No." He leaned forward, his mouth hovering above hers. "I think you'll sleep with me because you're my True Love and I'm asking you to." His lips brushed hers.

Letty bit back a moan at the brief contact.
"You're *always* asking me and I'm *always* telling you no." She reminded him, just to prolong the game.

"This time is different. I really do need you right now."

"Am I supposed to melt at that? Because, you could be more romantic if you said something about my hair or my eyes..."

"I *really* need you, Scarlett." His topaz gaze met hers and she saw the strain he was trying to hide. "Please." He said hoarsely.

...And Scarlett melted.

Chapter Nineteen

Scarlett's biggest problems are her *ideas*.
Bad folk should never get ideas. Ideas just confuse them.

Psychiatric case notes of Dr. Ramona Fae

He was going to die if he didn't have her.

Marrok tried to suppress his need, not wanting to scare her, but the wolf was trying to take control. The news that she *wasn't* determined to marry Prince Charming roared through him like fire.

Scarlett was sitting on his lap, allowing him to take the robe from her still damp body, keeping her magical blue eyes on his... and it was all he could do to stay in control. Despite his attempts to rein it in, he could see the black smoke of his wolf-form begin to appear on his arms. The wolf wanted out.

It wanted Letty.

In the dungeon, Marrok had ground his teeth and urged her to come against his hand. He'd been aching for her, but he'd known how important it was to move slowly. To tempt her closer. To try and be *gentle*. He still knew that it was the smart play. The long view. It was what Scarlett deserved.

But...

"I need you so much." He whispered. "I'll make it good for you. You know I will." His teeth nipped her lower lip. "Say yes, baby."

"Yes." She breathed. Instantly, his mouth slammed against hers and she gasped. "Oh *yes*." Her hands tugged at his clothes, as wild as he was.

Marrok could feel his body changing even as his mouth ravaged hers. In his wolf-form, everything was heightened. He could hear every seductive sound. He could smell her desire. He could feel her small movements, and see her perfect body, and --*God*-- could he taste her.

Marrok dipped his head to lick the side of her neck. "Mine." It was a growl.

She shifted, so she was facing him. Her legs parted, straddling his lap and she smiled up into the face of The Big Bad Wolf.

The innocent show of trust turned him on even more. The wolf wanted to be inside of her before she changed her mind. Its hands pulled Scarlett even closer and she whimpered. It didn't want to coax or take its time. The swirling edges of the wolf-form licked along her skin and his deepest animal instincts screamed to slam into her.

To just take.

No.

Marrok gave his head a shake, holding onto control. He wasn't an animal. What was he doing? She was too small. Too breakable. Too Good. What if he hurt her?

Suddenly terrified, Marrok pulled back.

Blue eyes met his, dazed with need. "You okay?"

"I'm scared." He said breathing hard.

"Of me?"

Only Letty would ask something so ridiculous. "No. Of harming you."

"You won't." She leaned up to kiss him. "You're always gentle with me."

Wolves had no idea how to be gentle. He tried, for her sake, but he probably sucked at it. She had such faith in him, though…

"Show me what you want and I'll do it." He vowed. "Give me a minute and I can get back to my human self." His eyes drifted down to her spectacular breasts. "Maybe two minutes."

"You don't have to change." Her lips whispered across his. "I like you this way."

Marrok groaned. "Thank God." The wolf came out when he was stretched to the breaking point with desire and he didn't see that abating anytime soon. "I had no idea how I was going to keep my word on that one." He stood up, carrying her towards the bed. "Tell me if I'm too rough."

"Ditto."

God, he loved her.

Her legs wound around his waist and her lips found his as he tumbled them onto the mattress. For an endless moment, everything was perfect. She was sweet and yielding and tasted like heaven. Pillows and blankets were shoved aside as they devoured each other. He needed her more than oxygen. It was what he'd been fantasizing about for weeks. He could have her and she would let him.

…Then what?

He'd never done this with someone he loved. Everything felt different. Better and hotter and so much more important. But what if it *wasn't* different. What if she didn't feel it too? What if she just left afterwards like the others?

He couldn't recover from that.

Uncertain, Marrok eased back and tried not to notice how radiant she was. It just made everything more confused. He needed her so badly he was shaking and the wolf was still vying for total control, but he was suddenly nervous.

"Marrok?" Letty tilted her head so she could maintain eye contact when he would've glanced away. "It's alright. I won't hurt you."

He flinched. This time it didn't sound so ridiculous.

"If you're not ready, we can wait." She assured him in the most caring voice he'd ever heard. "Do you want to stop?"

"Christ no." That was the last thing he wanted. The wolf wanted to howl at the very thought. "Just... You'll stay when it's over?" No one else ever had. Not once they were finished with him.

"Where else would I go?" Her hand came up to his cheek. "Don't worry." The woman really did know his thoughts as soon as he had them. "You're safe with me, remember? This isn't because you're handsome. It's because you're *you*."

He swallowed. "Promise?" The word was out before he could censor it.

She nodded, blue eyes locked on his. "Looks actually don't matter quite so much to an ugly stepsister, you know."

"You're not ugly, Scarlett."

"And you're more than just a gorgeous face, Marrok. I promise." She hesitated and he sensed her getting another new and surprising idea. "Has anyone ever made love to you before?"

"From the time I was twelve I was being..."

Letty cut him off. "No." Her palm came up to his shoulder and she eased him onto his back, so they could switch positions. "Has anyone ever *made love* to *you*?" She rolled on top of him.

He shook his head, understanding what she

meant. "No." In every way that mattered, there was just Scarlett.

She leaned down to kiss him, looking flushed and tousled and smug. "Well, I'm about to."

Marrok gave a reluctant chuckle at her teasing grin. "Baby, I have been waiting *years* to hear you say that."

"You've only known me six weeks."

"I always knew you'd show up, though." He hadn't known her name, but he'd known that she'd come. "I never doubted that I'd find my True Love and that you'd save me."

She smiled. "You really think I saved you?"

"I know you did."

"Because *I* think we're about even." She moved against him and he saw stars. The woman was everything he'd ever dreamed of and more. "I never would've gotten out of the WUB Club without you, Marrok. In fact, since you would've been released in less than six months, I'm thinking you only escaped *at all* because you wanted to help me."

"You couldn't stay in there. It wasn't safe for you."

"See?" Scarlett slid down his body. "You're always trying to protect me, even when it puts *you* at risk. We're partners."

Marrok's eyes closed as her mouth trailed southward. "I would do anything to protect you."

"I know. It's part of you being gentle."

"It's part of me being insanely in love with you."

He felt the heat of her breath against him. "I think we're both right." She whispered.

One of his hands fisted in the sheets as her tongue danced across the tip of his straining manhood.

"*Jesus.*" His free palm tangled in her silky, shiny, soft hair and he tried to keep himself still. There was no way he could completely succeed, though. He urged her head closer to him. "Baby, I need you so much I really am going to go crazy if you don't..." He let out an agonized groan as she sucked him deep into her mouth. "*Letty.*"

No one had ever done this for him before. No one had ever cared enough about his pleasure. Obviously, he'd known it would feel awesome, but it felt *fucking awesome*. Better than anything ever had. The lush pink lips he'd been obsessing over for a month and a half sealed over him and he lost the capacity to think. He couldn't get enough oxygen into his lungs.

Marrok forced his eyes open so he could watch the shifting black mist that covered his body blend with her red tresses. It was beautiful.

She was beautiful.

"Every share circle, I spent the entire session picturing this." He got out. "I have a vivid fucking imagination and it didn't even come *close* to how incredible you are."

She lifted her head long enough to give him a playful look. "I *knew* you weren't paying attention to those stupid meetings. You talked a good game to Ramona about all that psychobabble, but I could feel your eyes undressing me the whole time."

"I was paying attention to what mattered."

"You know, half the reason Ramona hated me was because she was so jealous of the attention you paid to *me* and not to *her*."

"You think I should've paid *more* attention to that lunatic?"

"Hell no." Her eyebrows drew together. "You're mine. Even then, you were mine."

Marrok liked that answer. Possessiveness wasn't love, but it felt pretty damn satisfying to hear her claim him as her own. "I'm a hundred percent yours, baby. I have been right from the start."

"I know! Ramona was just *completely* out-of-line. *Such* a terrible doctor." Scarlett frowned. "And she didn't do anything to make you feel better about yourself with her unprofessional behavior."

"Well, I'm feeling fine, now." He tugged her lips back towards his throbbing erection, before she got distracted by another do-Gooding campaign. "Please don't stop."

She grinned at him and didn't stop.

Marrok enjoyed it for as long as he could, but there was no way he was going to last. He was too close. His jaw locked, struggling to hang on. "Letty?" He tried to focus. "I'm about to come."

Her head popped up, again. Going so long without talking must have been hard for his precious little chatterbox. "That's the whole *point*, dummy."

"I'm still not ready." Somehow, he found the strength to pull away from the warmth of her mouth. "Not yet." He flipped her around, so he was on top again. "First, I need you with me." He settled between her legs and was so damn grateful that she was his. "I need you."

"You have me." Scarlett looked straight into her eyes and smiled. "But, I'm still the one making love to *you*." She nodded as if precision on the point was vital. "I want you to feel safe with me."

"I feel a hell of a lot more than safe right now." He was going to lose control if he didn't get inside of her soon.

Be gentle.
Be gentle.

Be gentle.

"You know what I mean. It's important that you trust me to..." Scarlett trailed off with a gasp as he surged forward, seating himself deep within her damp heat. "*Marrok.*"

He had her.

Finally.

"You're the only person in the world I trust, Red." Marrok dropped his forehead against hers. She was hot and tight and perfect. He knew what it was to come home. "You're my wife."

She bit down on her lower lip, her body shifting to accept more of him. "Not so fast. You have to propose before we're..." She let out a breathless sigh as the next stroke went even deeper. "Oh yessss."

"I think I *did* propose. And that sounded like a yes to me."

She blinked. "You did *not* propose and I didn't say... God *yes.*"

He chuckled at that and increased his thrusts. "New thought: Since you're the one running this show, I think *technically* you should be the one doing the proposing."

"You expect *me* to ask *you* to get married?"

They were already married, as far as Marrok was concerned, so he really didn't see why there needed to be any asking, at all. "Don't worry. I'm not going to play hard to get." He dipped his head to suckle her breast.

She obviously had a lot more to say on the subject, but she was getting sidetracked by all the wicked things he was doing to her body. "You really are Bad."

"Told ya so." His teeth ground together, wanting to postpone his own orgasm. "Letty?"

"Mmmmm?" Full words were apparently beyond

her.

"Can I stop being gentle now?"

She frantically bobbed her head.

Hallelujah.

Marrok caught her leg and pulled it higher. At the same time, he dragged her farther under his massive form. The wolf was twice her size and it was hungry for her. The black mist licked against pale skin. He pinned her down, enjoying the small whimper of surrender. Both of her wrists were caught in his palm and her body was his for the taking.

"Wife." He breathed into her ear.

Dazed blue eyes met his. "Marrok."

It wasn't exactly what he wanted to hear, but it would do.

He rocked into her again and again. Scarlett gave a cry of passion, surging to meet his demands. As far as he could tell, she *liked* the ungentle him.

Thank Christ.

She was so close now and he was about to lose it. Marrok's hand slid down to where their bodies were joined and he deliberately brushed his thumb over her tight flesh. He'd been paying attention in the dungeon. He knew just how she liked to be touched.

Scarlett went taunt, her eyes wide. "Yes, yes, *yes!*"

The ripples of her climax pushed him over the edge. "Letty!"

And then all he could do was hang on and ride out the explosion.

***

"Marrok?"

"Yeah?"

"You okay?"

"I have no idea. I can't feel anything below my nose."

Scarlett grinned at that and pushed back a handful of his tawny hair. He was back in human-form, sprawled out on top of her like he had no intention of ever moving.

She knew the feeling.

"Did I hurt you?" He asked after a moment.

"No. Of course not. You were very gentle."

"Not at the end I wasn't."

She gave him a kiss. "You were a little *less* gentle, but I loved it." Even at the end, he'd been careful not to harm her. She never worried about him being too rough. Marrok always took care of her. Maybe because he understood what it was to be treated badly. To be hurt and unloved and discarded.

Even now, she could feel the tension coming back to his body. He had just given her everything he had, but he was still unsure. He was instinctively bracing for her to leave him. He couldn't help it. God only knew what he'd endured in his life.

Scarlett didn't take offense at his wariness.

In time, he'd see that she'd meant what she'd said. He was safe with her.

She snuggled closer to him, her palm finding his. "I have to work on a plan to destroy my stepsister, but I'm too relaxed to remember why." Their fingers locked together and she closed her eyes. "I'm going to take a nap and you're going to hold me. Deal?"

She felt him relax against her. "Deal."

Marrok positioned himself so he was lying between Letty and the door, like he wanted to protect her against any surprise invasions. Given Jana's tendency to attract enemies, it was probably a good guess.

He nuzzled her hair, his body curving around her. "So... was this really your room as a kid?" He asked after a while.

"Kind of."

From the direction his palm was going, napping was the last thing on his mind. "Well, that's *kind of* kinky, don't you think?"

She batted his hand away, just to torment him. "I think you're incorrigible."

"Oh come on... You didn't ever lay in here and daydream about some local Wolfball player ravishing your Good little self?" His teeth nipped her ear. "I'm imagining the reverse situation, right now."

"There aren't any local Wolfball players." Scarlett said staunchly. "My grandmother controls the Enchanted Forest and she doesn't approve of that barbaric so-called 'sport.'"

"Really? 'Cause she's got a Blu-ray of my highlight reel sitting on a shelf downstairs."

Scarlett sighed. "Fine. *I* don't approve of it. It keeps the wolves in virtual slavery."

"Yeah, but it also keeps us alive." He grew more serious. "Without the Four Kingdoms wanting us for their stupid game, where else would we go? The wolves would be hunted down. Take away the teams and the Good folk wouldn't exactly be voting for us to hone our natural abilities."

It annoyed her that he was probably right.

"Some of the wolves could survive without the sports. Become servants or whatever like the rest of the Bad folk. But, I'm pretty sure I would've been killed. People don't always like me."

"If it wasn't for my grandmother watching out for me and my stepfather being a Good folk, I'd probably be in the same boat. The only friends I have I made in the psych-ward. What does *that* say about me?"

He chuckled. "You're still ahead of me. I've never had a friend in my life."

"Except me."

Marrok kissed the curve of her neck. "Except you, baby." He whispered.

She tilted her head back to look at him. "Wait, wasn't Trevelyan your friend? He must have been, if he wanted you to escape with him."

"We watched each other's backs. The dragon and I were stuck in a room together, so we formed an alliance against the other inmates. I didn't see the 'friendship' going quite as deep as he did, though, since I wasn't about to help him blow the prison up."

"He wanted to blow up the WUB Club?"

"A fair-sized chunk of it." Marrok shrugged. "He figured we could just walk right out in the confusion. I might be a bastard, but I couldn't slaughter hundreds of people."

"Of course not!

"Yeah, well, the dragon wasn't so squeamish. He needed me to help him pull the plan off. When I refused, he went fucking ballistic. I don't think he'll be invited to our wedding."

"Well, you were right to tell him no." Scarlett assured him righteously. She thought for a bit. "How did he finally get out, if you didn't help him?"

"Dr. White is always looking for a new inmate to entertain her after hours. Trevelyan played along, until he saw some sort of opportunity to escape." Marrok made a face. "*Obviously* she wasn't going to report him missing right away. How would she explain it? I think he only let her live so she'd have to face all the speculative whispering."

"Horrible woman. I'm not at all sorry I wiped her memory." Scarlett muttered. "Still, the dragon didn't actually have a *bad* plan. I mean, ours was *better*. No way would I let you sleep with that bitch to facilitate our early release. But, his idea was sort of ingenious in its simplicity." She sighed. "It's wrong that someone so clever was locked away in the first place."

"Well, Trevelyan's evil, so it wasn't *too* wrong."

"Maybe he wouldn't have been evil if he'd been given the opportunity to be better."

"I doubt it. He was *really* evil."

"Alright maybe not *him*, then." Scarlett allowed. "But a lot of Bad folk are trapped by circumstance." She shook her head. "There should be a place where *everyone* can be safe. Where *everyone* can have a say and be recognized and not have to live their lives as second-class citizens." She met his eyes. "We all deserve a chance at a happily ever after."

His expression went soft. "God, I love you." He ran a hand over her hair. "You are so Good it breaks my heart."

"I'm serious. When you were younger, there should've been somewhere that would take you in and make sure you were protected. You would've been spared so much misery."

"And maybe then I wouldn't have found you." He shook his head. "My path led me to my True Love and that's the only place I've ever wanted to be."

"Yes, but you had to needlessly suffer to get here. What if our situations really *were* reversed? Wouldn't you want to create a better way, if it had been *me* who went through that pain?"

Something dark passed behind his eyes. "You don't want to know what I would do if our situations were reversed. Anyone who harmed you, I would kill three different ways before they even realized they were dead."

She laid a hand on his chest. "You don't think I feel that way, too?"

"It's not the same." He realized he was going to lose this debate. She could hear it in his voice. He wasn't quite ready to admit defeat, though. "And, you know, there are a lot of guys like Trevelyan out there. Not as sociopathically villainous, maybe, but still… Some Bad folk *deserve* to be kept away from the rest of society."

"Not all of them, though. They shouldn't be punished before they do anything wrong. You can't paint everyone with the same bigoted brush. Most people just need a chance."

"Why is it up to *us* to give it to them? I can see you're thinking we have to do something and…"

Letty cut him off. "Because of our children."

Marrok blinked. "Children?"

"Well, given the *explosiveness* of our encounter, I'm rapidly coming to the conclusion that you're my True Love." She was absolutely certain of it, in fact.

"No shit."

She ducked her head. "Well, if we have a baby," she cleared her throat, because it seemed a little forward to bring up a future, right now, "it'll be fifty percent wolf. Don't you think she should have a more secure life than you did? What if something happened to us and my family? Who would look after her?"

He didn't respond to that, but his hand settled on the curve of her stomach as if he was already shielding their child.

Scarlett kept going. "Baddies need a place, Marrok. And my grandmother is turning over the entire Enchanted Forest to me."

"You want to invite villains to live *here?*"

"Yes! You and I could do this. I know it." Bad folk already hid in the Enchanted Forrest. This would just legitimize things. "We could be a fifth kingdom that's a safe haven for *everyone*. We need to…"

A pounding on the door interrupted her rapidly developing plan.

"Letty?" Esmeralda called. "Come quick. Cinderella is about to appear on TV and she seems like one pissed off bridezilla."

Chapter Twenty

Prince Avenant's obsession with the "usurper" remains unchanged.
Forward progress is doubtful until he can learn to see the truth.
…And until he stops petitioning for the rest of the group (and me) to be
executed for treason.

Psychiatric case notes of Dr. Ramona Fae

Avenant stared fixedly at the screen as the perky reporter stood in front of his former palace. "Good Lord, they've ruined my kingdom. Where are the stocks? What are those God awful flowers doing everywhere? It's supposed to be a land of frozen menace, not a garden party!"

The Tuesday share circle was gathered around the television in Jana's family room, waiting for Cinderella's announcement. Scarlett had no idea what her stepsister intended to say, but she knew it was going to be trouble. In the meantime, there was nonstop coverage of the WUB Club breakout on every channel.

Which was trouble enough.

Their escape seemed to have inspired villains everywhere. It was the first time Baddies had ever openly defied the status quo and come out on top. All around the Four Kingdoms, Bad folk were in the streets showing support. The Tuesday share circle had their faces and names plastered on signs as people marched into town squares. Marrok's souvenir Wolfball jerseys were worn in solidarity. Other people painted their faces Bridge Ogre blue, much to Benji's delight.

Even Scarlett was surprised by the response. Trolls, witches, ogres, wolves and every villain in between openly defied authority to cheer for their fellow Bad folk. Unrest had been brewing in the Four Kingdoms for a long time, but now it was bubbling over.

"I'm here in the Northlands, getting a response about last night's horrible getaway." The TV reporter's trying-to-look-grave expression didn't quite work with her three pounds of precisely applied makeup. "Many people here are worried what deposed Prince Avenant might be planning now that he's free of the Wicked, Ugly and Bad Prison and, no doubt, looking for revenge."

Avenant couldn't have been more pleased with that intro. "You should be worried, peasants."

"One person who isn't concerned is *current* ruler of the Northlands." The reporter continued, her voice going up and down in TV news cadence. "Avenant was overthrown by beloved bookshop owner, freedom fighter, and honorary princess Belle..."

"Usurping *bitch!*" Avenant seethed.

"...And she's sure the former prince will stay far away from his homeland. Belle?" The reporter thrust her microphone forward. "Any regrets about crossing an escaped convict with a known penchant for vengeance?"

"No regrets, at all." The camera panned to a dark haired woman in a yellow dress. She looked studious and Good and absolutely no threat to anyone. But she'd kicked Avenant's ass during the Northlands' uprising. "Avenant was a beast of a man who deserved to be ousted."

It was a miracle the TV screen survived Avenant's rage. "A beast would have *fucking killed you* when I had the chance!"

Benji cringed at his volume. "Shhh! You're going to wake-up Dru." He chided, as if that wouldn't actually be a *positive* thing.

Drusilla was still in her mystical coma, sleeping sounding on the wicker sofa. She'd stay like that until Scarlett got her to Charming, no matter how loud Avenant ranted.

"Why *didn't* you kill Belle?" Esmeralda asked Avenant archly. "The girl doesn't even have any powers. Why couldn't you just freeze her and her stupid little rebels solid when they came for you?"

Scarlett glanced at him in surprise. That was a good point. Why *hadn't* he won the fight? Even if Baddies weren't used to winning, with his abilities Avenant should have at least triumphed over a librarian.

Avenant's jaw ticked. "It all happened very quickly."

Esmeralda smirked at that non-answer. "Well, I guess you'll go up there and kill Belle *now*, right? Since you've had time to *process* your failure."

"Oh, I'm going up there." His gaze stayed riveted on Belle. "But death is too quick for a usurper."

Esmeralda snickered. "That's what I *thought* you'd say." She looked over at Marrok. "Isn't that what you'd thought he'd say?"

"Yep." Marrok gave Avenant a knowing grin. "Poor bastard." He looped an arm around Scarlett's shoulders. "The Good ones are always a pain in the ass."

"Shut-up, Wolf." Avenant and Letty chorused.

Marrok chuckled and kissed the top of Scarlett's head. "They're worth all the aggravation, though. Believe me. Having your True Love is worth anything."

Scarlett smiled up at him. The safer he felt with her, the more he relaxed. The man was delightfully open about his affection. It made her feel cherished. She cuddled closer to his side, the two of them taking up the floral loveseat.

Avenant spared Marrok an annoyed glare. "I'm *not* one of you mindless animals. I don't need a True Love. And, if I *did*, it wouldn't be some proselytizing usurper."

"If you say so."

On the TV, Belle kept talking. "Avenant is too smart to come back to the Northlands. We're not even seeing the rallies of Bad folk here that are popping up in the other kingdoms. He knows he doesn't have any friends left."

"I don't need any goddamn friends, either!"

"You have us." Benji assured him.

Avenant glanced over at him and, for once, didn't make a cutting remark.

Scarlett was a little bit touched. Under all the snarking, the Tuesday share circle really was learning to bond. Ramona would be so proud.

"I'm sure Avenant realizes his best chance of survival is staying far away from here." Despite her confident words, Belle's brown gaze reflected worry. Obviously, the woman knew who she was dealing with.

"I will never stay away from what's mine." Avenant said quietly.

"Anything you want to say to the ex-prince?" The reporter prompted as the segment wound down. "If he's watching, what do you want him to hear?"

"I want to tell him..." Belle hesitated, trying to find the right words. "Don't." She finally decided.

"Don't?" The reporter had clearly been hoping for something juicier.

Belle nodded and looked into the camera. "Avenant, just... *don't*."

Avenant stepped closer to the television, all his attention on her face. "She knows I'm coming for her."

He whispered to no one in particular.

Esmeralda took up a little song. "Avenant and Belle sittin' in a tree..."

"By the time I'm done with her, she'll be *hanging* from a tree." Avenant scoffed. "You're all right. I should've killed her. I'm *going* to kill her."

Somehow Scarlett doubted that. The prince of the Northlands was obsessed with the usurper, but not in the way all the WUB Club doctors and psych-tests thought. When he looked at Belle, his cold blue eyes didn't shine with hatred or a need for retribution.

Well, okay, maybe they *did*.

But, much deeper than that, there was just... longing.

"Lunchtime!" Jana called, striding into the room with a platter of food. "I thought you kids might be hungry, waiting for Cinderella to show her scrawny face."

"Sandwiches!" Benji's expression lit up. "What kind?"

"Fresh little pig." She patted Marrok's head. "Specially made for my precious wolf, because they're his favorite."

Marrok beamed up at her, the fair-haired child of villainy. "Thank you, Jana."

"You should call me 'grandma,' dear. You're family now."

"He's not your grandson-in-law, *yet*." Scarlett reminded them pointedly. "He hasn't even proposed."

Marrok selected a sandwich and strove to look innocent. "I'm waiting for *you* to propose, Red."

"There's no way *I'm* going to be the one to..." Scarlett stopped her protest short as Cindy finally appeared on the television. Not a blonde hair was out of place and her fake eyelashes fluttered prettily. She was wearing her most "serious" pink dress. All the rose-colored lace made her look like a frosted cupcake.

"She's really supposed to be the beautiful sister in your family, huh?" Marrok snorted. "Everyone in the Westlands must be blind."

"Citizens of the Four Kingdoms, this is your beloved Princess Cinderella." Cindy smiled sweetly and Scarlett knew the arrogant expression was meant for her. "I'm sad to say that the recent uprising of prisoners and Bad folk has forced me to take drastic measures to protect all the Good citizens of my kingdom."

"It's not *your* kingdom!" Scarlett shouted.

"The sickness of insurrection has even infected my dear Charming." Cinderella continued in a sorrowful tone. "My men caught him conspiring with the enemy and I've had no choice but to lock him up for his own protection. But, worry not, Good people. *I* am in control of the Westlands, now. And our wedding will go on as planned."

"Aw shit." Marrok sighed. "This just got more complicated."

"I'm sure this rebellion is being led by my ugly stepsister Scarlett." Cinderella blinked back phony tears. "I can't help but feel partly responsible for her horrible, horrible actions."

Just looking at that deceitful bitch filled Letty with rage.

"Dearest Scarlett," Cinderella made an appeal straight to the camera, "I'm asking you to please turn yourself in before this goes any further. Don't make me strike back against *all* the Bad folk who you've led astray. Don't make me come after Drusilla and your crazy-house friends and even your mysterious grandmother." She accompanied the word "mysterious" with an eye roll.

Rumors circulated about Scarlett's family, but, for obvious reasons, no one had ever filled Cindy in on Jana's real occupation.

"You don't have to come after me, dearie." Jana muttered. "I'm coming after *you*."

"Why, I'll even have to punish that beautiful wolf of yours, Letty. If you push me, I'll have to see him suitably… punished." Cinderella gave a smile gleaming with all her sexual weirdness. "Marrok certainly looks like someone who could be rehabilitated with a *firm* hand."

"She's threatening you." Scarlett got to her feet and glanced at Marrok. "You specifically."

"I heard her." He didn't sound worried about it. "I'm confident you can keep me safe."

"But, how would she know to threaten you *specifically* unless she knows you're mine?" Scarlett's mind was racing. "Someone must have told her about us."

Marrok's head tilted in thought. "Dower." He surmised after a moment. "It couldn't have been Dr. White, so it must have been him. Asshole was bound to get caught. I told you to let me kill him." He ran a palm through his hair. "*Shit.* Dow knew we were coming here."

"Oh man…" Esmeralda groaned. "Letty, could Cinderella find your grandmother's house?"

"I knew we shouldn't have brought that interloper along." Avenant put in. "You all heard me say it."

"Get to the basement!" Jana ordered.

"All I want is you and Drusilla, Letty." Cinderella cooed from the screen. "If you just do the right thing and surrender, you have my word as a princess that the rest of your minions will be spared. I have no desire for any violence. All I want is peace."

...And that's when the flying monkeys dropped the first firebomb.

***

Scarlett was thrown backwards as the blast blew out the wall of the living room. Her body went flying, hitting the floor in a heap. She lay there, unmoving, as all hell broke loose.

"*Letty!*" Marrok's whole life flashed before his eyes. He ran for her, not even processing the fire and shouting and deafening explosion. "No, no, no, *no*." He dropped to his knees beside her and pushed back a handful of shiny red hair so he could see her face. "Baby? Look at me. Jesus, don't leave me." His fingers found her pulse and he almost cried in relief when he realized it was beating.

She was alive.

For now.

Marrok scooped her up in his arms. He looked around and saw that the whole cottage was going up in flames. "Jana, where's the basement?" He roared.

"This way." The Jabberwocky was already yanking up a trap door in the kitchen and herding Benji down a hidden ladder. The bridge ogre had Dru draped over his massive blue shoulder. Esmeralda was right behind him.

Wherever Jana was leading them, Marrok trusted that it was the best plan. Who knew this place better than her? Marrok handed Scarlett to Avenant. He could tell she was beginning to come around and he wanted to comfort her, but he had to do something first.

She'd want him to get that damn shoe.

"Protect Letty." He ordered and sprinted for the stairs.

"Where the fuck are you going?!" Avenant bellowed.

Marrok ignored him and took the steps three at a time as he raced upstairs. The monkeys were still bombarding the house with smaller firebombs. Cinderella must have told them to level the place. He reached Scarlett's bedroom just in time to watch the thatched roof get destroyed. Every piece of furniture in the room was knocked to its side.

Including the end table where the glass slipper sat.

Luckily, years of Wolfball gave Marrok good reflexes. He dove forward, his palm outstretched... and the shoe tumbled right into his grasp.

Touchdown.

Above him, the monkeys shrieked in agitation, spotting him through the burning roof. The holes in the ceiling were now bigger than whatever remained of the straw. Marrok gave the chimps a taunting wave and dashed from the room.

If it actually *had* been Scarlett's glass slipper, he would've been happy to see the damn thing splinter back into sand. But since Letty wasn't planning to wear it to her dream wedding with Charming, he had to rescue it for her. Drusilla's only chance to wake-up was a kiss from her True Love. Letty would be crushed if her sister was left stranded in a coma and Prince Not-So-Bright would probably need proof that Dru was his destined bride.

With the shoe cradled against his chest, Marrok sprinted back into the hall. Rather than waste time on the stairs, he gripped the railing with his free hand and swung himself over the balcony. He only had seconds before the entire place was incinerated. He dropped to the first floor in a graceful crouch, already moving back towards the kitchen.

His entire roundtrip couldn't have taken more than two minutes, but, while he was gone, Letty had woken up. He could hear her furious voice as he neared the trapdoor.

"Get your hands *off* me, you son of a bitch!"

"Marrok told me to watch you!" Avenant shot back. "And, for some reason, I'm listening to him."

"I don't care what he said! I'm going to drag my True Love down here, whether he likes it or not!"

She'd finally called him her True Love.

Marrok beamed and headed down the ladder, slamming the trapdoor behind him and sealing it tight. No way were the monkeys getting through that. The whole place seemed to be lined in steel. "Letty? I'm here."

"Oh thank God." She headed for him, the relief in her voice quickly turning to anger. "What were you thinking, you idiot?! You could've been *killed*. Why in the hell...?" She trailed off as he held up the glass slipper, her expression somewhere between surprised and incensed. "You went back for *that?*"

"You said you needed it."

"Well it's nothing compared to how much I need *you*." She gave him a shove. "I can't believe you would risk yourself for a damn shoe! Do you have any idea how stupid it was to...?"

Marrok stopped the lecture in the most effective way possible: He kissed her. His mouth sealed over hers and she gave that little gasp of pleasure that he loved. Her body leaned into his, her lips parting in acceptance, and all was right in his world.

"Tell me I'm your True Love." He whispered when he finally raised his head.

"You already know that you are."

"Tell me anyway. I like the words."

Scarlett looked at him. "You're my True Love, Marrok. And I'm yours." Blue eyes narrowed. "But if you ever pull a stunt like that again, I will brain you. Got it?"

"Got it." He gave her another quick kiss and felt completely safe for the first time in his life. "Got *you*."

"Jackass." She batted him away, but he could see her trying not to smile. "I have to go check on Dru. Try to behave for five seconds." She headed over to her sister, who was stretched out on the floor.

"Well, there goes another house." Jana said philosophically. "Good thing I hated the joint. I usually live down here." She sat down on a box of hand grenades. "At least, it's got some style."

Marrok looked around for the first time and saw that the space wasn't really a basement so much as it was a bomb shelter. A series of recessed lighting lit the room, which was filled with supplies. An interconnected series of tunnels led off in various directions, providing escape routes. Computers were setup along one wall, along with a huge stockpile of food and weapons.

Having the Jabberwocky for a grandmother-in-law just got better and better.

"I loved that house." Scarlett sighed. "Something *else* Cinderella ruined."

"So, we'll build another one." Jana waved a dismissive hand. "I've gone through like six of them so far. Every one of them just the same as the last. I even have identical furniture down here someplace. They're just cookie-cutter masks. You know that."

"*This* house was really special, though." Scarlett

glanced over at Marrok and he could see her thinking about their time upstairs.

He gave her a wink. "It wasn't the house, baby. It was the company."

Her mouth curved.

"So what do we do, then?" Avenant complained. "Stay here and help you rebuild? I have a kingdom to conquer and a low tolerance for grime." He ran a finger along a massive crate of bottled water, making a face at the dust.

"Now we fight back." Marrok told them. It was all so clear. "If Cinderella can use the media, so can we."

"The media?" Scarlett squinted at him like he was crazy. "What do we know about the media?"

"Red, I have my own *fan club*. I know how to get people's attention. It's the reason I wasn't tossed in a pit to die long ago." Marrok turned to Jana. "Do these computers link us to the outside world?"

"Of course."

"Then we're going to do a public service announcement."

"About what?" Jana scoffed. "*Not* firebombing? Does anyone really need an explanation on why that sucks, especially for the innocent homeowners? You think insurance covers winged gorillas?"

Esmeralda frowned. "We could rat Cinderella out as a raging bitch, but I doubt anyone would believe us without proof. Not with ---ya know-- all the lying we've done and crimes we've committed."

"We could do a video on why we don't like monkeys." Benji volunteered. "Because, I really don't like monkeys anymore."

Avenant looked interested in Marrok's plan, which had to be a first. "I'd be happy to go on camera and give a speech to the masses. I have *much* to say on why my enemies should be crushed."

"No." Marrok kept his attention on Letty. "We're going to talk about giving Baddies a place to belong. The seven of us can't stand up to all the Good folk in the Four Kingdoms forever. But if we had *more* people here and on our side, we'd have a force."

Scarlett paused in the act of covering Dru with a cozy blanket. "Yes!" Her eyes lit up. "With a force of Bad folk, not even Cinderella could stop us."

"Aren't Marrok's online fans mostly horny teenage girls and brain dead jocks?" Esmeralda complained. "How are *they* going to help?"

Jana frowned. "Hang on, *I'm* part of his online fan club."

"And I appreciate that, but it's not just my fandom who's paying attention to us. You saw the news." Marrok gestured upwards. The TV was probably a molten mass of melted plastic by now, but they'd all watched the protesters on its screen. "Good folk have pushed people to the edge. Right now, every villain in the Four Kingdoms is standing on a ledge and waiting for an excuse to jump off."

"An inspiring image." Avenant deadpanned.

"All I'm saying is they want a leader… and we have one to give them."

"Really?" Scarlett asked hopefully. "You'll film something about the Enchanted Forrest being a…?"

He cut her off. "Oh no, not me. *You*."

"Me?" She blinked, her excited grin fading. "Wait. No. Why can't *you* do it?"

"Because, no one in their right mind would follow any idea *I* have. You've seen my psych-tests. I'm crazy."

"We're *all* crazy! And we're working together, so

this whole thing is *our* idea."

"Working together? Absolutely. *Our* idea? Not so much." He snorted. "Even if it does save our asses, *my* ideas generally don't involve turning our backs on multi-million dollar criminal enterprises in favor of do-Gooding."

"Wait, *what's* this idea?" Jana demanded.

Scarlett disregarded that. "Marrok, you said yourself, you're used to being in the spotlight." She tried a persuasive smile. "And you're so talented at it. It *has* to be you."

"Flattery won't work unless you're trying to lure me into bed." He informed her piously. "Besides, I might be the most famous one here, but *nobody* can convince Bad folk to do crazy shit like you can, Red."

The rest of the Tuesday share circle nodded.

"We'd still be locked up if it wasn't for you, Letty." Benji gave her a shy smile. "You saved us."

"Letty is good at saving people." Marrok moved to kiss Scarlett's temple. "Even when they don't deserve it. This will be a piece of cake for her."

She didn't look so sure. "We're partners, Marrok. And you're so much more likable than I am. *You* should be the one to..."

Marrok cut her off. "You are a *thousand times* more likable than me. Ask anyone."

"I would agree with that." Avenant agreed.

"See?"

"What does *he* know about being likable?"

"Hey!"

Scarlett ignored Avenant's protest and looked around at the others. Marrok could see her resolve strengthening at their expectant expressions. "Alright, here's what I think." She took a deep breath. "We escaped together and we should finish it together. If we do this media thing, we *all* do it. Side-by-side."

Esmeralda rolled her eyes. "Cue the inspirational music."

Scarlett arched a brow. "*Or* we could just cower in the shadows and let all the Good folk think we're afraid of them. That they've won and that we're hiding. You like that idea better?"

No one liked that idea better.

"Is that what a badass witch would do?" Letty pressed. "Or the rightful Prince of the Northlands? Or an insatiable bridge ogre? Or the infamous Jabberwocky?" She shook her head. "I think *those* people would fight every fucking Good folk who's trying to destroy us. Who locked us in cages, and told us were weren't pretty, and stole our magic, and abused us because we weren't powerful enough to fight back. Today we proclaim our freedom and we bring our enemies down. Today, we take *back* our happily ever afters."

Jana stared at her. "Damn... That's a good speech, girl."

"Told ya." Marrok shrugged. "She can talk people into anything. It's like a super-power."

"Oh, *fine*." Esmeralda sighed. "Hell, I'm always up for starting a war. Let's do this." She waved a hand over her face and glamored herself a makeover, complete with fresh black lipstick and a dramatic cone-shaped hat. "But if we're going on camera, I want to look my best when I tell all those Good folk to kiss my shapely green ass."

Chapter Twenty-One

It's trite but true: There are no good Bad folk.

Psychiatric case notes of Dr. Ramona Fae

It happened so fast that Scarlett wasn't sure exactly what to make of it.

The speech she gave was basically a slightly polished version of what she'd told Esmeralda. About happy endings and freedom and stopping the oppression of Bad folk. Once she got started, it was surprisingly easy to list all the reasons why Baddies deserved rights, too. It was a subject close to Scarlett's heart.

"I'm not saying it will be easy, but we *have* to change the laws in the Four Kingdoms. We have to be counted and equal and *heard*. Working together, we can achieve that. It'll take time, but we can get it done. And, in the meantime, we've made a deal with the Jabberwocky."

Behind the camera Jana had rolled her eyes, but she hadn't interfered. Letty had taken control of the family business and, even if she wasn't totally onboard with the new management initiatives that Letty had planned, Jana was still thrilled to see her granddaughter taking command and inciting riots.

"As of right now, the Enchanted Forest is a fifth kingdom." Letty had said proudly. "We're free. Bad folk and Good folk are welcomed here, but all of us have the *same exact* rights and rules. Anyone who doesn't like that can talk to the Jabberwocky's Lollypop Guild Mafia and their sledge hammers."

"They can talk to all of us." Marrok had put in from beside her.

The other members of the Tuesday share circle stood around them and they'd nodded, too.

Scarlett had smiled at them and kept going. "So far, all we have is a whole lot of land and work and ideas. If that sounds good to you, you're welcome to come join us. If you want to stay in the Four Kingdoms, that's fine, too. I'm not going to rest until *all* the lands welcome Bad folk, so you can wait it out and I'll get to you." She'd paused. "Except for the Westlands."

"Here it comes." Esmeralda had drawled.

"Because, Cinderella?" Scarlett had stepped closer to the camera, her eyes intent. "I have the glass slipper and I *know* it doesn't fit you. You have no right to that kingdom. All this time you've been lying and I can prove it." She held it up. "Guess who this *does* belong to?"

"It that thing really just *glass?*" Avenant had rolled his eyes. "Jesus, for all this trouble, you'd think it'd at least be made of diamonds."

Letty had marched towards Dru, who was sleeping in Benji's grasp. "Let's do a close-up for the folks at home, Grandma. They can see who the *actual* princess is and who's been a duplicitous bitch." She carefully lifted her sister's limp toes into her hand and slipped the shoe into place. The glass effortlessly molded to Drusilla's foot.

Perfect fit.

Jaws had dropped all over the Four Kingdoms.

"Dru is Charming's bride." Benji had murmured. "She really is."

"Damn right she is." Scarlett had flashed the camera a triumphant grin, imagining Cinderella's scream of rage. "Too bad, Cindy. The castle and tiara and the handsome prince belong to my sister. ...And we're going to take them all back."

That would have been a great and dramatic ending for her PSA. But, of course, Avenant couldn't let someone else have the last word.

"We're also going to kill Belle." He tacked on as if Scarlett had just forgotten to mention that step of the plan.

Scarlett and Marrok turned to glower at him.

"Oh for God's sake..." Esmeralda had snapped and, thanks to their subpar editing skills, that's where the video ended. Still, it was certainly good enough work to convince everyone watching that Cindy was a phony.

And that the Enchanted Forest was a real up and coming neighborhood.

From the moment their video hit the internet, people started arriving. More people than Scarlett had ever anticipated and she was an optimistic girl by nature. More than the winged monkeys could ever hope to stop. The flying apes beat a hasty retreat as they were massively outnumbered. Also, they might have realized that Cindy wouldn't be in a position to pay their salaries for much longer.

When it was safe to go back to the surface, Jana led them through a network of tunnels that brought them to a cheery glen where it was easy for the other Baddies to find them. Scarlett quickly saw that Marrok had been right. The Bad folk thought of her as their leader, now. They shook her hand and gathered around her and listed all the reasons why she was an inspiration.

But it wasn't really about *her*.

The discontent had been simmering for so long that all they needed was a spark. Someone to tell them that it was time to stop the oppression. Witches, trolls, wolves, ogres, goblins, cats, and every other species ostracized and despised for simply being different poured into the Enchanted Forest. Baddies from all over the Four Kingdoms listened to her message and... believed.

They believed that she was going to lead them.

Scarlett wasn't sure what to make of that. Hell, night was falling and she wasn't even sure where they were all going to sleep.

Unsure of what to do in a kingdom with no houses, she'd put Avenant in charge of setting up some sort of temporary shelter. He was intimidating enough that he somehow scared the new Baddies into digging up some Renaissance Faire-style tents. As per his exacting instructions they were now being set up in neat concentric circles, while he stood with his arms crossed over his chest and snapped out orders.

To ensure that Avenant didn't drive their citizens to a rebellion on the very first day, Letty put Esmeralda in charge of protecting the new arrivals from his "leadership." She'd put her grandmother and the Lollypop Guild in charge of security. And she put Benji in charge of watching Dru and of organizing some dinner for the troops. Thanks to Jana's paranoia, they had supplies in place to feed an army and plenty of blankets, but it was just the tip of the iceberg. They needed beds. And a school for the kids. And buildings with roofs. And some kind of store...

Letty needed to start making plans.

First, though, she needed to get rid of Cinderella. Her stepsister would be out for blood now, with or without her team of soaring simians. If Scarlett didn't do something to stop her, Cindy would destroy them all.

Marrok glanced down at her. "You have that look on your face, again."

"What look?"

"The same look you had right before you whacked Ramona with the chair. The 'I've-made-up-my-mind-to-do-something-crazy' look."

Scarlett sighed. The man really could read her thoughts. She took his hand and led him away from the others so they wouldn't be overheard. "I need to go to the Westlands tonight."

"No, you don't."

She wasn't sure what to make of that. "Yes, I *do*. Cinderella is going to come after us. We've bought maybe a day or two, but she'll want revenge. I just outed her to the world. She'll never take that lying down." Letty shook her head. "I have to stop her."

Charming had been kidnapped and his palace guards had done zilch to save him. No other volunteers were dashing to the front of the line, either. Apparently, Scarlett was the only one who would stand against Cindy and her army of rats.

"You're not just going to start walking towards the Westlands, Letty."

"I *have* to." She turned to meet his brooding gaze. "Why are you fighting me on this?"

"Why am I against the idea of my wife wandering into a trap? Let's start with all the sex I won't be having when you're dead and work our way up to the fact that organizing all this was *your* idea," he waved a hand around the makeshift camp, "so you need to be here and organize it. You're not leaving me with this mess."

"I'm not leaving you, at all."

"Oh, so *I'm* invited on this suicide mission?" He arched a brow. "Thanks."

She blinked. "You want me to go alone?"

"No, I don't want you to go, at all. You don't think

Cinderella will be expecting you to show up and try something crazy? She's met you, Red! She's going to have her men scouring the Westlands for you."

He was probably right. That didn't make her feel any better. "You're supposed to be on my side."

"When haven't I been on your side? *At* your side?"

"Right now!" She was hurt by his sudden change in attitude. Marrok was usually the one who pitched in and made all her plans possible. "Are you regretting becoming mixed up with this?"

"I'm in love with you, Scarlett." He said simply. "I will spend the rest of our lives beside you, getting mixed-up in crazy shit and loving every minute of it. But, I'm thinking 'the rest of our lives' should last at least a week. So, we're not going to the Westlands without some kind of strategy."

"I have a strategy: I'm going to walk into the castle and kill that bitch."

"I meant a strategy with like maps and stuff."

"Did I need a map to get us out of the WUB Club? *No.*"

"We had the element of surprise in there. Here, you announced what you plan to do all over the internet."

"That was your idea!"

"It got rid of the monkeys, didn't it?"

She nodded. "And next we'll get rid of Cinderella. Everything will be much more peaceful when she's gone. I promise."

"Around you nothing will ever will be 'peaceful,' baby." He dipped his head closer to hers, his hand coming up to caress her face. "Seriously, if you want to rescue Charming and save the kingdom, we'll do. I'd do anything for you, no matter how embarrassingly noble.

But, we need to do it *right*."

She made an aggravated sound, her defenses crumbling under his touch and annoying logic. "I guess we could setup surveillance of the castle first, if it would ease your mind."

"It really would." He kissed her. "Now, hurry up and figure out how we can pull this off without getting killed, so I can get you naked, again."

Scarlett let out a sigh. God, he was just impossible to resist when he got all flirty and gentle. "You're very hard to stay mad at."

"Tell that to my coach. I've spent weeks at a time in a cage, because he found it so simple to stay mad at me."

"I'd be glad to tell him. Right after I shoot the bastard."

Marrok chuckled and kissed the top of her hair. "God, you're adorable. I would help Cinderella keep the Westlands forever before I risked losing you."

She dropped her forehead onto his shirtfront. "Since I can't very well go anywhere without you, I don't think it'll come to that."

"Well, you *could* go. I'd just have to follow you."

"No, I couldn't." She lifted her gaze to his. "None of my ideas would work without you there to help me. We're partners. It would be pointless to even try and conquer the Westlands without you beside me." She hesitated. "Actually, it would be pointless to do anything without you beside me, Marrok."

Topaz eyes stared into hers, promising her everything. "Now would be a good time to tell me you love me." He murmured.

Letty made a face, feeling awkward. She'd never said those words to anybody before, because it had never been true before. "You already *know* I love you."

"Tell me anyway. I like the words."

Her awkwardness faded at his dazzling smile. "I love you." She said sincerely and went up on tiptoes to brush her mouth against his.

He kissed her deep. "Again." He ordered hoarsely.

"I love you." She nipped his lower lip. "I'd have bludgeoned you to death with my feelings journal long ago if I wasn't totally smitten with you, Wolf. Instead, I just documented how much you irritated me in excruciating detail."

He looked delighted. "My feelings journal is fifty-some pages of dirty limericks and conjectural sketches of your naked body. It's a real work of art."

"I'll bet."

"Hey, do you have any idea how challenging it is to rhyme 'Letty' with a new word in each poem? There's only so many times we can make love on a jetty or you shout 'I'm ready!'"

She snickered as his mouth trailed down her neck. "Just because I love you, doesn't mean I don't also hate you."

He moved to nuzzle her temple. "There was also one with you in a teddy. That was my masterpiece."

"This dress I'm wearing is the current extent of my wardrobe. Cinderella just turned everything else to ash, including the rest of my underwear. So, I don't think you'll be seeing me in a teddy anytime soon."

"God, Cindy really does need to die." He decided. "You're the brains of the outfit, Red. Go ahead and think of a plan."

"Why do you sell yourself short, even when you're just joking around?" She frowned at him. "I'm not the brains of this. You've had just as much to do with us getting this far as I have."

"What did I do?" He scoffed.

"You showed me how to disable the security cameras. How to handle Dr. White. How to get into the dungeon. How to get *out* of the dungeon. How to cut the power. How to deal with the wolves. How to do the PSA..." She shook her head. "You've saved me about fifty times, so far."

He looked bemused. "You saved *me*, Scarlett. In so many more ways than that."

"We saved each other. I told you, we're partners."

Marrok watched her for a beat, his expression going grave. "I really do love you." He finally whispered.

"Keep saying it. I like hearing the words, too." She paused meaningfully. "In fact, now would be a good time for you to propose."

He grinned. "And steal your big moment?"

"I'm not going to be the one who proposes! Why do you keep saying that?"

"Because, I'm pretty sure that *my* part of the partnership is the seducing you part." His mouth found the curve her throat, again. "*Your* part is the everything else part."

"Your part is going to be a colossal failure then, since I'm not about to sleep with you out in the open and Avenant is never going to waste one of his precious tents on us." Still, she couldn't resist tilting her head to give Marrok better access. "His royal pain-in-the-ass-ness is mad because I told him we won't help him kill Belle."

"Well, let's just kill her, so we can have some privacy and I can do Bad things to your Good little body."

"We're not killing Belle! That poor girl was

completely justified in kicking Avenant out of the Northlands and you know it. He's a tyrant. Besides, he doesn't even *want* her dead. All his whining to the contrary, Avenant just wants *her*."

"Yeah, I noticed that, too. But, I really want to rip that dress off you, so I'm willing to play along with his mania and..." Marrok's teasing trailed off, his gazed fixed on something over her shoulder. "Shit." He quickly set her away from him and straightened his clothes.

Scarlett turned and spotted her grandmother headed towards them. She had no idea why Marrok bothered to stop their make-out session for Jana. Knowing her grandmother, she would've just cheered him on. "Something wrong?"

"I told her I was going to help you with the Cinderella plot. I don't want her to think I'm trying to get you into bed, instead."

"You *are* trying to get me into bed. And it's working."

"I know, but I want your grandmother to see me as husband material. I'm supposed to be helping you plan, right now. If she doesn't think I can be a real part of this business, she'll take you away."

"Marrok," Letty moved her head, forcing him to look at her, "*no one* could take me away from you. I swear to you, I'm yours for forever after."

He let out a long breath. "I know you are." He touched her hair. "I just want to be worthy."

"You are!" She rolled her eyes when he remained visibly unconvinced. The whole conversation struck her as ridiculous. "Come *on!* You can't possibly think *I'm* too good for *you*."

"I know you're too Good for me." He intoned.

"That's..." She almost said insane. "That's *untrue*.

You are so smart and funny and charming and protective and loyal..."

"I'm handsome." The way he said it, the words weren't bragging or even prideful. They were almost like a curse. "That's all I've ever been."

"You are handsome." Letty agreed. "But that's *not* all you are. Do you think I'd sleep with someone just because he was handsome? Would I tell him I loved him? Is that all you think *I* am? Someone that shallow?"

His eyebrows drew together. "No! Of course not, Letty."

"Do you not trust me?"

"I trust you more than I trust myself."

"Then believe me when I tell you you're worrying over nothing. We're supposed to be together. You're the one who convinced me of that, remember?"

"I know, but..." He ran a hand through his hair. "I just feel like something's going to go wrong. It can't be this easy."

"You think this has been *easy?*"

"I think a whole lot of people should be keeping me away from you and nobody is. Not even you. That seems very fucked up. Nothing has *ever* gone this right for me."

"Well, my grandmother certainly isn't going to keep us apart. In fact, she's probably coming over here to talk to *you*. She likes you *waaaay* more than me."

"No." He shook his head, taking the comment seriously. "Jana and I both love you more than anything. She's trusting me with you. I have no clue why."

"Because she knows you'll die for me."

That got his attention. "Yeah." He said starkly. "I would. Without even a second thought."

Tears filled her eyes and Letty cleared her throat.

"So, when our daughter brings home her True Love, are you going to care what he looks like? Or are you going to care that he'd give his life to keep her safe? Which part seems 'all he is' to *you?*"

Silence.

"Because to *me*," Scarlett continued, "it's a lot more important that he loves her and makes her happy. My grandmother feels the same way and *that's* why she's your biggest fan." She paused. "Also, she really *is* your biggest fan. That's probably coming into play. She has your trading cards and everything. I think there's a calendar of your team down in the tunnels if..." She trailed off with a squeak as he yanked her forward.

Marrok's arms crushed Letty against his chest. His huge body curved around hers, holding tight. He didn't say anything. He didn't have to.

Scarlett leaned into his embrace. "I would die for you, too." She whispered after a long moment.

"I'll kill you if you even try it."

She snorted. "You really are a poet."

He kissed the top of her head. "You're just lucky 'Letty' doesn't rhyme with 'pain in the ass.'"

"Marrok?" Jana called, getting closer to them. "You'd better come over here. I don't like the looks of one of our new arrivals."

"See?" Letty arched a brow at him. "Told you she was looking for you and not me. *You're* teacher's pet."

He winked at her and headed over to Jana. "New guy bothering you, huh? Want me to kill him? Because, I can kill him."

"God, I like you." Jana pinched his cheek and Marrok smiled at her.

"We're not killing anyone on the very first day." Letty told them. It was sweet to see the two of them bonding, but, left to their own devices, they'd probably be scheduling public executions by nightfall. "What did this guy do to upset you, Grandma? It couldn't have been anything *too* terrible or you would've taken care of him yourself."

"That's true enough." Jana agreed. "But, he's still gonna be a probbbb-lllem." She was doing that sing-songy thing with her voice. That never boded well.

Letty sighed. "Alright, let's go *deal* with the problem, then." As they walked towards the tents, she took hold of Marrok's hand and he gave her fingers a squeeze. Whatever this "problem" was, she was sure they could...

Her thoughts skidded to a halt as she came face-to-face with one of Cinderella's rats.

Gustav stood with his arms crossed over his chest, bruises covering his body. Someone had taken his weapons, but he was still dressed in a palace guard uniform. From his stiff posture and the way his eyes were cutting around, Scarlett could tell he was terrified.

So was she.

She still had nightmares about Cinderella's henchman dragging her away.

Marrok glanced down sharply, feeling Letty freeze. "Are you alright?" His eyes slashed back over to the rat and he quickly pieced it together. "Son of a bitch. Is he one of Cinderella's pets? One of the men who arrested you?"

Scarlett nodded.

"Told you he was a problem." Jana chimed in.

Marrok muttered another curse, his hand smoothing over Scarlett's hair. "Wait here, baby." He stalked towards Gustav, his eyes going cold. "You miserable little fuck. You show up here after you put your goddamn hands on my *wife?*"

"I really like him." Jana stage whispered.

"Scarlett said we could all start over." Gustav backed up a step as Marrok drew closer. "She said all Bad folk were welcomed in the Enchanted Forest now."

"She didn't mean *you*." Marrok seized him by the front of his uniform. "What the hell are you doing here?"

"He's a spy." Jana gave an "obviously" sort of hand wave. "Cindy sent him here to infiltrate us."

"No!" Gustav's beady eyes widened. "She has no idea I even left. She'd kill me if she did."

"She'd have to wait in line."

Gustav swallowed at Marrok's threat and looked over at Scarlett. "I'm sorry for what happened at the ball. I am. But, I heard your speech and I thought that this was my chance to get away from Cinderella. You're the only one she's afraid of. I can help you stop her."

Jana glanced at Marrok. "He's lying. I hate liars."

"Me too." Marrok nodded and hefted the rat straight off the ground. "Let's go feed him to the trees."

"I can help you!" Gustav shouted again. "Please, just hear me out. I swear, I hate Cinderella more than you do! I'll do anything to see her destroyed."

Scarlett's attention stayed fixed on his battered face. "Did Cindy beat you?" She asked quietly.

"Of course she did! She's an evil, violent bitch, who keeps us as slaves. She had the other men do this because I told her it was impossible to recast the spell on Charming. It *is* impossible! Once a spell is broken, it can't be…"

"Charming remembers?" Scarlett interrupted excitedly. "He knows that the slipper is Dru's? That's why Cindy locked him up?"

"Yes! He's refusing to marry Cinderella and she's

going crazy." Gustav's tone grew more fervent. "Even if you do kill me, at least I'll die free. Her fucking hands will never touch me or force me to play any of her perverted games..." He trailed off with a shudder, his eyes dropping in shame.

Oh Jesus.

"Marrok?" Scarlett cleared her throat. "Love, let him go."

"He's lying!" Jana insisted.

"He's not lying." Scarlett had seen that exact same expression on Marrok's face when he talked about his past. She glanced over at her True Love and knew he recognized it, too.

Marrok dropped Gustav to the ground.

The rat straightened his uniform, still not looking at them. "I just want to be free." He repeated in a shaky voice. "I can't ever go back there."

Scarlett took a deep breath. "You won't." She promised. "You're safe here with us."

Gustav glanced over at her like she was an angel sent from heaven. "Really?" He whispered, his voice thick with emotion.

Jana rolled her eyes in disgust.

"Really." Scarlett said.

Marrok sighed. "Letty," he backtracked and leaned down closer to her ear, so they could speak privately, "I see what you're thinking, but *no*."

"He could've been you." Her palm came up to touch his cheek. "Marrok, how could I ever turn away someone who could've been *you?*"

"You don't have to turn him away. *I'll* do it."

"He needs our help. The whole point of this is to protect people." She slowly shook her head. "And Cinderella *does* force the rats to sleep with her. I told you there was something weird going on. She hits them and treats them like dirt and..."

"And all that's probably brainwashed them into following her every order." He interrupted. "Your grandma's right. Cindy sent him here to spy on us."

"I don't think so." Gustav looked too grateful and relieved to be faking this. He was presently trying to hug Jana. Hopefully, he'd live through it.

Marrok wasn't giving up. "You're thinking about *my* past? Well, I'm thinking about *yours*. This guy helped drag you off to the WUB Club, Letty. He sure didn't try to help *you* when *you* needed it."

"I know." She bit her bottom lip. "I can forgive him, though."

"Why would you *ever*...?"

"But, *you* were in the WUB Club. How else would we have found each other?"

Marrok's eyes narrowed at that argument and she knew she'd won. "That was a really underhanded card to play, Red."

"What can I say? I'm Bad." She shrugged. "Besides, you were just telling me that we needed more information before we invaded the Westlands. Gustav can help us."

"Are you kidding? I don't trust a damn word he says."

"He hasn't *gotten* to say anything, yet." She arched a brow. "Seriously, you're always claiming I can talk people into things. Just let me *talk* to him. You're standing right here with me. What's the worst that could happen? We can always kill him later, but we can't *un*kill him once he's dead."

Marrok made a sound of frustration that Scarlett took as another victory.

She gave him a quick kiss. "Thank you." She marched towards the rat and got straight to the point. Who knew how long she had before Marrok and/or Jana snapped. "Who's helping Cinderella with the spell on Charming? She doesn't have any powers, so she must have hired someone to do the heavy lifting. Who is it?"

"Trevelyan." Gustav said instantly. "Cinderella's working with the dragon."

Chapter Twenty-Two

Even for a crazy person, Trevelyan was crazy.
It was impossible to predict or understand him. Personally, I was glad when he escaped and we were rid of him, once and for all. The man's feelings journal was the stuff of nightmares,

Psychiatric case notes of Dr. Ramona Fae

Even on her wedding day, Cinderella was harassed.

She shoved aside the useless Baddie stylist who was doing a half-assed job on her hair and glowered at the dragon in her heart-shaped mirror. "I paid you a fortune and the spell didn't work! *That's* the bottom line here. I don't care about your idiotic excuses, I just want results. *FIX HIM!*"

Trevelyan wasn't impressed with her *completely logical* orders. The man was a disgrace to magic. "Once a spell is broken it can't be recast." Even in his human-form, his voice sounded like a dragon's, seeping out like a low rumble of thunder. "Everyone knows that."

As usual, Trevelyan wore an ankle-length trench coat with decorative flames embroidered along the bottom hem. It molded around his muscular body like a second skin. With his exotic features and long ebony hair studded with silver beads, he really was stunning.

An asshole, but stunning.

Cinderella had considered taking Trevelyan to bed, just to add some variety to her life, but he was impossible enough to deal with when he had his clothes *on*. God only knew what he'd be like naked. Besides, what if dragons mated in their animal form the way wolves did? Cinderella enjoyed some erotic pain as much as the next princess, but fucking an actual dragon might prove difficult even for her.

"A second spell *can* be done." She insisted. "You're just too chicken shit to try it."

"Your majesty, please." The troll hairdresser tried to stick some more pins into Cinderella's golden coif. "Let me just finish..."

"Get out!" Cinderella surged to her feet and all but threw the hideous woman from the room. She was so sick of Bad folk disrespecting her. She slammed the door shut and angrily shook out her golden curls in a fit of spite.

Where the hell was Gustav? He'd been missing since the other mice had punished him with that well-deserved beating. That had been last night, though! That pussy should've been back on his feet and ready to serve her, again. Why did she have to do *everything* herself?

Trevelyan's vivid green gaze stayed fixed on her. "If I do anything else to Charming, it will probably turn his brain to scrambled eggs."

"Like he's such a fucking rocket scientist, now?" Cinderella retorted. "I'll take my chances."

"I won't."

Cinderella hurled a hairbrush at the dragon's stupid head. "You're so goddamn *useless!*" He didn't even bother to duck as the brush sailed passed his skull. That only made her angrier. "What am I supposed to do, huh? Marry that asshole from his cell in the dungeon? My dress will get *filthy!* Did you even think about that?"

"A bigger problem will be getting him to say 'I do' when the only word he seems to be screaming is 'Drusilla.'"

"Bastard." She wasn't sure if that was directed at

Charming or Trevelyan, because it certainly applied to them both. "You told me it was *Scarlett* in that garden. If I'd known it was Dru, I could've broken her weeks ago."

"I didn't tell you it was Scarlett. I didn't even know their names. You smuggled me into the castle, because you knew that shoe wouldn't fit you, and I tailed Charming until I saw him put it on his destined bride." He arched a brow. "I described it all to you and *you're* the one who said it must have been Scarlett."

"I thought it was!" Why did everyone want to blame Cinderella for their own failings? "You said it was a homely redhead and naturally I thought of Scarlett. Dru's such a little *nothing*. How could I even guess Charming would want her?"

"Well, either way, I can't respell him."

"If you're so concerned about Charming, maybe you should consider that there are worse things for him than spending the rest of his life as a drooling idiot."

"Like marrying you?"

"Like *making* him marry me." She snarled. "Because, he's *going* to be my beloved groom if I have to break every bone in his body to get him down the aisle." She shook her head in disgust. "This is all your fault. Charming's been fighting me this whole time, because he still subconsciously remembers Dru. You should have cast the spell *before* he slept with her. The True Love bond wouldn't have been so indelible."

"And miss the little porn show they put on? Where's the fun in that?"

"You did it just to screw me over!" Cinderella raged. "You *knew* he'd sense I wasn't his True Love. You *deliberately* made it even harder for me to convince him, by letting Dru touch him. Admit it!"

"Yeah, well, I don't like you."

"Then why the hell are you here!"

He lifted a shoulder in a shrug. "Your check cleared."

There *had* to be more to it than that. He wanted something. Otherwise he would've just ignored her summons, like he had the dozens of other times she called. From the second he'd unexpectedly shown up this morning, she'd felt Trevelyan's restless energy.

Like he was... waiting.

He kept talking, ignoring her suspicious frown. "Look, my point is, I know which girl had that glass slipper on, even if I wasn't sure on her name. Trust me. I saw a lot of her in that garden. Charming isn't after Scarlett. He wants Dru."

"Drusilla is *nothing*." Cinderella reiterated. "Less than nothing. The flies on the crap of nothing. So is Charming. They'd *never* get together if it wasn't for Letty. *She's* the one who's trying to bring me down. *She's* the one I have to worry about."

"Scarlett interests me." He said softly. "I'll confess, I was satisfied being the only inmate to have broken out of the WUB Club. The distinction had a certain cachet. But, now that my record is tied, I find I have a lot of questions on how she pulled it off. No one understands the difficulties of that place better than I do. How the hell did she even get across the Lake of Forgetting?"

Cinderella made a face. "She stole a boat."

"A boat?" His eyebrows climbed. "That's it? That actually *worked*?"

"Disgusting, isn't it? I'll see everyone in that hospital dead, I swear to Jesus. Incompetent morons."

"A boat." He still seemed amazed. "I never thought of that. Why didn't I think of that? It's so..."

"Stupid? Childish? *Evil?!*"

His mouth curved. "Clever."

Cinderella didn't appreciate the new gleam in his eyes. "She's not *clever*, she's a duplicitous bitch. You saw her traitorous internet video, inciting my citizens to turn against me."

"I saw it. For a clever girl, it doesn't make much sense. No one with a brain would buy any of that sentimental bullshit about justice and sharing." Trevelyan snorted. "I'll give her the benefit of the doubt, though. Maybe she's planning to lure other Baddies to the Enchanted Forest so she can rob 'em."

Cinderella's lips pressed together. "She's planning to ruin my wedding. *That's* what she's doing."

"Well, you have mice all over the Westlands, poised to execute her if she shows her face." He paused. "A face that isn't *so* ugly for an ugly stepsister, now that I think about it."

"She's a hideous monster!"

"The wolf doesn't think so." Trevelyan's tone changed. "Pretty clear from that video that he'll be with her if she shows up and Marrok isn't a man you want to cross. My guess is you're gonna have one hell of a reception on your hands."

Cinderella glanced over at him thoughtfully. Did he and the wolf have some kind of history? Maybe that was the dragon's game. Maybe he was trying to get hired on as an assassin.

She tested the waters, not wanting to appear too eager, even though she was desperate. "If you refuse to cast another spell on Charming, the least you can do is stay and help me carry out the wedding, then. I might just need the extra protection from party-crashers."

"I want a bonus, if I'm the bouncer."

"Sure." After all, Charming's royal bank accounts were about to become joint, thanks to the Westlands' community property laws. "Kill Letty and anyone else who gets in my way, and you'll have more gold than you can carry."

"I have something else in mind." He said softly. "The woman. She really… interests me."

"Scarlett?" What the hell was going on that every hot guy in the Four Kingdoms wanted an ugly stepsister? First Marrok and now Trevelyan?! The whole world was in chaos! "Fine. Help me and you can do whatever you want with her." Cinderella promised. "Rape her, torture her, question her… I don't care. She's all yours."

"Good. I've been waiting for her to show up for a long time."

God, it went against all the laws of nature that someone as beautiful as Trevelyan would desire *Letty*. Wasn't it enough that she already tricked Marrok into panting after her? Now Scarlett had *two* gorgeous men, while Cinderella's loser fiancé plotted to leave her at the altar! Hopefully, Trevelyan really did mate in dragon-form. It would serve her stepsister right.

"Well, you can't keep her for long." Cinderella warned. "She has to die or she'll just keep causing problems."

"I just need her long enough to destroy Marrok."

Ah-hah! It *was* about the wolf. "What did he do to piss you off?"

"Marrok chose to stay in that fucking prison rather than help me. He *forced* me to touch that bitch Snow White in order to get out of there." The dragon's voice turned venomous. "And now --after all his bullshit-- *now* he chooses to escape. That's a betrayal."

"Not to defend him, but Scarlett can talk people

into anything. He probably didn't have a choice." It would be a shame to see someone as pretty as Marrok die for Scarlett's crimes.

"Oh, he had a choice. And he chose disloyalty over friendship. Now, *I* choose to take away the only person he loves. I promised him he'd regret screwing me over and he's about to know *exactly* what I meant."

"You believe that crap about Scarlett being his True Love?" Cinderella snorted. "I don't. I figure she's using a spell on him."

"Oh, I believe it. For five goddamn years, I've waited for an opportunity to get back at the bastard. Then today, he goes on the web and posts a video starring the one thing he can't live without." Trevelyan gave a cold smile. "He'd always talk about finding his True Love. He was *sure* that she was out there. I knew all I had to do was wait and he'd reveal her to me."

Yeah... It was never wise to make an enemy of a dragon. They had magical powers, delicate egos and long memories.

Cinderella rolled her eyes. "...So you're going to kill Letty, then?" She summarized. That was all that really mattered and Trevelyan looked ready to list a thousand more grievances he'd stored up against Marrok.

"Eventually."

"Yeah. Fine. Have fun with her first. I don't give a shit. Just so tomorrow dawns with Scarlett dead and me wearing my crown, I'll be happy."

He smirked. "And shouldn't every bride be happy on her wedding day?"

Chapter Twenty-Three

> Today in group, we tried a team building exercise.
> There were three fatalities.
>
> *Psychiatric case notes of Dr. Ramona Fae*

Marrok shifted the duffle bag full of weapons he'd gathered from Jana's vast arsenal and glowered up at Charming's ridiculous blue castle. "I hate this plan."

"So do I." Esmeralda agreed. "We just broke out of an impossible-to-break-out-of fortress and now we're breaking *into* an impossible-to-break-*into*-fortress." She shook her head. "What's wrong with this picture?"

"At least you two have nowhere better to go." Avenant scoffed. "I should be halfway to reclaiming my throne from that fucking usurper, by now."

"Or just halfway to *fucking* the usurper, by now." Esmeralda taunted. "Admit it. You're *totally* crushing on the librarian." She snickered when he sent her a look of frozen death. "Oh don't be mad. I think it's sweet. You can bring Belle some roses... right before she has you locked up, again."

"I *told* you, I'm going to kill the woman."

"Before or after you beg her for a date?"

"Both of you be quiet." Scarlett hissed. "Tomorrow, we can work on convincing Avenant's True Love not to arrest him on sight. Right now we need to concentrate on Charming."

"That usurper is *not* my...!"

"Shhh!" Scarlett ordered right over Avenant's protest. "Now, does everyone understand the plan?"

"The plan I hate, you mean?" Marrok arched a brow at her. "Yeah, I got all the stupid, risky details of it screaming in my head like a funeral dirge, as a matter of fact."

He'd been trying to talk her out of this disastrous idea all night. Once Gustav had showed up, Scarlett's creative energies had been unleashed, though. Nothing was going to talk her out of this, short of chaining her up.

Which Marrok had actually considered.

Christ, if Trevelyan was involved in this, it was going to turn into a bloodbath. What was the dragon up to? Marrok couldn't get their last meeting out of his head. The dwarf guards pulling the dragon away, while he shouted threats. Swearing that he'd have revenge for Marrok's "betrayal." Promising to take away everything that Marrok loved.

"You two work on creating the distractions out here." Scarlett told Avenant and Esmeralda, just in case they'd forgotten their assigned roles. Which, honestly, was a good guess, knowing them. "Start in exactly ten minutes. Make sure whatever you do is big enough to draw the guards' attention."

Although they were bickering, annoying, idiots, even Marrok was a tiny bit moved at how readily Avenant and Ez agreed to come to the Westlands and lend a hand. Being part of the Tuesday share circle was like being a part of a screwed-up, criminally-inclined family. Even when they didn't like you, they were still there to help you blow shit up.

It was touching.

The four of them were huddled in the royal garden of the Westlands, hidden by some oh-so-special singing fountain, waiting for Gustav to return. The rat had gotten them this far, but while he went to clear the next leg of their journey, he'd left them hiding in the most aggravating spot in the Four Kingdoms. That did nothing to improve Marrok's opinion of the guy.

The singing fountain wouldn't shut-up.

Show tunes, pop hits, opera... It just. kept. singing. If Marrok owned this ugly castle, he would've torn the damn thing out and put up a basketball court. Was there no place else Gustav could've stashed them?

"Meanwhile, Marrok and I will find Charming." Scarlett continued. "I know the layout of the castle and Gustav's making sure the guards don't bother us as we sneak in. We'll go through the servants' entrance, so we should be able to..."

"What about the dragon?" Marrok interrupted. Letty wasn't getting how dangerous it was to have Trevelyan around. "What are we going to do if a fire-breathing monster with unmatched magical powers attacks?"

Scarlett grinned. "You're going to stop him." She said with total confidence.

Marrok rolled his eyes. "I hate this plan."

"It's going to work." She insisted.

Not unless he did something insane. One-on-one, there was no fucking chance Marrok was going to be able to stop a dragon. It was sweet that Scarlett thought he could do it, but it was literally impossible. If it came down to a fight, there was just one option: Letty had to run. It was the only way either one of them would survive. He could just imagine how well she'd take that news, though, so he wasn't sharing it until he absolutely had to.

Marrok sighed. "I'm just saying, if I die before I get to live out my 'you and vanilla pudding' fantasies, I'm going to be pissed."

"Honestly, Wolf." She sent him a look of mock

disapproval. "Do I seem like a *vanilla* girl to you? Think big. Think *strawberry*."

Just like that, the game was over.

Marrok's mouth curved in total, desperate love and he knew that Letty had won. There was no way he was going to be able to hold out for her to propose. He'd waited as long as he could. Marrok was opening his mouth to ask her to please-for-the-love-of-God marry him, when Gustav came scampering back over.

"Okay." The rat was out of breath as he crouched down beside them. He had to raise his voice to be heard over the serenading water. "I sent the guards at the door away. They still think I'm in charge, so they listened to me just like the others." He'd been ordering guards out of their path all morning. "You have to hurry and get in there, though. Charming's not in the dungeon, anymore. Cinderella had him dragged upstairs for the wedding."

"If this is a trap, I will kill you." Marrok promised him, refocusing on this terrible plan. "And if I'm dead and I can't kill you, *they'll* kill you." He jerked a thumb at Avenant and Esmeralda.

"I can kill him, now." Avenant volunteered.

"Nobody's killing Gustav." Scarlett must have said that fifty times so far. She smiled at the rat. "Good job. Go back to the Enchanted Forest and stay safe, alright? And thank you."

"Thank *you*." He gazed at her in adoration. "You've saved my life."

Marrok would've mocked the rat's gushing, but he tended to agree with it.

"Nonsense. You saved yourself." Letty patted Gustav's hand and headed for the side of the castle. The girl wouldn't rest until she'd saved everyone.

Marrok followed her, grateful just to get away

from the caterwauling fountain. "Cinderella really sings all the time?"

"Yep."

"No wonder you hate her."

"It's aggravating, right?" Scarlett glanced back at the loud water feature with a frown. "I have no idea where that thing even came from, but, if it were my castle, I'd get rid of it."

"We really do think alike." Marrok caught hold of her hand. "Listen, when we get in there, you stay right beside me, alright?"

"Where else would I be?"

The two of them quickly reached the base of one of the castle's soaring turrets. Charming's ancestors had apparently all been six year old girls. They'd designed the entire Westlands to be full of flowers and rainbows. Everywhere, in every direction, there was nothing but neatly manicured gardens and identical cottages. All the manufactured perfection was topped off by the stupid palace. The whole fanciful structure was a nightmare of pastel colors and carved cherubs.

"So you grew up here?" Marrok whispered as they made their way through the arched door of the servants' entrance and into a long corridor. Since most of the staff was Baddies, no one had put much effort into making this part of the castle as pretty as the outside. Marrok found the lack of frolicking dolphin statues a welcomed change.

"I grew up in the village. But, my stepfather was an ambassador to the royal court, so I spent a lot of time running around this place with Charming and Dru."

"And Cinderella?"

"No, she liked to spend her time shoplifting, scrubbing floors, and strong-arming everyone to vote for her for homecoming queen." Scarlett made a face. "I still say she looked fat in that dress."

"Have I ever told you it *completely* turns me on when you're bitchy?"

She slanted him a grin. "And I've noticed you get turned on *a lot*. What does that say about us?"

"It says we were made for each other." When they reached the end of the hall, Marrok put an arm up so she'd stop. He peered around the corner and saw the whole place was teeming with servants heading up and down a staircase.

"We have to go that way." Scarlett whispered. "If Gustav is right and Cinderella's preparing Charming for the slaughter, she'll take him to the throne room. It's the gaudiest spot in the palace. Perfect for her gaudy wedding. Those stairs are the only way up there."

"Wonderful." He considered their options. "Are you sure we can't just rescue Charming tomorrow?"

"He won't live to see tomorrow." Letty said flatly. "That's why the servants are rushing around. Cindy's prepping for the reception and the execution to follow. Trust me. She'll chop his head off the second that ring is on her finger."

Shit.

Marrok sighed. "Serious question: Will the Westlands care if she decapitates their prince?"

"Of course they'll care, but how can they stop her? Cinderella's rats have overthrown the guards and everyone else is cowering in their houses for fear of being branded traitors."

"Not *everyone* else. Just the Good folk. The servants are still here." He gestured towards the stairs. "Baddies are all over the castle, because no way is a princess painting her own fingernails." He arched a brow.

"So, the question is, do the Bad folk of the Westlands think Charming is worth saving or will they let him die?"

Scarlett chewed her bottom lip. "Charming works with me to improve villains' rights and he's been employing some of these people for years... But, I don't know if they'll risk themselves to help him."

"Well, *I* know we're not going to be able to avoid every Bad folk in this palace. Even with Gustav calling off most of the rats, we'll be spotted by someone. So, the 'sneaking' part of the plan is over."

"So what do we do?"

"So we don't sneak." He met her eyes. "If we can't be sure the Baddies will side with Charming, I'm pretty damn sure they'll side with *you*."

***

"I hate this plan." Scarlett did her best to appear outwardly calm, but her heart was racing. "Everyone's staring at me."

"That's the point." Marrok's fingers stayed locked around hers as they walked side-by-side down the middle of the hall. "Just keep moving and everything will be fine."

She tried to focus on the stairs, but all she saw were the wide eyes of the servants they passed. People froze in their tracks at the sight of them.

This was never going to work.

"Marrok, we have to get out of here. Someone's going to raise the alarm and we're going to get caught and shipped back to the WUB Club. I know it."

"Baby, Good folk would be too afraid to let you back in there. The next riot would be seen from space." He gave her palm a reassuring squeeze. "Look around."

"I am, but..."

"Scarlett, *really* look around. These people don't want to turn you in. They're on *our* side."

She blinked and glanced around with new eyes. This time, she noticed that all the hairdressers and maids, seamstresses and footmen were... smiling at her. No one was rushing to call for Cinderella or report the break in. Instead, they looked thrilled. Several people actually reached out to pat her shoulder in greeting as she passed by.

Clearly, Cinderella hadn't endeared herself to the Bad folk of the castle.

"Miss Scarlett." Antonio, the palace baker, beamed at her. "Thank God! You've come to save our prince." His fuzzy green face reflected staggering relief. "Cinderella had him dragged upstairs, screaming that they'd either be having a wedding or his funeral. We've been watching the ceremony on TV and it's like a horrible nightmare. You have to stop her!"

Letty gave the tree ogre a reassuring smile. "Marrok and I have it all under control." She headed up the stairs. If her confidence still wasn't a hundred percent, at least she was doing a better job of faking it. Besides, so many people were counting on her to fix this that she really didn't have much of a choice but to succeed. "Don't worry. We're about to cause some trouble."

Marrok's mouth quirked. "We should make that our new family motto, Red. Seems everywhere we go we start something fun."

"You have some seriously bizarre definitions of fun."

Scarlett led the way towards the throne room. All around them the trappings of the Westlands' wealth glinted and shone. Marble pillars lining the halls. Gold leaf shining on every door knob. Waterfalls of crystal dangling from the chandeliers.

Marrok arched a brow as they passed a twenty foot tall portrait of Charming posing beside his favorite horse. "Nice place Dru's going to marry into."

She snorted. "You wouldn't think so if you'd ever tried to sit and watch TV here. It's impossible to find a relaxing piece of furniture." She looked around and made a face. "I would never live someplace specifically designed to make people feel uncomfortable."

"Does that mean you won't be building me a castle in our new kingdom?" He pouted. "Because, your grandmother said I could be prince of the Enchanted Forest. She's going to steal me a crown and everything. We have it all planned."

Scarlett rolled her eyes. "The two of you should be kept far apart."

"Oh, don't be jealous. You know you're my princess, baby."

"There aren't going to *be* princes and princesses in our kingdom. We're about equality."

"Did we vote on that? I don't remember voting on that."

She refused to be amused by his teasing. "Would you please concentrate on saving your soon-to-be brother-in-law?"

"I'm a multi-tasker. You should know that by now." Still, Marrok unzipped the duffle bag slung around his shoulder and began skillfully sorting through the weapons. "And let's not call Charming 'my' anything, okay? I still don't like the guy."

"You've never even met him."

"Yeah, but I'm holding a grudge that you were

engaged to him."

"I was never *really* engaged to him, though."

"Turns out I'm unreasonable and don't give a shit about that part. In fact, I *also* blame him for the fact I spent the past six weeks tortured with your lie about that damn glass slipper."

"I didn't technically lie. It was more like an omission..." Scarlett trailed off with a frown as Marrok dug what looked like a glass vial from his bag and shoved it into the pocket of his cargo pants. "Do I even want to know what that is?"

"Probably not." He looped a military-style gun around his torso and hesitated. "I need you to promise me something."

"Of course. Anything."

"If you see Trevelyan start to turn into his dragon-form, you *run*. Got it?"

"Absolutely not." She made a scoffing sound. "Have you gone crazy for real? I'm not about to run away and leave you..."

He cut her off. "Baby, you *have* to run. If you trust me to stop him, then you need to get out of the way first."

That didn't sound good. Her eyes narrowed. "What aren't you telling me?"

He gave her an innocent look. "What do you mean?"

"I can see on your face that you're hiding something. What is it?"

Marrok studied her, apparently weighing his options. "Have you ever seen a dragon?"

"No. Why?"

"They're... big."

"How big?"

"Oh, pretty big."

"*How big?*"

He sighed. "About fifteen feet. Give or take."

Scarlett stared at him.

Marrok arched a brow at her. "So, that's why you listen to me and *run*, alright?"

"Oh my God." She gave her head a clearing shake. "Okay, wait. Time out." She stopped walking and held up her palms in a T-shape. "Fifteen *feet?*" Her voice went shrill. "You can't fight a fifteen foot long dragon, Marrok! There's no way my plan is going to work without you dying!"

"I told you I hated this idea. Usually, you come up with much better ones."

"You didn't tell me *why* you hated it, you idiot!" She gave his arm a frustrated whack. "We're not doing this. Let's get out of here, before anyone else sees us."

"Gustav said the wedding is already starting, though."

"Do you think I give a shit about that wedding, right now?" Scarlett seized him by the elbow and tried to herd him back downstairs. "Move it."

"Letty, hang on. If we just change a couple of details, this can all still work."

...And that's when Esmeralda and Avenant started setting off their very loud distractions.

"Oh no!" Scarlett sent a frustrated look towards the windows. "They're early."

"*Again.*" Marrok scowled. "Fuck. We should stop including them on these missions if they can't figure out how to tell time."

Scarlett's mind buzzed with frantic ideas for escape. There was no way anyone in the Westlands was going to miss the gigantic fire blazing where their courthouse once stood. Two seconds later the "Good folk only" country club went up in flames, followed by the statue of Cinderella that had just been erected in the town square.

The explosions *had* been part of the plan. They were meant to draw attention away from the palace, but that was *before* Letty realized they needed to cancel this whole idea. They'd just alerted Cinderella to their presence and they were too close to the throne room to hide for long. How were they going to get out of the kingdom without a confrontation? A confrontation they couldn't *possibly* win.

This was a disaster!

"Red?" Marrok's voice went serious as he saw her panicking. "We can't turn back. This has to happen *now*. I will take care of Trevelyan. I promise."

"All fifteen feet of him?!"

"I wouldn't have brought you in here if I didn't know we could do this, baby. All you have to do is *stay away from the dragon*." Topaz eyes burned into hers. "Trust me."

She swore under her breath. "I *do* trust you, but I'm not going to just let you face him all by yourself. I'm your True Love, damn it! It's my job to save you from your own suicidal craziness."

He slowly grinned. "Remember that because…"

Whatever he'd planned to tell her was cut off by Cinderella's armed rats bursting out of the throne room and heading straight for them.

Chapter Twenty-Four

Sometimes I wonder why I counsel these patients to work together. I shudder to think what would befall this world if all the Bad folk were ever smart enough to organize themselves.

Psychiatric case notes of Dr. Ramona Fae

"Scarlett!" Cinderella smiled cheerily as her men dragged Letty and Marrok across the parquet floor of the throne room. "Welcome to my wedding. I *soooo* hoped you'd be here to witness my special day."

As much as Scarlett detested the woman, even she had to admit that her stepsister made a beautiful bride. Cindy was decked out in a four foot wide wedding dress, studded with enough pearls to choke every oyster in the sea. Her blonde curls fell in perfect ringlets, covered with a nearly transparent lace veil. Perched on the tippity top sat the diamond tiara of the Westlands. Hundreds of twinkling diamonds glinted mockingly as the rats hustled Scarlett and Marrok forward.

Charming's eyes lit up like he'd been rescued as soon as he saw them. Apparently, he missed the fact that they were all screwed. "Letty, how's Dru?"

He tried to move closer, but he was tied to one of the room's countless marble pillars. A metal dog collar and chain gave him about two feet of slack, which was just enough for him to reach the golden altar beneath a flower covered trellis.

The whole room was decorated in various shades of pink, with about two hundred empty chairs arranged in neat rows. Not many guests wanted to show up to a wedding that was really a hostage situation. Along the far wall, a huge banquet was set up, including a half dozen ice sculpture swans and an incredibly lovely wedding cake. It stood twelve tiers high, a masterpiece of sugar flowers and lattice work.

Bizarrely, though, it looked like someone had punched a hole in the intricate decorations, straight through to the chocolate of the fifth layer. The frosting on Cinderella's fist sort of limited the assault suspects. Her stepsister was mad at a *cake,* but *Letty* was the one who'd been committed. Unbelievable.

"Dru's fine." Letty assured Charming, trying to sound calm. "Or she will be when you're together, again."

"They'll have to be reunited in whatever hell Bad folk are sent to, because none of you will ever live long enough to see it happen here." Cinderella laughed. "God, this just couldn't have worked out any better." She glanced up at the man standing next to her. "Looks like I didn't need you after all, Trevelyan. You're lucky I'm a princess of my word. Letty is all yours."

Scarlett's eyes traveled over to the dragon and she swallowed. Even in his human-form, the man looked formidable. Black hair fell to his waist, framing the deep angles of his exotic face.

His green gaze found hers and held it. "Hello Scarlett. I've been waiting for you."

Marrok's jaw ticked. "What the hell is this about, Trev?"

"It's about you betraying me." Trevelyan arched a brow his attention still on Letty as he answered. "Did you think I'd just forget about that, Wolf? I told you I'd have my revenge." He glided closer. "And for a debt this high, you can only pay with your most valuable possession."

Letty tried to shift away as he lifted a hand to caress her hair. The feel of his fingers made her cringe.

It took eight rats to hold Marrok back despite the magic inhibiting restraints they'd put on his wrists. Even the guards holding Scarlett released her to rush into the fray. "You son of a *bitch*. You touch my wife and I'll see you fucking dead! I swear to God."

Trevelyan ignored that. "At first, I wondered what you saw in an ugly stepsister." He mused. "But, soon I saw it, too. The spark she has." His thumb traced down her cheek. "You look in her eyes and you see nothing but life and purity and *ideas*." He leaned closer to her and inhaled deeply. "I bet she tastes like Goodness is always supposed to, but never does."

Scarlett was afraid to even look in Marrok's direction for fear of what he might do if he saw how scared she was.

"Can we cut down on the creepiness?" Cinderella requested. "It's wrecking my wedding." She waved a hand towards the altar. One of the rats was acting as officiant, a gun in one hand and book of wedding prayers in the other. "Jack, skip to the 'I do' part."

He obediently flipped ahead in the vows. "Do you, Charming, underserving prince of the Westlands, take the regal and glorious Cinderella as your rightful princess and…?"

"Never!" Charming cried, cutting him off. "You might as well behead me right here, because I'll never marry anyone but my True Love. Drusilla, wherever you are, I am yours!" He shouted the last part at the rat videographer and Scarlett realized that Cinderella really was broadcasting this whole wedding over the news.

Her eyes narrowed thoughtfully.

Cinderella whacked the back of Charming's skull. "What was that? I didn't quite hear you."

"I said... Hey!" His words ended in a shout as the rats wrestled him to the ground and shoved a gag in his mouth.

"I think he said 'yes.'" Cinderella decided as Charming thrashed around on the floor. "See? That was definitely a nod."

Charming emphatically shook his head.

"None of this is legal." Scarlett looked at the TV camera. "Cindy is taking over this kingdom by force. Once she's done here, she'll be coming after the others. She'll be coming after *all* of you."

"Every other kingdom in this land would be *thrilled* to have me as their princess!" Cinderella seethed. "I'm the only one worthy of a crown." She looked back to Jack. "Continue with the service!"

"Do you Cinderella, benevolent and magnificent princess of our dreams, take this undeserving wretch to be your doting husband and slave?"

Cinderella smiled sweetly. "Until death do us part." She promised and daintily dabbed at her eye with a pink handkerchief.

Trevelyan went back to taunting Marrok. "Did you know your woman was Good before you claimed her? You must have. Even I can see it. How does it feel to fuck a Good folk just because you *want* to?" He paused for a beat. "Wait. Don't tell me. I want to be surprised when I try her for myself."

"Oh, Letty's full of surprises."

Scarlett's gaze cut over to Marrok, picking up on his tone. Golden eyes met hers and she knew exactly what he wanted her to do. For whatever reason, Marrok wanted her to piss off Trevelyan and she was happy to oblige.

She really could read the man's mind.

"I don't believe that anyone is all Good or all Bad." She told Trevelyan in a serious tone. "It's that kind of thinking that keeps all of us trapped."

"No, it's *me* who's keeping you trapped." Cinderella retorted. "And once you're gone, I'm going to see the rest of the cowering Bad folk in the Enchanted Forest trapped, too. Trapped in prisons far away from here, where their ugly faces and wicked schemes and Bad smells can't bother me *ever* again! They can rot there, along with every other bastard in this kingdom who's stood against me."

Letty kept her voice loud enough so the audience at home could easily hear. "Well that proves my point, doesn't it? Good and Bad folk are all on your hit list. We're not so different after all." She kept her attention on the camera. "Anyone who doesn't want to be ruled over by a temperamental beauty queen --anyone who thinks we're better than that-- should probably do something about it."

Trevelyan rolled his eyes. "You're kinda preachy, aren't you?" He took hold of her arm. "No matter. We can probably find *something* to do with your mouth."

"*Stop talking through my beautiful ceremony!*" Cinderella shrieked.

Everyone ignored that.

Letty wrenched back against the dragon's hold. "Do you think I'll *ever* submit to you?"

"Absolutely you will. Everything you did for Marrok, you'll do for me. Count on it." He reached for her again.

Scarlett's foot slammed into his leg. The kick couldn't have hurt him *that* much. He topped her by at least ten inches. But his expression still darkened at her resistance. She felt a surge of satisfaction at that.

Marrok gave a derisive snort as Trevelyan swore in pain. "The woman is half your size and has her wrists tied. How can you possibly be losing?"

"Shut up!" Trevelyan bellowed. He stabbed a finger at Marrok and Scarlett could see a green mist begin to move along his skin. The dragon was coming out. "Every night, locked in that cell, I'd listen to you talk about your True Love. About how you would give *anything* for her. About how she would save you."

"She will."

"She *won't*." Trevelyan hissed. "That's what I'm about to prove. *Nothing* is going to save you, Marrok. After what you did to me, you don't deserve to be saved."

"I didn't do a damn thing to you." Marrok shot back. "I just knew killing a hundred people was a bad idea. Seems like that would be pretty fucking obvious to anybody with a brain in his head."

"Everyone pay attention to *me!*" Cinderella shouted.

No one did.

"You didn't have my back." The angrier Trevelyan got, the heavier the transformative smoke grew around his form and the less attention he paid to Scarlett. His body got bigger by the second. It elongated, becoming larger and eerily dragon-shaped. "I had to sleep with that bitch Dr. White, because *you* wouldn't help me get out of there. Do you know how degrading that was for a dragon?"

"I'm about to have you all killed!" Cinderella screamed. "The canapés will be ruined if I don't get this damn wedding over with soon. Is that what you want? To spoil my reception?!"

"You slept with Snow White because you *wanted* to, Trev." Marrok retorted, clearly not giving a damn about the temperature of the hors d'oeuvres. "Letty and I managed to escape without climbing into her bed." He shrugged with the same taunting grace that had made Scarlett want to punch him a thousand times in share circle. "Or maybe we're just smarter than you."

"Bastard." The furious word was accompanied by a drift of smoke from between Trevelyan's lips. It could only be a precursor to fire. "We'll see how funny you are when you're stripped of the one thing that's ever given you hope." He was fully a dragon now. His huge body loomed over Scarlett, his clawed hands reaching for her.

She quickly backed away from him, her eyes finding Marrok's.

If you see Trevelyan start to turn into his dragon-form, you run.

Damn it. Letty had no idea why he'd told her that earlier or what he was up to, but she trusted him. Marrok had backed plenty of her ideas. Whatever his plan was, she was going with it.

Scarlett took off running.

"Stop her!" Cinderella screamed.

Trevelyan gave a harsh laugh, watching as Letty raced down the aisle between the empty folding chairs. "Where do you think you can go that I won't catch you, woman? No place is safe from..."

Marrok moved. The rats stumbled back as he shook them off and surged forward. He must have been sandbagging his struggles earlier to draw them away from Letty, because he had no problem throwing them all aside. Marrok drove his weight into the shifting mist of Trevelyan's midsection, sending them to the floor. Trevelyan gave a roar of outrage.

"Jesus, the wolf really is crazy." Cinderella declared.

For once, Letty almost agreed with her. Nobody sane would tackle a dragon.

She reached the door and anxiously turned back to watch the fight, trying to decide what to do. Trusting Marrok was one thing, but no way was she going to stand by and watch him slaughtered. Fifteen feet of enraged monster was too much for anyone to face alone.

Sure enough, Trevelyan was getting the upper hand. He was too big. Marrok couldn't even turn into his wolf-self because of the magic inhibiting bindings on his wrists. He was tied-up and helpless. There was no way he could win against a gigantic dragon who hated him.

Scarlett started back towards the men, her heart pounding in her throat. "Marrok!"

"I should have killed you years ago!" Trevelyan had his hands around Marrok's neck. "Die knowing I'll be finishing off your woman as soon as I'm done with you. You've lost *everything* and there's nothing you can do about it, Wolf!"

Marrok's gaze locked on Trevelyan's. "If you think that, you haven't met my True Love."

Scarlett saw a flash of something in his palm and she realized it was the weird vial he'd put in his pocket earlier. The rats had taken their guns, but they hadn't noticed that little tube. She heard the crack of glass against the wooden floor. What the hell was Marrok...?

Whoosh!

A cloud of purple smoke enveloped both men, quickly spreading backward to cover the rats as well. Scarlett's eyes widened. It was the same mystical fog that the WUB Club used. The same mystical fog that had knocked Dru out. The same mystical fog that put people into goddamn comas.

...And Marrok had just let it loose.

That was why he'd made her promise to run. That was why he'd drawn Trevelyan's attention by pissing him off. Marrok must've gotten some portable version of the purple smoke from her grandmother's weapon cachet and he hadn't wanted Letty to be hit with it, too. He'd been protecting her. Which meant, this had been his plan to beat the dragon all along.

No wonder the idiot didn't tell her about his idea. She never would have agreed to anything so dangerous!

Scarlett gave a panicked cry as Marrok collapsed. Trevelyan toppled over beside him, his body shifting back into human-form. The rats were falling, too. The gas was doing what Rumpelstiltskin had always insisted it would do and flattening everyone in its path. Within seconds, Cinderella, Jack, Charming, and Letty were the only ones left conscious in the entire room. Even that small dose of purple smoke had knocked out everyone else.

Letty's whole world stopped as she gaped at Marrok's motionless form. He wasn't moving. He *couldn't* move. He was trapped in magical sleep.

"*Marrok!*"

"Great." Cinderella threw up her hands in frustration. "There go our witnesses." She looked over at Jack. "Can we finish the ceremony without witnesses?"

"It's your kingdom now, highness. We can do whatever you decree."

Cinderella beamed. "Well, *finally* the world makes sense, then. Keep going with the vows."

Scarlett ignored that inanity. She raced forward, all her attention on Marrok. The concentrated burst of purple smoke was dissipating quickly, which was fortunate since she wasn't thinking clearly enough to wait.

"Marrok?" She collapsed to her knees beside him. "What kind of kamikaze bullshit was that?! *Huh?!*" Scarlett stared down at his still face and tried to breathe. "Don't do this to me! When you said you'd die for me, it was supposed to be metaphorical! Open your eyes. *Please* open your eyes." She shook his shoulder trying to rouse him. "*Marrok.*"

He had to wake-up. She couldn't survive without him. He was her True Love.

Scarlett froze.

Wait... *He was her True Love*.

Letty could've cried as relief flooded her system. She could fix this. The purple smoke wasn't permanent. It could be cured with True Love's kiss! Suddenly, Marrok's plan didn't seem quite so suicidally stupid, after all. He'd set this up because he'd known she could awaken him again.

She leaned over, her mouth finding his.

This had to work. If it didn't, she'd beat him to death in his sleep. The smooth warmth of his lips beneath hers caused her insides to dip. Even unconscious, the man was addictive. If she lost him, she had no idea what she would do. Marrok meant everything to her. He was...

...kissing her back!

He was kissing her back!

Within seconds, Marrok was awake and participating in the embrace. One big hand came up to tangle in her hair, pulling her closer. Scarlett found herself smiling widely as he tugged her down on top of him.

"Oh thank God." She drew back to touch his cheek with her palm. "Don't you *ever* do something like that, again! You almost gave me a heart attack, you jackass! You don't get to plan anything else without telling me. What would've happened if something went wrong?"

"What could've gone wrong? You're my True Love." He grinned. "I knew you'd save me."

Scarlett looked into his clear golden eyes and saw total trust. How could she be mad at someone who had such complete faith in her? She shook her head. "You and I are just destined to save each other forever, I think."

"All the more reason you should propose soon."

Scarlett nearly laughed. There just wasn't a better time to do this than when they were surrounded by people in mystical comas, and Cinderella was trying to take over the world, and Charming was chained to a pillar. She and Marrok didn't do anything the traditional way.

"Are you sure you want to be my husband? Even after this?

"Baby, I'm *positive*. I vote we go home to the Enchanted Forest and corral a non-rodent minister, right after we're done here." He gave her another kiss, his voice dipping lower. "And, by the way, I'm *already* your husband."

Scarlett kissed him back. "I know." She used the jagged glass from the broken vial to slice through the binding on her wrists. "Don't go anywhere. I'll be right back with your proposal." She handed the glass to him so he could free himself and quickly stood up, heading for her stepsister.

"Uh-oh." Cinderella watched her advance and began to look worried. "Jack, skip to the 'pronouncing us man and wife' part."

"Highness, I think we should get out of here before..."

"Just do it!"

He glanced back down at his wedding script, his voice racing over the final words. "By the power vested in me by her resplendently majestic Cinderella, I... *Shit!*"

Scarlett stopped the ceremony by punching the bride.

Jack caught Cinderella as she careened backwards. The two of them went tumbling into the floral arch above the altar. The whole rose-covered monstrosity tipped over in a crash of pink petals and crystals.

"Have you lost your mind?!" Cinderella cried. Shoving Jack away, she stumbled to her feet. She batted the crushed flowers from her hair with an agitated hand, blood trickling from the corner of her mouth. "You're ruining my wedding. Letty!"

"You sicced a dragon on my True Love, stole my sister's prince, locked us in prison, burned down my grandmother's house, and tried to kill us with flying monkeys." Scarlett shouted back. "To hell with your tacky wedding!"

"Tacky?" Cinderella gasped. "Do you know how much these decorations *cost?* This wedding is befitting a true princess!"

"You aren't a princess!" Anger was coursing through Scarlett's body, driving her onward. "*Drusilla* is the princess. *You* are the psycho who's kidnapped her groom."

"Dru's nothing but an ugly stepsister. She doesn't deserve Charming or my palace!"

Scarlett hit her again.

"Highness!" Jack gasped at Cinderella fell to the floor. His beady eyes narrowed at Scarlett. "How dare you strike the ruler of the Westlands, you bitch..." His insult stopped mid-word as Marrok leveled a gun at him.

"I wouldn't." Marrok advised.

Jack's mouth slammed shut so fast his pointed teeth clinked together. He raised his hands in surrender.

"Coward!" Cinderella gave him a shove.

Marrok grabbed a set of keys from Trevelyan's belt. The dragon wasn't waking up unless his True Love arrived and, honestly, that didn't seem real likely. For all intents and purposes, he and the sleeping rats were incapacitated forever.

Stepping over the dragon's eternally slumbering body, Marrok headed for Charming. "Here." He tossed him the keys to the dog collar and chain. "Get out of there. You have a bride to save."

Charming quickly freed himself. "Nothing can stop me from reaching Drusilla, now." He proclaimed grandly. He gazed at Letty and Marrok in deep gratitude. "I owe you *everything*."

"No shit." Marrok agreed.

Scarlett rolled her eyes at that typical display of tact. "Charming, you and Dru belong together. Of *course* we'll do whatever's necessary to see you reunited and happy. We know what it means to have a True Love, don't we, Marrok?"

Marrok flashed her a smile. "We sure do, baby."

"*I* am Charming's True Love." Cinderella screeched. "You may have ruined this wedding, but I'll have another and another and *another* until I have him!" She darted for the exit, her tiara sitting lopsided on her head. "Nothing will stop me from having what's mine! No matter what I have to do, I'll..."

She threw open the door and ran straight into dozens of pissed off Bad folk.

Scarlett grinned as Cinderella's escape was

blocked by all the people she'd treated like dirt. Letty couldn't have been a hundred percent sure that her pointed remarks to the camera would inspire anything, but she'd hoped.

Now, Bad folk were standing up for themselves. Not allowing Cinderella to take what was theirs. Stopping her from fleeing justice. Cindy tried to backup, her eyes wide with horror, but there was no place for her to go.

"You're headed to jail." Scarlett watched as her stepsister was seized by Charming's staff. "Take it from someone who knows: It's not the honeymoon spot you've fantasized about."

"You can't do this to me!" Cinderella seethed. "*I am Princess of the Westlands!*"

"Actually, you're about to be prisoner number one of the new and improved WUB Club. Don't worry. I have it all planned in my head. We don't torture and starve people anymore, but it's a hell of a lot harder to break out." She stalked over to grab the crown off Cinderella's head. "And I'll be taking *that* for my sister."

Cinderella gave a shriek of indignation as she was dragged away.

"Well, that was fun." Marrok came to stand beside Scarlett and arched a brow. "So... Something you want to ask me?"

She glanced up at him and bit back a smile. "You already know what I want to ask you."

"Tell me anyway. I like the words."

"Oh alright." She heaved a mock sigh. "Do you want to marry me or not?" She demanded, paraphrasing the same words she'd used to convince him to escape the WUB Club with her.

He pretended to think it over, looking amused. "It depends. Can we have ice swans at the reception?"

He gestured towards Cinderella's buffet table, where the stupid sculptures were already beginning to melt.

"Nope."

"Well, what do you know... We really do think alike." He hugged her close and let out a contended breath. "I am yours, baby." He whispered in a more serious voice. "I'd die to marry you."

"Well, there's always the possibility you *might*." She wrapped her arms around him and gave him one last chance to make the rational choice. "There will probably be a lot more days just this weird in your future. Dangerous, insane things just happen around me. Felonious grandmothers, and founding kingdoms for Baddies, and escaped mental patients. Are you really prepared for all that?"

"Yep."

"Good." She gave him a smacking kiss. "Because, I'd just talk you out of it if you tried to leave me. I'm pretty good at convincing people to do crazy stuff, you know."

"Trust me, I'm not going anywhere, Red." His hand wrapped around hers, holding tight. "You are my very own happily ever after."

Epilogue

Every person in the Northlands adored their generous prince.
He brought sunshine into their grim lives.
Even if those peasants didn't deserve it.

The Official and Authorized Biography of Prince Avenant

The dream came as it always did.

Every night since Avenant escaped, Belle relived the same memory, as vivid as it had been all those years before. She was back at the auction, watching her family's possessions get sold to the highest bidder.

It was the only way to settle the debts that her parents had left, but it meant that everything she had -- everything that was familiar and safe-- was being ripped away. Belle sat silently on her father's armchair, which would only be hers for another few moments, and wished she could feel hatred for the people preying on her misfortune.

All around her, her neighbors meandered through the house, scrutinizing her belongings and appraising their worth. Dimly she heard comments about the quality of a rug or the weight of a silver candlestick. A few people had the decency to lower their voices. Most didn't bother.

Belle was too numb to even feel violated by the mercenary invasion.

She just wanted it to be over.

She had no idea where she'd go after the auction. There was no place for her to stay that night or any night after. Her parents had been beautiful flighty people, who'd expected their innately bookish daughter to be the same. Because she'd tried to make them happy, she didn't have a job. Didn't have any money. All of her friends were actually her parents' friends and beautiful flighty people didn't make deep connections. Belle was all alone.

She was too numb to care about that, either.

She was beaten.

A butterfly was flitting in the garden outside the window. She watched it through the glass, mesmerized by its dance through the flowers. So much of the year, the Northlands was white and cold. The brief days of summer always seemed like magic with their warmth and color. If her parents had to die, at least their final memories were of the strong sun and brilliant greens surrounding them.

The auctioneer was loudly listing off the key features of her mother's art collection. It all sounded like white noise. Someone held up a painting of abstract shapes that Belle had always hated. So had her mother. But, the artist had been the height of fashion two years before, so of course she'd bought the biggest canvas in his studio. Belle watched as it sold for a tenth of what her mother had paid for it and didn't feel a thing.

"What a hideous painting. Honestly, you're better off without it."

Belle turned to see Avenant standing beside her chair. Of course, he'd show up to gloat when she was at her lowest. She was just surprised that she hadn't seen him enter. Usually, she was morbidly aware of his presence. It went to show how far gone she was in her depression.

"I should've known you'd come." She muttered.

"Yes, you should have." To celebrate her misery, Avenant wore the white and gold regalia of the palace, complete with the circular crown of the prince. His

stunning face surveyed the goings on with a sardonically amused expression. "How could I miss the social event of the season?"

Belle watched as her father's chess set went on the block. He hadn't played, but the game had been a decoration in the study for as long as she could remember. She had a brief flash of moving the pieces around the board as a child while her father laughed.

It sold to the obnoxious neighbor down the street for fifteen gold pieces.

Avenant made a scoffing sound at the price. "Everyone here is astoundingly cheap."

"If my parents had been cheaper, maybe I wouldn't be in this mess." The family china was up next. Belle turned her head away, not wanting to see it go. It was one of the few things she had left of her grandmother.

"Are they really going to sell one object at a time?" Avenant checked his watch. "This will take forever."

"Feel free to leave if my poverty is cutting into your busy schedule."

"Not until I have what's mine."

"Nothing here is yours, Avenant."

He arched a brow at her. "We'll see about that." He turned towards the auctioneer and raised an imperious hand. "Six million." He called casually.

Belle's attention snapped back to him. The last bid on the china had been forty gold pieces. Was he out of his mind?

The auctioneer clearly hoped so. "Six million, Prince Avenant?" He repeated eagerly. "Well, I don't think anyone will go higher on this lovely lot of..."

"Six million for all of it." Avenant interrupted.

"The furniture, the house, the garish plates. I'll take everything." He looked around. "Anyone want to up my bid?"

No one did.

It was double what the estate was worth. Enough to pay off the debt and then some.

Avenant was going to win it all.

"You really are a beast." Belle whispered.

Avenant ignored that. He smirked as the auctioneer's gavel came down and he bought everything she owned. "See? All mine." He headed over to the mantle where the first place trophy Belle had received in high school debate still sat. "This should have gone to me." He picked it up, his eyes glowing with triumph. "Now, I finally have it."

Rage filled her.

For the first time since her parents died, Belle was consumed with honest and real emotion. It felt wonderful. "I won that debate and you know it, you bastard!" She surged to her feet and advanced on him.

All their lives, the two of them had been locked in an endless conflict. Belle wasn't even sure how it had happened. In school, they consistently scored one and two on every assignment and activity, so their only competition had been each other. It led to an unhealthy rivalry. Why the hell had Avenant joined the debate club if not to screw with her? Why had Belle volunteered for the dance committee if not to try and block his chances at being prom king?

The one-upmanship hadn't faded when they reached adulthood. It was like they sought each other out to continue their private battle. Avenant loomed over her, smiling smugly and holding her trophy… and, in that second, Belle knew she wasn't beaten.

She would never surrender to this man.

"Belle, you know I won that debate." He goaded. "The judge on the end was swayed by the length of your skirt, not your arguments."

"Well, you bribed the other judge, so I figure it all evens out." She tried to grab the trophy back from him, but he held it out of reach.

"Don't be such a sore loser." He taunted. "It's mine, fair and square."

"You son of a bitch! You think you can just steal my life away and I'll…"

Avenant cut her off. "Oh, I don't want the rest of this stuff." He waved a hand around to indicate the fortune in lands and fixtures and objets d'art he'd just purchased. "Keep it all."

Belle blinked. "…keep it?"

"Well, what would I do with low quality furnishings?" He glanced over to the auctioneer. "Send someone to the palace to collect your money and return the woman's belongings."

"Of course, sire."

Avenant looked back at Belle. "See? I can be gracious in victory. You should be used to that by now."

He wanted to take everything from her and then just give it back? Just to prove he could? Just to revel in her humiliation? He honestly thought she'd let him get away with that?

"You're going to regret this." She vowed softly.

Icy blue eyes gleamed as he studied her furious face. "I doubt it." He touched her flushed cheek with the back of his fingers and chuckled when she shoved him away. "I got exactly what I wanted." He gave the debate trophy a spiteful waggle and headed for the door. "Now, if you'll excuse me, I'm late for polo."

Only he could make her this angry. Everyone was gaping at her and Belle didn't even notice. She grabbed a vase from a nearby table and pegged it at his retreating head. "I hate you!" She raged, not caring if she was arrested for attempted regicide.

He ducked to the side so the porcelain projectile sailed passed his skull and shattered against the wall. "I technically owned that vase. I'd charge you for it if you had any money to..."

She cut him off. "I will see you rotting in a hole somewhere if it's the last thing I ever do! I swear to God, I am going to beat you so badly you'll never *be able to come back from it!"*

His mouth curved with all the cold authority of winter. "Impossible. No matter what you do... I'll always *come back."*

Belle's eyes snapped open, her heart pounding in her chest. She sat up on the mattress, her eyes quickly scanning for danger. For the moment, she was safe. Her bedroom was quiet and empty... A bedroom she only owned because Avenant had bought it back for her at that horrible auction. She'd successfully overthrown the Northlands and taken Avenant's crown, but she'd never been able to sleep in the castle. She didn't even want to. In some fundamental way, that would always be his.

And he'd be coming back for it.

He'd be coming back for *her*.

She'd seen Avenant on TV when Cinderella was carted off to prison. Charming had stood there, with a healthy and awake Drusilla beaming by his side, and proclaimed that everyone who'd escaped from the WUB Club was pardoned. They could either stay in the Westlands and be treated as honored friends, or they could return to the Enchanted Forest with Scarlett and

Marrok to help build a new kingdom based on equality. Either way, the future for Bad folk was suddenly wide open. Nothing would be as it was before. Everything had changed.

Avenant had listened to the speech... and slowly smiled.

Belle drew her legs up to her chest and dropped her forehead to her knees. She knew that expression. He wore it whenever he was about to take their rivalry to a whole new level of Bad. Already, she could feel him plotting in the shadows, waiting for an opportunity to strike. Nothing would stop him from...

The phone beside her bed rang and Belle jolted. Her eyes slowly traveled over to it, dread filling her. She didn't recognize the number on the caller-ID, but she knew who it was. Insane as it was, she could *feel* him.

Reluctantly, she picked up the receiver and said one word. "Don't."

"Why shouldn't I?" Avenant demanded from the other end. "Give me one reason not to."

Her insides clenched at the deep sound of his voice. "Because we both went too far the last time and this time it'll be even worse."

"Worse than me rotting in that goddamn prison? I don't see how that would be possible, even for someone with your penchant for treachery."

"It wasn't my fault you were sent there!"

"Bullshit!" His tone got even more incensed. "You wanted to play hardball, so *fine*. No more half-measures. I'm going to get my kingdom *back*, no matter what I have to do."

"You could have a hundred other kingdoms." She tried. "You could live in the Westlands. You could stay in the Enchanted Forest. You could go to another land and start over completely."

"No." The word was unequivocal.

"Damn it, if you come here..." She squeezed her eyes shut and tried to stay calm. "Just *don't*."

"Give me. a reason. not to." He repeated darkly, spacing the words for emphasis.

"They'll be more fighting. More bloodshed. Hasn't there been enough?"

"Well, that's easily fixed. Surrender to me."

Her teeth ground together. "I'm not going to surrender and you know it."

"Then get ready for a war. I'll have what's mine, even if I have to melt the entire Northlands to claim it."

"There's nothing here that's yours, Avenant."

"We'll see about that, won't we?" He slammed the phone down.

Belle winced at the sound. She slowly replaced the receiver and sat quietly in the dark. There would be no reasoning with him. Despite everything, he blamed her for what had happened. He had magical powers, a short fuse and he wanted vengeance. This would be their final competition and she had the horrible feeling that she wasn't going to win.

The beast was coming for her.

Don't miss the next book in the Kinda Fairytale series:

Beast in Shining Armor

Beauty vs. Beast…

Contestant One: Avenant is a handsome prince with a dark side. There's a beast inside of him, always waiting to get out. All his life, he's been labeled a monster and he's done his best to live up to his Bad reputation. His parents hated him, his fairytale kingdom fears him, and now he's been dragged into court. Again. His newest legal troubles are all because Belle Ashman stole his throne. The beautiful bookshop owner is the one woman Avenant longs for. The two of them have been in competition since childhood and the contest just became winner-take-all.

Contestant Two: Tired of Avenant ruining her dates, firing Mother Goose, and tearing down Humpty Dumpty's wall, Rosabella Aria Ashman decided to depose the tyrant. Eight months ago, Belle led a rebellion and had Avenant thrown in prison. Now, the Beast has returned, demanding his kingdom back. Avenant might be gorgeous, but he's also arrogant, selfish and he's been mean to her since kindergarten. This time, Belle's determined to vanquish him, once and for all.

The Ultimate Showdown: In the farthest corner of the Northlands, there is an impenetrable labyrinth. Made of ice and stone, no one has ever entered it and emerged alive. Now, Belle, Avenant, and other storybook contenders for the crown are heading into the maze. Whoever solves its riddles gets the kingdom. In order to win, Belle and Avenant are going to have to work together. Considering their lifelong feud, that would be challenging enough, but they're also dealing with an angry minotaur, an unknown killer, miles of twisting corridors… and the fact that these two mortal enemies might just make a perfect team.

Now available!

Printed in Great Britain
by Amazon